Unfinished Muse

R.L. Naquin

Bottle Cap Publishing

Edited by Sara E. Lundberg

Cover design by Yocla Designs

Published by Bottle Cap Publishing

Other Works by R.L. Naquin

Published by Bottle Cap Publishing:
Transmonstrified (short story collection)

The Mount Olympus Employment Agency Series
Unfinished Muse, Book 1
Unamused Muse, Book 2 (October 2015)
Uninspired Muse, Book 3 (December 2015)

Published by Carina Press:
The Monster Haven Series
Monster in My Closet, Book 1
Pooka in My Pantry, Book 2
Fairies in My Fireplace, Book 3
Golem in My Glovebox, Book 4
Demons in My Driveway, Book 5
Phoenix in My Fortune, Book 6

For Kevin, who is the heart of every new project
and gets the first book in every series.
Without you, I'd be stranded in a cubicle,
dreaming of being a writer.

Chapter 1

I'd owned that potted philodendron for two years without it ever uttering a word—so naturally, I ignored it when it finally spoke up.

To be fair, I wasn't in the mood to talk to anybody, let alone a figment of my imagination. Over lunch, I'd dumped my boyfriend, Freddy (it's not you, it's me, I hope we can still be friends), then finished out the rest of the work day at my crappy call-center job before packing up the stuff on my desk and telling my boss that I quit (it's not working out, I'm not a good fit, you'd be better off finding someone more suitable for the position).

I left the house that morning with a boyfriend and a job, then returned home single and unemployed. I supposed the last straw that changed everything came when I opened the door to the coat closet and the partially finished quilt I'd been working on for five years in short, fruitless spurts fell out and attacked me. Half the pins had come loose over time, and some of the blue satin squares flapped at me as I bundled it all up and shoved it into a garbage bag to throw away.

Once I'd tied the bag shut in an act of finality, something inside my gut shifted and flipped over. My ears popped, and my arms broke out in goosebumps.

And that's when the plant spoke up.

"Well, there you go," she said in a shushing, grandmotherly voice filled with disapproval. "Nowhere to go from here but up."

I saw the leaves rustle when the voice spoke. I'd been looking right at it. If someone were playing a practical joke, it beat the hell out of me who it could've been. I didn't actually have any friends in this town. I wasn't very good at friendship, frankly. I'd only been in Topeka for nine months—plenty of time to go through three boyfriends, but not nearly long enough to make a friend. Friends required more effort.

That didn't make me sound like a very nice person, even to myself.

"I suppose we're moving again," the plant said in an aggrieved tone. "I dry out on those long car rides, especially when we go to the higher elevations. I didn't think I'd ever recover in Denver."

I'm losing my freaking mind. Plants don't talk. I've had a hard day. Maybe my blood sugar is low. I should eat something.

If I ignored Phyllis the philodendron, maybe had some protein, she—*it*—would stop talking and everything would go back to normal. A hot bath, maybe a glass of wine. Lots of people imagined crazy shit after a terrible day.

Right?

Phyllis didn't stop talking while I was in the kitchen. But she did shout so I could hear her over the sizzling of the grilled cheese sandwich frying in the skillet.

"Mark my words, Wynter. You'll be glad you finally hit rock bottom in the end. Now we can really get to work."

I flipped the sandwich and opened a bottle of chardonnay I'd shoved in the back of the fridge behind the moldy lunchmeat and the leftover spaghetti.

"Your whole life will open up to new possibilities! Wait till you find out what's ahead!"

I filled a bulbous glass and gulped down half the liquid.

"I know you can hear me in there, Wynter. Ignore me all you want, but you can't hide from your destiny."

I drained the glass and refilled.

"Honey, I know this is hard for you to accept, but the sooner you do, the sooner we can get you started on your way."

The fire alarm went off, and I yanked my smoking sandwich off the burner. After throwing open the door and the kitchen window, I waved a potholder at the screaming alarm until it stopped. Two neighbors popped their heads out their back doors and gave me questioning looks across the inner courtyard.

"It's okay!" I yelled at them. "Just burned some toast. Sorry!"

My landlady, Mrs. Terwilliger, scowled, shook her head, and slammed her door. Mark something-or-other, who lived directly across the courtyard, gave a friendly smile and shrugged before going inside.

Or was it Mick? No, maybe it was Mike. I was terrible with names.

"See?" Phyllis said. "I knew you were listening. Otherwise, how did you set your kitchen on fire? You were standing right there."

I refilled my wine glass and realized I'd already emptied three quarters of the bottle. I stuck a pinot grigio in the fridge. My bad day had progressed into a truly awful night. I grabbed my glass, my bottle, and a granola bar and left the charcoal-and-cheese sandwich to cool in the sink.

"Ah, you're back," Phyllis said. "That's not all you're going to eat, is it? A bottle of wine and a granola bar? Oh, honey, you really have given up, haven't you?"

I charged through the living room and around the corner without comment or pause. While I ran hot water in the tub, I ate my granola bar and reveled in the fact that I could no longer hear a voice yelling at me from the other room. Either getting a little food in me had done the trick, or the sound of running water drowned out the voice that had to be coming from my own head and not from a potted plant someone at a farmers market had given me for free two years ago.

When I shut off the tap, I discovered it wasn't the granola bar silencing the voice. It had definitely been the sound of the water.

The voice was quieter, since it came from the other end of the apartment, but still easy to hear. "You're not going to drink that entire bottle in the bathtub, are you? That's not going to solve your problems, you know."

I refilled my glass, chose a mystery novel I'd been meaning to read, and turned on the radio. Loud.

Once I sank into the hot water, the tension melted, and I closed my eyes. The music covered the disconcerting voice I still heard through the bathroom door, and my head buzzed pretty hard from drinking so much so fast. Without the bossy voice distracting me, pictures of Freddy's sad, puppy face flashed behind my closed eyelids.

I frowned. Dealing with a talking plant had been less upsetting than thinking about the breakup.

Mind you, it wasn't like I'd never had the same exact breakup conversation several times before. That didn't make it any easier. But what's the point of continuing to go out with someone when you know it's not going to last forever? Freddy was really sweet, but we'd already had All the Conversations. Once the initial giddiness burned off, we didn't have a damn thing in common.

Try explaining that to a guy, though. They never understood. It was easier to try to convince them you were broken in some way. Hell, maybe I *was* broken. Maybe it really was me and not him. Still, I didn't see the point in putting all that effort into a relationship if I didn't want the guy to eventually move in with me or walk down an aisle or share babies. Freddy was vanilla ice cream. I wanted mint chocolate chip. Was that so much to ask?

Still, I'd done a crappy job of breaking it to him, judging by his reaction. I felt like a total bitch. And proving what a nice guy he was, he still picked up the tab at lunch and offered to drive me back to work.

But honestly, he was a little too clingy, calling several times a day, even when I was at work. He wanted more of me than I was ready to give. Two months was too soon to start having serious conversations about refrigerators. *Refrigerators.* Seriously. I didn't have anything edible in mine besides ice and a few slices of processed cheese. Asking me what kind of refrigerator I wanted in my future house was like asking which rocket ship I wanted for a hypothetical trip to Venus. Or, you know, whether I wanted to breastfeed or bottle feed someday. I figured we had maybe three more dates, tops, before he asked that one.

His horse was so far ahead of my cart he was about to lap me.

Plus, I never did quite understand what he did for a living. He said he was an actor, but in the few months we were together, he never talked about rehearsals or invited me to a show he was in. He didn't appear to be hurting for money, though. It all seemed a little weird.

I wrung out a washcloth and folded it into a rectangle to drape over my eyes. The radio DJ made some crack about a local politician, then the air went dead for about fifteen seconds before the new song started.

The brief silence was filled with what sounded like a raunchy sea shanty being sung from my living room by someone's maiden aunt. I pretended not to hear it.

After an hour or so, the water was too cool to be comfortable, the wine was gone, and my stomach was telling me to get my ass into the kitchen and make it some pie. Or at least order a pizza. I'd never even opened the novel I'd brought in with me. Concentration was seriously lacking.

My head spun when I stepped from the tub. I tucked a towel around my middle, shut off the radio, and stuck my head out the door.

The singing had stopped, at least. Cautious, I tiptoed down the hallway clutching the empty glass and bottle.

Nope. No talking plants here. I'm not in the least bit crazy. I stepped into the living room.

"Oh, there you are!" Leaves shivered above the plain terracotta pot. "I was worried you'd dozed off in the tub."

I froze for a second, then ducked into the kitchen. The empty bottle made a loud clank when I dropped it in the trash. Noise seemed like an excellent response to what was going on in my head. The pan in the sink banged on the porcelain with satisfying volume, though the charred

10

sandwich made a disappointing thud when I tossed it on top of the dead wine bottle.

The knowing voice of my conscience, now in the handy form of a talking plant, shouted an admonishment at me from the next room. "You should really start recycling your bottles if you're going to drink that much, dear."

I rolled my eyes and banged the pan around the sink while I scrubbed black crusty stuff and melted cheese from the cheap non-stick surface. Through the doorway behind me, the voice cleared its non-existent throat and belted out an off-key rendition of "I Am a Pirate King" from Gilbert and Sullivan's *Pirates of Penzance*. Disturbing didn't begin to describe the sound of a grandmotherly voice singing about sinking ships and doing dirty work. Especially when the voice couldn't possibly exist, so must be something my brain was regurgitating.

Because the plant couldn't really be talking, right?

I placed the pan upside down on the counter to dry, wiped my hands on a moderately clean dishcloth, and turned to face my own insanity.

The plant I'd been calling Phyllis since she was a scrawny branch with a few dry offshoots went quiet. I moved with slow deliberation into the living room and stood before the perfectly normal plant. With tentative fingers, prepared to pull my hand back at any sign of sharp teeth or suckered tendrils, I poked at the dirt in the pot.

"You're dry," I said. "It's supposed to rain tonight. Fresh air should do you some good."

"What are you doing, Wynter?" The branches quivered, and a leaf dropped from a stem. "Do be reasonable, sweetheart. If you don't like operettas, I'll sing something else."

I didn't respond. Why should I? It was all happening in my head, so my delusion already knew what I had in mind. Trying not to show fear, I grabbed the dish beneath the pot and carried the whole thing out the back door into the courtyard, placed it beside the door, and went inside.

The silence was amazing.

And a little lonely, now that I didn't have a made-up problem to distract me. I checked my phone and saw that Freddy had left two voice messages as well as a text that said "Thinking of you."

I sighed and left the phone on the counter without listening to the messages. The text was sweet, in a way, but I'd never gone back to a guy I'd broken up with, and I didn't mean to start now. The ones who kept trying after the breakup were even less likely to get me to give in and try again.

I turned off the ringer. If Freddy wasn't done trying to convince me to *work on our relationship*, he'd be calling back. I'd rather miss a call than ignore it. One action was without knowledge, the other was deliberate. If I didn't know about the call, I didn't feel as much guilt over not taking it.

I plopped on the couch and turned on the television to veg over some sitcom doomed for early cancellation. I didn't really follow the plot and got lost halfway through. Mostly, I was distracted by the idea that I'd have to go looking for a new job come Monday, or pack up all my stuff and move in with mother. Again.

I cringed at the idea of living with Mom again. I was twenty-four. I shouldn't have to keep moving back home. And my mom leaned well toward the bonkers side, so there was that.

One of the characters on television pulled out a box of the same cereal I'd seen advertised during the commercial break.

I wrinkled my nose. "Product placement." I clicked off the television. It was early for a Friday night, but my day had been draining. All I wanted was to crawl into my bed and hide until at least tomorrow. Besides. I probably needed to get dressed, since I'd been wrapped in my towel long enough that not only was I dry, but so was the towel.

I sighed and unfolded myself from the couch, running my fingers through my short, blonde hair and leaving it spiked around my head. By morning it would probably be flat on one side from the pillow.

After throwing on a tank top and a pair of underwear, I deserted the towel in the middle of my bedroom floor and crawled under the covers. My eyes burned from weariness.

I managed to doze for a few hours before the courtyard erupted in a rap song. A loud rap song.

I listened for a moment before I realized it was the theme song to *The Fresh Prince of Bel-Air*, as sung by someone's beloved Nana.

I groaned and wrapped the pillow around my ears.

A few seconds later, a window facing the courtyard lit up and someone yelled for quiet.

My mouth went dry. *Oh my God. They can hear it, too.*

I scrambled out of bed and pulled on a lavender kimono I sometimes used as a bathrobe, then ran for the back door and flung it open.

In the glow of Mrs. Terwilliger's porch light, my philodendron bopped its leaves to the beat of its own song. "…to the cabbie, 'Yo, homes, smell ya later!'"

"Wynter, is that you singing?" Mrs. Terwilliger yelled across the space.

"No ma'am!" I yelled back, then hissed between my teeth and lowered my voice to a whisper. "Would you stop it! You'll get me evicted."

I snatched up the singing plant and rushed inside. As soon as I closed and locked the door, she stopped singing.

"You know, it's cold out there, Wynter. That was a mean thing to do."

"Waking up my neighbors was mean, too," I said. I shifted my feet, self-conscious about talking to a plant now that the plant could talk back.

"Can we stop with the games now and discuss this like rational adults?" Every word she uttered was accompanied by a shushing sound of leaves rubbing against each other.

"It's the middle of the night."

There was a long pause before she spoke again in a tight, disapproving voice. "It seems to me you have nothing better to do anyway."

"Don't you judge me. You're a freeloader hanging around all day while I work at a crappy job taking shit from customers. I got tired of people yelling at me. Don't I deserve better than that?"

"Do you think you do?"

I opened my mouth to argue—as if arguing with a houseplant were the most natural thing to do in the middle of the night—then snapped my jaw shut, frowning. "Are you trying to psychoanalyze me?"

"Do *you* think you need therapy?"

"Are we playing the question game?" I tilted my head at her.

"Would the question game help you make better decisions?"

"Can you help me make better decisions?"

"Yes. Yes I can."

I grinned. "I win. That wasn't in the form of a question. Thank you for playing." I poked at her soil. "You're still dry. I guess the weather girl was wrong." I put the pot in the empty sink and sprayed water on the soil. "I'm going to let you sit here and drain for the rest of the night. While you do that, I will be sleeping. If you wake me up, I will chop you into tiny pieces with kitchen scissors. Do you understand?"

"Yes," she said in a mopey voice. "Though I'm not in the least bit afraid of you. Get some sleep, and we'll talk in the morning. We have a lot to discuss."

I nodded. "I guess. Goodnight…hey, what do I call you?"

"You've been calling me Phyllis for two years, dear. Why would you change that now?"

I tried not to think of all the intimate moments I'd spent both with and without boyfriends in front of this self-aware plant. "Goodnight, Phyllis."

As much as I was eager to get back to sleep, I never did manage it that night. I was too afraid I'd wake up in a white room with padded walls.

Maybe an institution would have been easier than what Phyllis had in store for me. Apparently, she had my whole life already planned and had been lying in wait for me to hit bottom.

And now that I'd done it, she was more than ready to take over.

Chapter 2

After a long, mostly sleepless weekend spent arguing with a philodendron and dodging questions from Mrs. Terwilliger, I found myself standing on the sidewalk in the worst part of Topeka, bright and early Monday morning.

With a houseplant tucked under my arm.

The street was fairly empty of vehicles and pedestrians, which was good, since Phyllis was so excited to have browbeaten me into all this she hadn't shut up the whole way there.

"Are you sure you have the right address?" I asked, shifting her to the other arm. "The only businesses in this area are meth labs and prostitutes. I wasn't especially good at chemistry in school, so I hope you didn't drag me here to meet my new pimp."

She made a tutting noise, interesting for someone with no tongue. "Stop fussing, Wynter. Just do what I say. You'll see."

All I *saw* was a homeless dude whip himself out and pee on the side of the building she wanted me to enter.

At one time, the place might have been full of doctors' offices or accounting firms. Now it was a single-story mess of peeling gray paint, boarded-over windows, and cracked concrete.

And she wanted me to waltz in there like I had an appointment.

Spend a weekend arguing with a plant. When you finally lose, you'll walk into the pits of hell rather than continue the argument.

I squared my shoulders, lifted my chin, and walked past the homeless guy shaking himself dry and tucking back in. I averted my eyes and didn't return his greeting. At the threshold, I hesitated a moment, then pushed the door open.

With the first step inside, everything changed.

The door closed behind me, and I blinked in the sudden brightness. I stood in a round atrium bustling with people. Several stories above me, the ceiling rose to a glass dome. Everything was white and shiny and clean, and hallways led off in several directions. A bank of elevators opened and closed with people pouring out and more taking their places.

In the center, a reception desk held court, surrounded by couches and chairs for people to wait in comfort.

"Over there, dear," Phyllis said. "We need to get you checked in."

I supposed she meant the reception area. I didn't ask. My jaw hadn't yet learned to reconnect my lips.

We stood in line and waited our turn. I'd been so busy taking in the enormous—and impossible—building, I hadn't looked at the receptionist yet.

"Don't stare, dear, it's rude," Phyllis said. "Put me on the counter, please. I'll take care of everything."

I closed my mouth and did as I was told. This entire situation put me so far out of my element, I might as well have been at a cocktail party on Mars.

"Patrice," Phyllis said. "How wonderful to see you, dear."

Patrice wore small, mirrored sunglasses and a cleavage-baring, hot pink blouse that set off her green skin. Her dark green dreadlocks coiled around her ears with one or two skinny locks dangling over one eye. I called them dreadlocks in my mind because there was no way I would admit to myself that the woman had a head full of live, moving snakes.

"Phyllis," she said with a remarkable lack of hiss in her voice. "It's about damn time you got here." She looked from the plant to me and back again. "Is this her?"

"It is, yes."

Patrice fixed me with what I was sure was a stony stare through those glasses. I may not have finished college, but I sure as hell knew a gorgon when I saw one. Not that Medusa was real, of course. I looked away in case my apparent lateness was cause for giving me that look over the top of her rims. Forget Mars. I was all the way out on Jupiter, and the cocktail party had turned into a lecture on alien economics.

"Took you long enough," Patrice said. She handed me a clipboard with a pen attached by a silver chain. "Fill out this paperwork and bring it up when you're done."

"Thank you," I said in a near whisper, eyes to the floor. I clutched Phyllis against my chest and made a beeline for the farthest chair from the desk.

I settled into the seat, hands shaking, and put Phyllis on the table next to me. "What *is* this place? Why didn't you warn me what to expect? How is any of this possible? Are we even *in* Topeka anymore?" I rattled off

16

questions, hoping for answers, but also hoping some sort of understanding would click in my brain so I could think coherently.

A faun in dress shirt and tie trotted past, and I felt my brain shrink away from the elusive understanding I so desperately wanted.

"If I'd explained it first," Phyllis said, "you either wouldn't have come or wouldn't have believed me. Knowing you, a little of both. Just fill out the paperwork. You don't want to make Patrice angry."

No. No, I did not.

The top of the form gave me the name of where I was, at least. Finally, some sort of clue: *Mt. Olympus Employment Agency*

I filled out the form the best I could. My name was easy—Wynter Greene. I'd had a lot of minty-fresh jokes throughout my life, but now that I was an adult, I didn't have to deal with it as much. The standard address, date of birth, and social security questions rounded out the first section. No problem.

Section two was where things went a little sideways. They wanted the names of my parents. Who asks for that on a job application? I shrugged and put down my mom's name, Cora Greene. I left the father question blank. I had no clue. Every time I'd tried to ask my mom about it, I got a different story.

"Check the box for which parent is the superior deity?" I frowned at Phyllis. "What's that supposed to mean?"

"Leave it," she said. "Let them sort it out."

Section three was where I expected them to ask about my previous jobs. Or school. Or qualifications of any kind. Nope. They wanted to know if I could fly.

I dropped the pen and held up my hands. "Phyllis? What am I supposed to do with this?"

Her leaves quaked and she chuckled. "Answer 'no' to all the abilities questions, but in the write-in portion, tell them you're good with plants." She laughed at her own joke.

I didn't find it funny at all. "Crazy-ass job application," I muttered under my breath. "And a talking plant who won't help me."

I left nearly everything on the form blank. I didn't know if they were joking or serious, and I didn't want to come off sounding like a lunatic. Though the fact that I had to hand the forms to a gorgon while a lady with flowers growing out of her hair waited in line behind me kind of gave weight to the idea that the application questions were serious.

Or that I was lying on the street somewhere with head trauma, and this was the weirdest dream ever.

I bit my lip and squinted at the page in my hand. Yeah. That had to be it. Head trauma. I decided to proceed as if the whole thing were an entertaining product of a vehicular accident involving a family of ducks, a carload of clowns, and a careening melon cart. That could cause anybody to slip into a coma featuring a colorful dream cast of bizarre characters.

My cheeks tightened with my strained smile as I handed over the clipboard.

Patrice pushed her sunglasses up her nose and sniffed. "Not a lot of information here." She yanked the papers from the metal clip and shoved them into a folder. "Follow the copper line to Thebes for orientation and further instruction. Next, please."

She slammed a stamp on the outside of my folder and set the whole thing on a tall pile. The flower-haired lady shoved me out of the way and threw a broken stick on the desk. "I'd like to make a complaint," she said. She and Patrice both gave me a pointed look.

"Oh, sorry," I said and went back to where I'd left Phyllis on a table, talking to a rubber tree. "I have to follow a copper line to Thebes."

"Of course, dear," Phyllis said. "Everyone has to start with orientation. You go on along, now. Pick me up when you're finished. Sadie and I have a lot of catching up to do."

Sadie shook a fat leaf in my direction. "Don't dawdle, sweetheart. You don't want to miss the donuts. That's the best part."

I scowled and turned away, examining the floor. Thin metallic lines crisscrossed everywhere in a complex pattern I'd assumed was part of the design. I could see now they all led in different directions.

Can't believe she's deserting me to talk to a potted tree.

With my head down to follow the copper line, I saw less of the crazy stuff around me, which was soothing. I saw my own feet encased in low-heeled black pumps. I saw other perfectly normal feet cross my path. If I passed a root or hoof or claw along the way, they were easier to accept than seeing the full bodies they were attached to.

In the back of my mind, I worried that Thebes was a very long trip, considering it was on the other side of the world. Where, exactly, I wasn't sure, but it was part of Greek mythology, so it had to be pretty far away. I crossed the atrium, went down a hall, turned right, and the copper line stopped short in front of a door with the word *Thebes* painted in copper across it.

So, not halfway across the world. Just someone being clever with the names of their conference rooms.

"Hold on to your butts," I said, taking a deep breath and pushing the door open.

Immediately, I could tell I'd missed the donuts portion of the meeting. In fact, the refreshment table on the left-hand wall was deserted, and everyone was already seated and facing the wall on the right. Until I walked in talking to myself, anyway. At that point, a room full of people swiveled their heads around to see who the disruptive, late girl was.

The person they'd been paying attention to was a diminutive, frail-looking woman, old enough to be my grandmother or possibly my great-grandmother. She wore a pink tracksuit embroidered with odd symbols on the cuffs and collar.

"Is this orientation?" I asked, trying to squeak above a whisper.

The tiny woman pursed her lips until her red lipstick was nothing but a thin slash. "How many more are they going to send me last minute like this?" She threw her arm in the air in the universal symbol of "whatever, fine." She flicked her hand at a seat in the front row. "Sit down. I was about to start."

I ducked my head and hurried to the chair, my cheeks burning. All around me, people clutched notebooks and pens, ready to take notes. I was late to class and unprepared. Any second, she would probably give us our final for the semester. I glanced down at myself, certain I'd be in nothing but my bra and underwear. When I saw my skirt and blouse, I frowned in disappointment. Not a dream. This total suckfest was absolutely for real.

I dug through my purse as quietly as I could so as not to attract further attention. Fortunately, I'd gone through a stage where I thought I wanted to write poetry, so I had a pen and mini notebook with me. I flipped past several half-finished sonnets to a blank page.

"Now that we're all here," the small lady said, "we'll begin." She cleared her throat. "I'm Mrs. Moros, and you'll be spending the next few days with me. At the end of the week, you'll get your work assignments, provided you make it through orientation and testing."

Ah. So there is a test. I knew it.

She rested her hands on her hips and paced while she spoke. "You're all here for the same reason: you've hit bottom. Every last one of you has managed to screw up your life."

A rumble went through the crowd, and people gave each other sideways glances.

"No," she said, raising her voice. "Don't go looking at your neighbor to see who's the bigger loser. You're all losers in my book."

Somewhere in the back row—which honestly was only five rows back—someone sniffled. Part of me wanted to object, but the rest of me had to stifle a laugh. Yes, I'd quit my job, but that didn't make me a loser. For one thing, I didn't get fired. I left on my own terms.

This wrinkled, bossy little stick figure doesn't know anything about me.

She swung around and stared at me. "That's one," she said.

"What?" She couldn't have heard me. I didn't say anything out loud.

"Guard your thoughts, Wynter. You'll want to have more self-control than that if you're ever going to make anything of your wasted life." She spun around and marched off to say something probably equally chilling to a bald guy at the end of the row.

I sat dumbfounded, my arms prickling with raised hairs. Mrs. Moros knew my name.

And she'd heard exactly what I'd been thinking.

Chapter 3

Over the course of that week, I had several opportunities to regret having quit my crappy call-center job.

The rest of that first morning, I sat as still as I could in my chair while Mrs. Moros droned on about the company, its heritage, and more times than I cared to count, how pathetic we all were.

The second time she said it, my gut clenched and my jaw tightened, but I did my best not to think anything that might get me into trouble. The woman was seriously scary, despite her tiny size and wrinkled exterior. The fact that I had to guard my thoughts was scary all by itself. What kind of place was this?

The kind of place with a gorgon for a receptionist, that's what.

By lunch, my head hurt, my stomach gurgled, and my ass felt like I'd been riding a horse cross-country. Sitting still wasn't really my thing, but every time I'd squirmed, she nailed me back in place with her beady little eyes.

Of course, I didn't think about it that way as she did it. She'd have heard me with her wicked mind-reading skills. Seriously scary-ass woman.

She let us go at noon with the admonishment that we needed to be back by one. I had no idea where we were going, but I followed the crowd out the door and down the hallway. We took a winding path through the building, past columns, across a rotunda, and through a pair of glass double doors marked Ambrosia.

I knew ambrosia was supposed to be the food of the gods from Greek mythology. I got it. I also thought it was a mean joke. No matter where you were, cafeteria food should never be referred to as ambrosia. Not even in jest.

I grabbed an orange tray and placed a fruit cup on it. I watched as a redhead with short, bouncy curls ordered the brown stuff in the back row of silver containers. The cafeteria worker scratched underneath her hairnet and plopped a spoonful of mystery meat on a plate.

"Next." She eyed me with suspicion, as if she thought I might try to custom order something.

I pointed at a container of chunky orange stuff. "Is that macaroni and cheese?"

She grunted. "Yes. You want it?"

"Yes, please." That should've been safe, right? Hard to make mac and cheese gross.

She plopped a generous helping on the plate and handed it to me over the sneeze-guard. The motion pulled at her sleeve and revealed her scaly wrist. I swallowed hard and took the plate. As I moved down the line, I glanced back and saw a snaky tail undulating behind the woman. Not behind. Attached.

I shivered and grabbed a bottle of water and a dinner roll.

"That's a lot of carbs," the redhead said as we waited behind the cash register.

I made a face. "Nothing else looked edible."

She lowered her voice so only I could hear. "I don't even know what I chose. I was so freaked out by the woman behind the counter, I just pointed blindly."

We moved forward, and it was her turn at the register. When she was done, she waited for me to pay for my own.

Without a word, we found an empty table and sat together.

"I'm Jillian Bean." She took a tentative bite of the brown muck on her plate.

"Your name is Jillian Bean." I kept my face blank. I knew I was being juvenile, but I couldn't stop it.

See, Wynter? This is why you don't have any friends.

She smiled. "Yes it is. Go ahead. I've been called Jilly Bean most of my life. It stopped bothering me when I was nine."

I smiled back at her. "I'm Wynter." I paused and lowered my voice. "Wynter Greene."

She gasped. "No! Oh, we're going to be good friends. You must've gotten even more crap than I did."

I nodded and bit into my roll. It was hard, dry, and nearly broke my tooth. "At least yours is less straightforward and kind of cute. Mine's just stupid."

She shook her head in a dramatic way. "Parents can be so cruel."

A middle-aged bald guy and a short Asian kid slid their trays on our table and sat.

"I'm Hal. We talking about our parents?" The bald guy cracked open his water bottle and took a swig. "Because Elmore and I have been trying to figure out the mysterious genealogy that landed us here." He stabbed at a piece of meat on his plate and held it aloft with his fork. "What the hell is this?"

I looked at the three of them, as diverse as three people could get. "I'm still kind of vague on what the hell we're all doing here. Or even where *here* is."

Hal wiped his mouth with a paper napkin. "It's pretty simple. Apparently, we're all descendants of Greek gods or heroes, and we all suck at life. That's kind of a good news, bad news thing."

I eyed Elmore, who was shoveling brown muck into his mouth. "None of us look especially Greek. Anybody know who the god in their family is?"

Jilly shook her red curls. "My parents are both completely normal humans disappointed in their daughter's lack of direction."

Hal shrugged. "My parents are long gone. They died in a car accident when I was sixteen."

Elmore came up for air and sipped his Coke. "Adopted." He went back to eating.

Jilly made a face, then slid her plate of goop over to him. "What about you, Wynter? Parents?"

"One. My mother is eccentric, but hardly godlike. I don't know anything about my father. I never knew him." I tasted my macaroni and cheese. It was gritty and had some sort of meat-like substance in it. I slid the plate to Elmore.

I'd have to pay Mom a visit. She'd never given me a straight answer before when I asked about my father. But that would have to change.

For the rest of lunch, we all avoided talking about the second thing that had apparently put us there—our supreme, rock-bottom sucktitude. I didn't blame any of them for not bringing it up. I didn't much feel like talking about my ongoing battle with quitting everything I touched.

Including my disgusting lunch. I ate the peaches out of my fruit cup, but nothing else looked like anything I recognized. Even the peaches were questionable.

They tasted a lot like regret for having missed the fabled donuts earlier.

On our way back to Thebes, we passed through the lobby. Phyllis still sat on a table next to the rubber tree plant, both of them waving their leaves in animated conversation. Patrice looked my way, and I ducked my head.

At any moment, I'd wake up from this bizarre dream, late for work at my crappy call-center job, knowing I still needed to break up with Freddy over lunch. That had to be the answer, because none of this was real. It couldn't be.

I averted my eyes as a winged lion with the head of a woman sauntered past pushing a mail cart.

Nope. Not real. Not possible.

And yet, with no other plan, I continued forward, following my new acquaintances back to the conference room labeled Thebes. Because, why the hell not? If nothing else, the nasty mac and cheese had left a very real taste in my mouth to prove its existence.

We all returned to the seats we'd been in earlier, and Mrs. Moros waited while we got settled.

"For the rest of today," she said, "we'll watch a filmstrip that gives a history lesson. You need to be acquainted with the gods and goddesses in order to understand the various departments."

Filmstrips? What year are we in, 1960? What are we, twelve?

She swung around and glared at me. "That's two."

I slunk down in my seat. I didn't know what happened at *three*, but it couldn't be good.

Mrs. Moros scowled and paced as she spoke. "Tomorrow you will return here to receive the first of your placement tests. Throughout the week, you'll be assessed for your knowledge, abilities, and intelligence."

She stopped pacing and managed to glare at the entire room at once. "I don't expect all of you to make the cut."

Without another word, she flipped a switch. The room went dark, and a movie started.

It wasn't a Hollywood blockbuster, but it wasn't an actual filmstrip, either. I really did feel like I was back in high school. Mrs. Moros left, and we watched a movie. If I were in school, I'd assume she went for a smoke.

Since I wasn't in school and this place was weird as hell, I thought it was more likely that she'd left to trick us and was actually in the room, invisible, watching to see who paid attention.

Paranoid? Sure. But a snake lady served me a vile lunch, and I walked past a sphinx coming back to the room. A little paranoia was warranted.

The movie went over all the basic Greek gods, which I mostly remembered from school and stories Mom read to me when I was little. Then it explained the mission of the Mount Olympus Employment Agency.

First, to guide humans to their greatest good. And second, to provide a life purpose to the bastard children of the gods.

Bastard. Nice. I'd thought that word had gone out of style other than as a general name for people who cut me off in traffic. I'd have to try it out in front of Mom and see if it helped me get any more information out of her about my father.

I didn't know what I'd expected. More call center work, I supposed. General office drone stuff. Maybe placement in a retail location. I didn't know for sure. When I heard *employment agency*, I assumed it would be temp work. This was something else altogether.

The departments were familiar, but only from stories, not as actual jobs. The Furies department dispensed justice. The Fates department was responsible for planning—though I was hazy on what they planned. The Muse department provided inspiration. Graces, Oracles, Dreams, Cupids…my head spun with all the possible jobs I might be placed in. None of them seemed inviting. And the sad truth of it was, I wasn't particularly good at anything.

Chances were, I'd wash out and be assigned to the cafeteria. If that happened, Phyllis was getting a good pruning.

When the movie was over, the lights came on by themselves, and we all looked around. Mrs. Moros wasn't in the room, and she'd given no instructions as to what to do. We waited. Gradually, first in whispers, then a little louder, the crowd grew restless.

Hal was the first to make a decision. He hauled himself out of his chair, stretched, then gathered his things. "We waited. I know it's only three, but I'm done. See you folks in the morning."

The door swung shut behind him, and we sat frozen with indecision. One person wasn't enough to cause a mass exodus.

A woman with dark hair and thick glasses stood and gathered her purse. "My kids will be home soon. If she's not going to give us further instructions, I could use the time to scrape some dinner together." She turned to a younger woman next to her. "You need a ride?"

Before the two women were out the door, three more people were packing up to go.

I didn't want to be the first to leave, but I sure didn't want to be the last, either. I waited until a group of five was walking out and ducked into the crowd. Nobody stopped us. It seemed ridiculous that I worried some supernatural creature would come storming after us waving a spiked club for leaving orientation early, but the possibility wasn't as out there as it would have been when I'd first arrived.

25

At the lobby, I split off from the group and grabbed Phyllis.

"There you are!" Her leaves fluttered at me in a disconcerting way. "What took you so long? The film should have been finished a half hour ago."

I blinked. "Nobody said we could leave."

Her voice was worried. "Were you the first to go?"

"No."

Her leaves rustled in a sigh of relief. "Good. You weren't the last, either?"

"No. Why?"

"You did well, then. It was a psychological assessment. There will be a lot more this week. Looks like you're doing great, though! Are you ready to go home?"

I tucked her under my arm, thinking of all the things one could do to damage a houseplant. Over-watering. Under-watering. Chemicals. Fire.

I bit my lip. Phyllis was a talker as long as it suited her. But when it came to information I might find useful, she hadn't said a damn word.

I could jam her down the garbage disposal. Drop her in boiling water. Borrow a cat and let it pee in her dirt.

I knew I'd never do anything to harm her, but it was comforting to think about it while I was mad at her for holding out on me.

Phyllis quivered with excitement. "See you tomorrow, Sadie!"

The rubber tree waved at us as we walked out the door.

~*~

I was not late on the second day. My hope was to get through the entire week without being noticed again by Mrs. Moros. I kept my thoughts as quiet as I could, took notes, and didn't squirm.

Fear is the ultimate motivator.

After another vile lunch on day two, our tiny captor sent us to Crete for our first real assessment tests. Not the real Crete, of course. It was a huge lecture hall with writing surfaces that folded out of the armrests. The right armrests, not the left.

Which meant, as a lefty, I had to turn halfway in my seat to use the damn thing, but that wasn't anything new to me. I was a little disappointed that a company as old as Ancient Greece had the same lack of regard for the downtrodden left-handed souls of this world as did the American school system.

Mr. Randall, a skinny man with a mop of black hair on his head, controlled the room. He had an overbite, which left his front teeth peeking from beneath an excellent '70s porn 'stache. He spaced out our group of thirty-two, presumably so no one could cheat, and furnished us each with a thick stack of papers and a pair of number-two pencils.

Trying not to be too obvious, I glanced at my lap to be sure I was fully clothed. Yesterday had proved to be real, but today might as easily be a naked-testing dream. Unfortunately, my black skirt was right where it was supposed to be. Hard to believe I was actually disappointed not to be naked in public. Nope. I was going to have to take the Ancient Greece version of the SATs.

The first section of the test was on the gods, goddesses, and heroes of Greek mythology. Believe it or not, I did pretty well on that part. Mom had raised me on stories of angry goddesses, heroic deeds, and disobedient mortals, much like other kids were brought up on fairy tales. Staring at the questions on my sideways desk, it occurred to me that my entire life had been a series of clues to my mysterious heritage, and that maybe the reason I hadn't lost my mind over the crazy shit I'd seen the last few days was due to my mother preparing me for it all.

Really needed to pay her a visit.

My number-two pencil flew over the page and filled in the lettered bubbles. A) Perseus. C) Hera. D) All of the above. A) Andromeda. I wasn't simply doing pretty well. I was sailing through it. Mom was either getting flowers or a rant from me when I saw her. Probably both.

Long before Porn 'Stache Randall called time on the first section, I'd already finished and checked over my answers. A few people around the room groaned. Papers shuffled.

"Please turn your booklets to section two. Do not begin until I instruct you to do so." Randall the Whisker-faced clasped his hands behind his back and sniffed so hard I worried his moustache would disappear up his nose. He perched on the edge of a desk and stared at his watch long enough to make everyone uncomfortable in the silence. "Go!"

The first question in the new section popped the self-satisfied bubble of elation I'd been floating in.

Q1: *Under what circumstances would you reveal yourself to your client?* A. You and your client are already acquainted in everyday life. B. The client is in mortal peril. C. Revelation would assist in completion of the assignment. D. The given assignment is flawed and requires alteration. E. All of the above. F. None of the above.

I hovered my pencil between mortal danger, all of the above, and none of the above. How the hell was I supposed to know anything about company policy? The question didn't even mean anything to me in the first place. Clients? Revelation?

Greek mythology had been a fun little trivia quiz, but this made no damn sense at all. I thought I was training for some sort of office job. Possibly even factory or retail work. Clients? I sucked at working with clients.

The best I could hope for was to wash out before the end of the week so I wouldn't have to follow through with any of it. But then, I'd be back to where I'd started, with no job, no money for the next month's rent, and the very real threat of having to move in with my mother. Again.

I sighed and chose "All of the above." Then I erased it and chose "Mortal peril."

The rest of the questions weren't much easier or less mysterious. Several questions dealt with the etiquette of mounting a winged horse. Another wanted my opinion on love at first sight. Three questions were devoted to my possible knowledge of arts and crafts, and two had to do with Ouija boards and tarot cards.

There was no rhyme or reason to the section. None. And the answers could have been any of the choices given.

When Moustache Randy called time, I'd only made it through three-quarters of the section. On the bright side, that was it for the day. I'd expected more sections, but apparently two were enough.

We all filed to the front and handed over our bizarre tests and our number-two pencils. Oddly enough, Randall seemed more concerned that he should receive *all* the pencils than he was that the tests came in.

"Mr. Turnbrook." His beady eyes followed a short, blond man on his way out the door. "*Two* pencils, if you please."

Mr. Turnbrook—I thought his name was Steve, but I wasn't sure—rummaged in his back pocket and found the second pencil. "Sorry." His brow wrinkled, and he shrugged as if he'd genuinely forgotten but didn't see what the big deal was.

Randall sniffed again. That moustache must've had a hell of a root system to stay anchored like that.

Under Randall's watchful eye, I dropped both pencils into the box on the table and placed my test booklets and answer sheets in their proper piles. My steps were measured and careful as I left the lecture hall. If I didn't keep control of myself, I'd bolt down the hall, through the building, and out to my car—possibly cackling like a crazy woman the entire way.

A few people gathered in a group, griping in hushed voices. I grimaced at them on the way past to express solidarity, but I didn't stop. In the reception rotunda, I scooped up my potted companion and strode out the door without a word.

"Well, that was rude," Phyllis said as I shoved her into the car and wedged her in between the bucket seats so she wouldn't topple over in traffic. "You didn't even give me a chance to say goodbye to Madge."

I didn't have any idea who Madge was. As far as I'd seen, Phyllis had been sitting by herself on a shelf with no humans or plants around her. I didn't care enough to ask, though, and pulled away from the curb without a word.

"I had a lovely day, thank you for asking, Wynter." Phyllis slapped me on the arm with one of her braches. "I know you're listening. Don't make me sing to you, sweetheart. Tell me how your day was."

I glanced at her quivering leaves and back at the road. "It was a big, fat, stupid waste of time. How the hell should I know whether you're supposed to feed marshmallows to a flying horse after it's taken a dump? Why would I ever need to know that?"

Phyllis's leaves shook and she emitted an odd, high-pitched giggle. "Are you concerned about your score?"

I scowled. "No. I just don't see why they made me answer questions that made me look stupid."

"Oh, honey. Everyone looks stupid when they take that test. That's part of why they give it."

I snorted. "Excellent. You've dragged me into a workplace that intentionally demeans me. I might as well sling burgers. At least there I might retain some dignity."

Phyllis sighed. "Be patient, Wynter. By Friday, the assessments will be over and you'll get your assignment. I'm terribly excited for you!"

"It's only Tuesday. Can you at least tell me what to expect tomorrow?"

She was quiet for a moment. "I suppose it won't hurt to tell you a little."

"Thank you." Finally, we were getting somewhere. "More tests?"

"Of sorts."

I turned onto the turnpike and headed east. "What does that mean?"

"Tomorrow is a little different." She drew her words out, obviously stalling.

My grip on the steering wheel turned my knuckles white. "Different how?"

"Well…tomorrow is the physical challenge."

I dropped my head back against the seat. "Seriously?"

She sighed again. "Of course, dear. If they don't assess your physical abilities, how can they tell which jobs won't kill you?"

Chapter 4

An hour later, I pulled into my mother's driveway, grabbed my talking plant, and stepped out of the car.

On my way up the walkway, I nodded at a ceramic garden gnome riding a lawn flamingo. "Frank, good to see you, buddy."

For a split second, the sun glinted off the statue and made it look as if he'd winked. I glanced away quickly and kept walking. Frank gave no other indication of coming to life and answering me—he never had before when I'd greeted him but my understanding of what was real and what was make believe had become a little skewed. If my mother's tacky yard decorations were about to come to life, I didn't want to be around to see it.

A person can only take so many impossible things in a single week.

As always, I paused at the front door and debated whether to walk in or knock. Mom always made faces at me if she had to answer the door, reminding me that I have a key for a reason. But what if she had a boyfriend in there and they were getting freaky? Or she'd decided to become a nudist—again. Or had the furnace cranked up and was in her underwear doing hot yoga?

I raised my knuckles to knock, then changed my mind. Whatever my mother was doing, it was bound to be something most other moms wouldn't be doing. She'd think nothing of throwing the door open, stark naked, while the neighbors watered the lawn across the street.

She wasn't an exhibitionist, really. And she wasn't vain. She simply had this odd way of assuming that whatever she was currently into would be interesting—or at least considered perfectly normal—to everyone else.

I patted the flowerpot under my arm. "Well, Phyllis. We might as well find out what she's doing today. Brace yourself."

"I'm sure she's lovely," Phyllis said.

"Uh huh." I lifted my chin, bracing for the worst, then opened the unlocked front door and stepped inside.

No matter how much I prepared myself for what my mother might be doing, I was never fully ready.

The light in the living room was so bright I had to squint until my eyes grew accustomed to it. The overhead light was on, and every surface held a table lamp with the brightest possible bulbs screwed into them.

Mom was in the dead center of the room on her elbows and knees, nose nearly pressed into the carpet. Her lips moved, and she whispered something I couldn't hear. I waited for her to pause, not wanting to interrupt whatever the hell was going on.

I honestly couldn't even make a guess.

After a few minutes, she inched forward a bit, then sat up, stretching her neck. I pressed my lips together hard to keep from laughing.

Mom blinked at me through the thickest lenses I'd ever seen. Her eyes appeared to be three times the size of her head. "Wynter. When did you get here?"

"A few minutes ago." I stepped away from the wall I'd been leaning against. "Whatcha doin'?" I tried to keep my voice light and curious instead of loud and demanding.

Everyone who met my mom thought she was adorable and eccentric. Try living with her for twenty-four years. Exhausting was a more fitting description after that long.

Mom blinked her enormous eyes again and showed me the tweezers she held in her right hand. "I'm re-tufting the carpet. What else would I be doing?"

What else, indeed.

I squinted at the white shag carpet behind her and didn't see any difference. "Looks great. You must've been working at it for a long time."

She wiped her brow with the back of her hand. "I guess. What time is it?"

I glanced at the clock over the fireplace. "Four thirty. I got out of work early."

"That's nice. How are things at the bank? Did you get that promotion I told you to go for?" She pushed herself up from the floor, looking a little wobbly.

I shook my head. "I left the bank months ago to work at that call center. Remember?"

She stretched her arms in the air, then swung them side to side. "Okay. So how's the call center going?"

"I hated it and quit last week." My stomach knotted at the look on her face. Here she was crawling around on the floor with binocular glasses and a pair of tweezers fluffing her carpet one tuft at a time. B. But I was the one who was the disappointment.

She took her ridiculous glasses off and set them on a side table with the tweezers. "Oh, Wynter." She sighed and perched on the edge of the sofa. "I didn't change anything in your room. You can move back in anytime. But honestly, you've got to find something that makes you happy. Something you can stick to."

I held Phyllis close against my body and looked at my feet. "I found a new job already."

"Oh?" She didn't look up at me while she busied herself with the very serious business of spreading her magazines across the coffee table in a perfect fan. "What are you doing now?"

Should I tell her about my impossible new employer? What about the talking plant? Did she know about all that stuff? Surely she would have told me by now if she did.

"I started training at an employment agency yesterday."

That made her look up, and I watched her face for any signs she knew what I was talking about.

She frowned. "A temp agency isn't a dependable source of income, Wynter. What if the work dries up? What if they have nothing for you?"

"It's not like that, Mom. It's more like I'll be working for the agency. It's not temporary."

Mom gave me a long look, then shrugged. "You know best, I guess. I'll keep your room waiting, just in case."

"Thanks." My voice was quiet. She didn't mean to hurt my feelings, but she had. Hard to believe in yourself if even your mom expects you to fail.

I set Phyllis on a table and sat in the stiff, pink satin chair in the opposite corner of the room from where Mom sat.

She straightened the lace doily on the arm of the sofa. "Well, I hope you enjoy the new job. How's Freddy?"

I froze.

I shouldn't have come. Screw it. I'll grab my talking plant and leave. Maybe Mom will forget I was ever here.

In the end, I decided to ignore the question and pose one of my own, instead. "Mom, who's my dad?"

She tilted her head at me, a mild look on her face. "What an odd question, out of the blue like that. I've told you about him before."

Sure she had. And every damn time he was somebody different.

"It was a security clearance question on my job application," I said.

"Oh." She smiled and smoothed her yoga pants over her long, dancer legs. "Well, you know. He was a fireman named Vince. Vince Clothos. He died a hero, you know. Ran into a burning hospital and rescued twenty-three people—fourteen of them children—before finally succumbing to the flames." She sighed for dramatic effect, a faraway look on her face. "He had beautiful eyes. Green. Like yours."

"Mom, my eyes are blue."

She didn't alter her nostalgic expression. "Blue. Like yours."

Nope. Today was not the day I would get the true story of my conception. What I did know for sure, thanks to my new job, was that he was a Greek god—or at least a descendent. But had she known? She must have, raising me on Greek stories like she had. That couldn't have been a coincidence.

Could it?

I moved to the couch and took one of her hands in mine. "Mom, was there anything…special about him?"

She smiled. "Of course. He was very special."

"No, I don't mean like that. I mean, did he have any special, uh, skills? Could he do anything you wouldn't expect a person to be able to do?"

She blushed all the way to her blonde roots. "Nothing I think we should talk about."

That was so not what I meant. I gave up. Maybe next time she'd slip up and give me something useful about my father. If he was only a descendent of a god and not the god himself, maybe he didn't know anything about his lineage either. I sure hadn't.

I let go of her hand and tucked mine between my knees. "So. What made you decide to freshen up the carpet?"

"Oh, it was about time, is all. They say you should really do it once every three years, at the very least."

What the hell kind of magazines is she reading? I glanced at the array of periodicals on the coffee table. *Better Homes and Gardens* probably advised a good steaming, but not the crazy operation she had going.

Phyllis was silent through all of this. I picked her up and held her in my lap. She didn't move, but her presence eased some of the tension I was feeling.

Mom didn't seem to think it was odd for me to be toting a houseplant around. Maybe she figured I was picking up some of her eccentricity.

"Mom, do you believe in magic?"

She gave me an odd look. "I believe in the magic of love. And the way my flowers bloom every spring. A baby's laugh. Is that what you mean?"

I scrunched my face in thought. "Not exactly. Like, magical creatures. The ability to fly. That sort of thing."

Her expression looked worried. "Are you feeling well, Wynter? You're not coming down with something, are you? It's too soon to call in sick at a new job." She rose from the couch, hands fluttering. "Let me get you some Echinacea. I'll juice you a pineapple and some ginger."

"No. Mom. I'm fine." I tried to grab her as she brushed past me, but I missed. Shrugging, I got up and followed her into the kitchen. If Mom felt like I needed an immunity boost, she wasn't going to stop until vitamin C leaked out my ears.

I watched as she chopped the top and bottom off a pineapple, then cut away the skin and cored it before slicing it into spears. She rinsed a considerable chunk of ginger in the sink, as well as a pear, which she cut into quarters. Her hands worked in precise movements as she peeled a lime, then fed everything into a very loud juicer. Within a minute, she handed me a frothy glass of juice with so much fresh ginger in it, my mouth and throat burned when I took a sip.

I grimaced and my voice was strained. "Thanks."

She rattled around in a cupboard, opening bottles and jars, then handed me a handful of pills. "Take these."

There was no use arguing. It wasn't as if she was handing me a bunch of drugs. Mom was strictly a home-remedy girl. And with all the stress in my life, my immune system could probably have used the boost anyway. I tossed the pills to the back of my throat and sucked the spicy juice through a straw to help me swallow.

They didn't go down easily, but they went down. Having lived with Mom most of my life, I'd learned to swallow a lot of difficult things—supplements, cooked dishes I couldn't identify, and raw, squiggly things best left unnamed.

My stomach was like iron.

We returned to the living room, and Mom had me sit on the couch while she returned to crawling around on the floor with crazy-thick glasses and a pair of tweezers. I watched her for a while, sipping my juice and wondering how I managed to grow up as normal as I did.

I glanced at the silent philodendron I'd brought with me like a security blanket. Maybe I wasn't so normal after all.

I cleared my throat. "Mom. Do you remember when I got this plant?"

She lifted her nose out of the carpet fibers and blinked at me with her magnified eyes. She flicked her strange gaze at Phyllis and back to me. "No." She returned to tugging and twisting the thread she'd captured between her tweezers.

"Sure you do. Some lady came out of nowhere and gave it to me at the farmers market a couple years back. Then she vanished into the crowd. I told you about it."

Mom shrugged and spoke into the floor. "Maybe you did. I don't remember everything you tell me, Wynter."

No, that was true. Mom was more forgetful every year, it seemed. "Could you take a look at her—it—please? You're better with plants than I am, and I'm worried she's—it's—not getting everything it needs. Does she need more sunlight? More water?"

Mom made an annoyed sound and lifted her head. "It looks fine. Nice and green. Bushy. No dry tips. You're doing fine."

I swallowed my irritation. "Could you just *look*?"

Grunting, she picked herself up from the floor and moved to the table that held my currently silent plant. Mom didn't remove her ridiculous glasses while she examined Phyllis in depth, touching leaves and prodding soil.

She frowned. "Well, that's odd."

My heart rate sped up. "What? What did you find?" I bit my lip, waiting for her to tell me my plant had a pulse or there were tiny feet and hands growing underneath the leaves. Something—anything—weird.

"Is this the pot it came in two years ago?" She held it in the air and peered at the bottom.

"Yeah. Why?"

"You've had it for two years in this same pot, and it never occurred to you to give it more room? The root system is so cramped, it's poking through the drainage holes on the bottom. You should be ashamed of yourself. I taught you better than that. I have no idea how this plant is even alive."

I felt terrible. I did know better, too. But for some reason, I'd never thought to transplant Phyllis. "Guess I got busy and didn't think about it."

Mom scowled at me. "You stay here. I'll be right back." She left the room, cradling Phyllis and murmuring to her. The back door opened and closed, letting me know Mom had gone out to her greenhouse.

I sipped my drink, consumed with guilt and wondering why Phyllis hadn't told me she needed more room.

Ten minutes later, Mom came back in the house with Phyllis seated in a much larger, much gaudier pot. Mom's fingers were dark with potting soil, and she smelled like fresh dirt and things that grow.

She handed Phyllis to me. "I gave her some fertilizer, too. See those pale leaves coming in? She needed nutrients. Still, you're doing a pretty good job." She patted my arm and smiled. "Keep it up."

I pulled the plant close to my chest. "Thanks for sorting her out for me." I kissed Mom's cheek. "Guess I'd better go home, since I've got work in the morning."

Mom walked out the front door with me, then stopped. She squinted at me, her expression vague. "How are things at the bank? Did you get the promotion?"

My heart sank. "No, Mom. I changed jobs. I'll come back soon and tell you all about it." I gave her a one-armed hug.

She frowned. "That's a shame. Your father was a banker. His name was John. John McClane. He'd have loved it if you'd followed in his footsteps." She shrugged. "Well, drive, safely!"

She turned and disappeared into the house.

I frowned at the yard gnome frozen next to me. "Look after her for me, Frank."

Mom was getting worse.

Chapter 5

Physical assessment didn't begin to touch what they put us through on Wednesday. We hiked the side of a mockup of the real Mount Olympus. We stood in a long line for the opportunity to push a foam boulder up a tall hill like the punishment of Sisyphus. We ran around a gym passing a flaming torch back and forth. So stupid. And the muscles in my ass were on fire after that boulder thing. It was heavier than it looked.

At least they gave us gym clothes and access to showers. Sensible or not, my heels were not built for extreme sports.

No matter how difficult it was, I kept my thoughts focused on the task, not on my aching muscles and pounding heart rate. Mrs. Moros was our testing instructor for the day, and I didn't want her yelling at me for thinking about how much it hurt. As Moros said several time to other students who weren't nearly as focused as I was trying to be, control your thoughts, control your life.

I was learning *something*, at least.

At lunch, my three new friends and I gathered in the cafeteria over tiny Styrofoam bowls of thin vegetable soup, shoe-leather roast beef drowning in lumpy gravy, mushy Brussels sprouts, and some sort of burned rice casserole.

None of us shared a bite with poor Elmore this time. As nasty as the food was, I was starving from all the exertion, and apparently so was everyone else. Elmore had to go back for seconds.

Jillian slumped in her chair. "I can't go back in there. I can barely walk."

Hal stared at his empty plate, glassy-eyed. "I ate all of it. What the hell? I can't eat like that. It's bad for my blood pressure, all that sodium and cholesterol. I'll have a heart attack if I have to run or climb one more step." He groaned. "That's it. They're trying to kill me—weed out the weak and the old." He used his napkin to mop the sweat from his bald head.

Elmore slurped his soup. "I heard the next part is all upper body stuff." He held up his arm. "I'm too skinny to lift, guys."

I listened to them complain while my feet throbbed and my ass ached in the uncomfortable booth. They sounded so defeated. I wasn't too happy either, but I wasn't ready to throw in the towel, yet.

"Come on, guys. This sucks ass. We all know it. But look around and out in the lobby. All those people survived it. We can, too. And if we try harder and complain less than most of the other people in our class, we're bound to get the better jobs, right?"

Jilly sat up a little straighter. "You think so?"

I nodded. "I do. Hal's right."

His eyebrows rose in surprise. "They *are* trying to kill us?"

"No. I think they're trying to weed out the weak people." I narrowed my eyes at my tablemates. "And we're not those people."

The second half of the day was no less strenuous than the first, but this time, Hal, Jilly, and Elmore formed a sort of pack with me, and we stayed ahead of everyone else. We were wolves, not sheep. We would not be culled.

Elmore's rumors had been correct. We did a lot of boat rowing the first hour, back and forth across a murky, dark river that had been hidden under the gymnasium floor. Hal did especially well and coached Jilly, Elmore, and me so we'd get the rhythm right.

The hour after that, we paired up and took turns holding or winding an enormous, heavy ball of thread that we couldn't allow to touch the floor or any part of our own bodies besides our hands. My arms quivered with the strain of holding it out for Hal to wind, and I dropped it twice.

The final hour saw us all in harnesses, floating in midair. At first, it was fun, and I thought the test was passive. The minute I relaxed to enjoy it, I flipped upside down, dangling six feet from the floor.

"Help!" I struggled to right myself, finally getting the momentum I needed to spin back around. It was a test of balance and core strength, and I had to focus to remain upright.

All around me, others flipped over, asses in the air and faces toward the ground.

Mrs. Moros strolled across the floor with a pointed stick, poking at bellies. "Up," she shouted. "Pull yourself back up. What are you, a mortal? You have the blood of gods and heroes in you! You should all be able to do this!"

Most of them figured it out—Elmore was already up, and Jilly was nearly there. Not everyone was close, though.

Hal wasn't far away from me, and he struggled, hands fisted and arms flailing, trying to swing around by sheer will.

"Hal. Stop." I waited until he relaxed and turned his head toward me. "Take a deep breath. Focus on your center. Breathe."

"I can't do it, Wynter." His face was bright pink from the blood rushing there.

"You *can*, Hal. Come on. Relax."

"One more try, but I swear, I'm done." He dropped his hands toward the floor and inhaled a few times.

"Use your stomach muscles to guide you. You can do this. It's more about balance than strength. Don't force it. Focus it."

Jilly had been close already, and my words may have helped. She flipped upright, grinning. "Hey! That wasn't so bad."

Elmore swung himself toward her and gave her a high five. "Nice going."

Hal strained for a moment, then relaxed. He drew himself up, as if sitting up in bed. "Oh." His eyes grew wide. "I did it." He relaxed too much and started for fall forward, but caught himself.

Mrs. Moros stood beneath me with her stick, head tilted a little. I kept my mind blank. She made a gruff sound, then moved to poke a few more people.

Some of the folks in our class never did get the hang of it. One woman, petite with dark skin and fantastic braids all over her head, was a natural. She made us all look like uncoordinated oafs. She did forward rolls and backward rolls. She swung herself to the wall and climbed to an overhead beam where she did a graceful pirouette and somersaulted off, allowing the harness to catch her.

I found out later she'd been a dancer until she gave it up to run off with some guy who eventually dumped her.

Rock bottom. Every one of us.

After an hour or so in the harnesses, right about when I realized I'd probably be saddle sore on top of everything else, Mrs. Moros hit a button and lowered us all to the floor.

"Go home." She moved through the class, unbuckling each of us. "Take some ibuprofen, a hot shower, and maybe ice the places that hurt the most. Get some sleep. Don't come back until Friday."

We glanced at each other in surprise, making sure everyone had heard the same thing.

Someone in the back of the crowd squeaked out the question we all wanted to ask. "We have tomorrow off?"

R.L. NAQUIN

She gave a curt nod. "Tomorrow the placement team will go over your test scores and evaluations. Friday morning you'll receive your assignments and be taken to your new departments."

"Unless we washed out," Hal whispered.

Mrs. Moros snapped her head around to glare at him. "No one washes out in my orientation class. Some assignments are simply more desirable than others." She spread her gaze over all of us. "If you think you're leaving the company now, you'll have to think again. I suggest if any of you are unsure of this, you spend your day off reading your copy of the contract you signed." Her words were clipped. "Nine on Friday." She turned and strode from the gym, leaving us all to wonder what the hell we'd signed.

~*~

I slept late on Thursday and woke up so stiff it took me ten minutes to achieve an upright position. After I grabbed some yogurt and made coffee, I sat down to examine the contract.

I hadn't read it. I freely admit I'd been stupid about that. But to be fair, I'd been scared to death of the gorgon who'd given it to me, and my houseplant had told me to do it.

Not an argument that would hold up in court, though. I was probably screwed.

The contract wasn't huge, so it didn't take long to find what I was looking for. In essence, I'd signed a three-year contract which gave them access to my bank account, credit cards, phone records, financial statements—everything. As long as I worked for the agency for the next three years, money would be deposited in my account. If I tried to break the contract, they'd take everything I had, including my car title and the lease to my apartment. I'd have nothing and have nowhere to live.

Harsh.

I scrubbed my face in my hands. Too late to do anything about it now. I gathered my spoon and empty yogurt container and took it to the kitchen, tossing a nasty look at Phyllis on my way past.

She'd been refreshingly quiet since I'd asked her about the contract on our way home the night before.

I tossed the container in the trash, rinsed the spoon, and set it in the sink. The kitchen was dark, so I pulled the curtain aside to let in some light. Movement caught my eye, and I peered into the courtyard.

That guy—Mitch? Mark?—stood outside his apartment with a bottle of window cleaner and paper towels. I leaned against the sink and watched his

42

muscles flex as he scrubbed at a stubborn spot on the glass of his back door. Did he always wear shirts that tight? Why hadn't I noticed him before?

Something made him turn and look at my window, and I froze. He waved his wad of paper towels at me and smiled. Not knowing what else to do, I grabbed the sponge in the sink and waved it back at him.

That's right. Standing here doing dishes. Not staring at rippling muscles. Nope. Just doing a little cleaning of my own.

The smile on my face felt strained. I hoped it looked genuine from across the courtyard and not like I'd swallowed a bug.

He turned back to his work, and I ducked out of the window before he could catch me watching again.

Honestly, he wasn't my type. First of all, I preferred blonds with power haircuts. His hair was a dark chestnut that fell over his eyes when he leaned over. I liked suits and ties, not jeans and tight T-shirts. Blue eyes, not dark chocolate.

I shrugged. Besides. I'd only broken up with Freddy less than a week before. I had enough problems without adding a guy into the whole thing. Especially not one that lived across the courtyard. They have a phrase for that: don't shit where you eat.

My relationship status needed to remain single for a little while before I made another spectacular mess of things.

I glanced at my phone sitting on the kitchen counter. No messages. No missed calls. Freddy had continued leaving voicemail, sending alternating angry and sad texts, and even pictures of himself with his dog. I'd kept to the one-week rule, but it hadn't been easy. I felt terrible, but honestly, I'd told him I wouldn't answer him. He simply hadn't believed me.

Now it was one day before the week was over, and he'd finally gotten the message.

I rubbed the front of my phone with the hem of my shirt, smoothing out the smudges and fingerprints. A tiny twinge of regret hit me, and I brushed it aside. Freddy wasn't The One. And even if there was no such thing as The One, Freddy still wasn't someone I could be happy with long-term.

I sighed and slid my phone in my pocket. Maybe he'd given up and wouldn't start calling again. Maybe he'd gotten the message finally.

The rest of the day I moved slowly. I caught up on laundry, soaked my aching muscles in the tub, and even ventured out to buy groceries to fill my refrigerator and cupboards.

I'd set Phyllis in the kitchen window to get some sun while I was gone. When I came inside, plastic bags cutting off the circulation in the fingers of both hands, Phyllis curled and uncurled her leaves as if I'd woken her from a nap and she was stretching.

Her greenery brushed together, making a soft shushing. "That was quick. Did you get anything healthy this time?"

I winced as I lifted my sore arms to put the bags on the counter. "I bought vegetables, among other things. I'm making progress."

"It's a start." Phyllis sniffed, which was a weird sound, coming from a plant. "You're not doing the planet any favors with those plastic bags, though."

I scowled and shoved a package of powdered sugar donuts in the cupboard. "If you're so worried about it, help me out. Remind me to take the reusable bags with me instead of leaving them on the table. Again."

She was quiet while I put milk and carrots in the fridge, but I saw her twitch a branch when the package of cookies came out of the bag. Eggs and a brick of cheddar cheese were fine, I supposed, but the ice cream seemed to be the last straw.

Phyllis groaned. "Honestly, Wynter. One bag of carrots doesn't mean you bought healthy food."

I ignored her and put away the rest of the groceries. "Now that you can tell me what you need, *do* you need anything? Fertilizer? More water? I felt terrible when Mom replanted you. Why didn't you tell me you were crowded in that old pot?"

Several leaves rose and fell in what I thought must be a shrug. "You'd figure it out eventually. We've been together for two years. You never leave me uncomfortable for long."

I didn't feel like I deserved her gracious attitude. I'd ignored too many things lately. "Well, make sure you tell me next time, okay? Now that you can talk, it should be for more than sea shanties and television theme songs."

"I don't see why you can't appreciate my musical gifts, Wynter. I'll have you know, I once trained with—"

She stopped so suddenly, I moved toward her and looked out the window to see what had stolen her attention.

Mark or Mack or whatever his name was, stood in the courtyard with his shirt off this time, spray painting a stack of old tires.

I slid Phyllis to one side of the windowsill to get a better look. "What the hell is he doing now?"

The plant spoke in a whisper next to my ear. "Do you suppose he's suffering from a brain injury?"

I didn't answer as I pressed my face closer to the glass. His muscles flexed when he stopped to shake the can. He turned and looked right at me, and I ducked under the cabinet.

"Well, now you've done it," Phyllis said, chuckling. "Now he'll think you're interested."

I groaned and covered my face. I'd just broken up with my boyfriend, started a new job, and found out the world was a much different place than what I'd always believed it to be. Getting cozy with the half-naked neighbor next door was not on the agenda. That was the last thing I needed.

In fact, all things considered, I probably needed to stay off the dating circuit.

Possibly for good.

Chapter 6

Friday morning my muscles ached worse than they had the day before. I sat in the same room we'd started in on Monday, in the same chair in the front row, and tried like hell not to squirm. If I could make it through the day without pissing off Mrs. Moros, I could say I survived boot camp.

We'd all arrived early, and Moros wasn't there yet. I turned in my seat and checked on my lunch buddies. Jilly had her hands in her lap, one hand clutching the other as if she was afraid they might fly away. Her normally cheerful face was sober. When she caught me looking at her, she forced a wan smile.

A few people over from her, Elmore sat slouched in his chair, arms folded, and one agitated foot jiggling over the opposite knee. He shrugged at me and jiggled faster.

Poor Hal looked defeated. He sat at the other end of the front row, shoulders sagging. He stared at a piece of carpet a few feet in front of him without looking up.

I frowned and faced front, wincing at my sore muscles. Was the job assignment thing that serious? Sure, I'd be stuck with it for the next three years, but it wasn't as if my entire life depended on where they sent me. Seriously. A job was a job—not that I'd ever lasted at a single job for three consecutive years. The longest I'd stayed in one position was four months at as a grocery clerk, and that was because I'd been dating my manager.

Everyone was acting like we were waiting to find out which ones of us would be chained to a rock and sacrificed to the Kraken.

I smirked. Good thing I wasn't a virgin. I'd make a lousy maiden sacrifice.

"Don't be ridiculous, Wynter." Mrs. Moros swooped into the room in time to humiliate me with her mind-reading mojo. "The Kraken is a pescetarian. He gave up maidens centuries ago. They made him gassy." She eyed me up and down over her rhinestone-encrusted glasses. "The purity of his meals was never an issue, though. So, your reckless lifestyle wouldn't have kept you safe, I'm afraid."

I slunk down in my chair and tried hard not to think anything else she could embarrass me with. I stared at the wall behind her and concentrated on pink elephants in tutus until her attention went elsewhere.

Mrs. Moros pursed her lips and graced the entire room with a sweeping scowl. "As the rest of you know, this day is going to affect your lives in ways you can't even guess at. I won't leave you in suspense. In a few moments, a human resources representative will bring us your assignments."

All around me were sharp intakes of breath and nervous shuffling. When I'd woken up this morning, I'd been more relieved to be done with orientation and testing. Now, thanks to the tension in the room, I realized I should have been more focused on where I was going next. My stomach clenched with the anxiety everyone else had already been feeling.

Better late than never.

Moros picked a piece of lint off the arm of her lime-green jogging suit and cleared her throat. "Ah. Ben. Come in."

A good-looking guy with dark hair and a pleasant smile stepped into the room with an armful of manila envelopes. "I'm sure everyone's been waiting for these all week."

A nervous twitter came from the small crowd.

Ben stood beside Moros. "Since I don't know any of you yet, I'll call out your names, and you can come grab your envelope. Feel free to open it up when you get back to your seat. I know how much you want to know where you're going."

The very first name Ben called was Hal's. Poor Hal sat frozen in his seat, eyes wide. After a moment, it was clear he wasn't going to respond. Moros elbowed Ben and lifted her chin toward Hal so Ben could walk the four steps over and deliver it himself.

Hal took the envelope with a shaking hand. He lifted the flap and pulled the paperwork out, his face a neutral mask. Once he'd read the top of the first page, he gave a single nod, slipped the paperwork back into the envelope, and sat staring at the wall with that same neutral expression.

I couldn't tell if he was relieved or about to face his death. He was unreadable.

The rest of the assignments went out quickly after that, and squeals of excitement mingled with groans of disappointment.

Elmore opened his envelope and let out a lungful of air. He grinned at me.

Jilly looked shocked, though not exactly unhappy, either.

Ben got to the bottom of the pile. "Wynter Greene?" He smiled as I took the package from him. "All right. Well, that's the last one. I'm sure you'll want a few minutes to look over your pack and talk to each other. Make sure you exchange information if you've made friends, since you're all going to different departments."

I took a deep breath, then pulled the papers from the envelope.

Congratulations! You've been chosen to join the Muse department.

I couldn't read the rest. A big yellow sticky note covered it. There was a handwritten message on the note.

Please see human resources immediately.

Was I in trouble?

I shoved everything back in its envelope and glanced around. Elmore and Jilly stood with Hal, patting him on the back and giving him brave smiles. I hurried over and joined them.

Jilly gave me a more cheerful smile than the one she'd been giving Hal. "What department did you get? I'm going to the Furies."

The Furies? They dealt in justice and revenge. Jillian Bean was the sweetest, perkiest person I knew. Why would they assign her to such a harsh job?

"Looks like I'm going to be a Muse." I turned to Elmore. "You seemed okay with yours. What'd you get?"

"Courier Service." He shrugged. "I have no idea what that means, but it sounds good to me."

Jilly elbowed me in the ribs and lifted her chin toward Hal. He hadn't moved from his seat and continued to stare at a section of the carpet, as if it might move if he looked away.

I squatted in front of him, making him look at me instead of the floor. "Hey. What's in your envelope? It can't be that bad, Hal. Moros said we can't wash out."

His tired blue eyes looked defeated. "She said that, sure. But I'm being transferred to the Underworld. I washed out, whether she wants to admit it or not."

I swallowed hard. I'd had no idea Hal had been having so much trouble. I knew most of the physical stuff had been rough on him. But he must've been pretty dismal on the written and psychological tests, too. Then again, who knew what criteria the people in charge here used? It was all a big fat mystery.

"Did it at least say what you'll be doing there? Maybe it's not so bad."

He shook his head. "I didn't read past the word *Underworld*. I don't think it matters."

I tugged lightly at the envelope under his palms. "Can I take a look?"

He handed it over without a response.

The paperwork inside was different from mine. Instead of the Mt. Olympus Employment Agency logo of a snow-capped mountain, Hal's stuff bore a flaming gate and the words *Underworld LLC* across the top.

The Orientation and Training team have thoroughly evaluated your qualities and skills and have determined you are a better match for our Underworld offices.

I supposed if I'd read that as the opening line, I might have been freaked, too. Poor Hal. I scanned farther down the page.

...and are pleased to welcome you to the Department of Welcome and Transportation, where you will be assigned the position of Ferryman.

I smiled. "Hal, this is actually pretty cool. I think you need to read the rest of it. I think you'll be happier than you thought."

Hal's hand shook as he took the paper from me and read the rest of the letter. He blinked. "I don't understand."

Jilly frowned at me. "What is it?"

I tried to show excitement so Hal would get that he hadn't washed out. "He's going to be the cool dude in the cowl who rows people across the river for a silver coin."

Elmore's eyebrows rose. "Dude, I would so love that job."

It occurred to me that Elmore would probably love any job they assigned him. How a guy like that could have hit rock bottom to end up in this place was beyond me. Then again, I couldn't imagine how Jilly had ended up there, either.

Hal, I could believe, though. And myself. I'd been on a rock-bottom trajectory for years. The only surprise was that it had taken me so long to finally hit it.

Hal sighed and slid his letter back in its envelope. "I guess that's not so bad. I probably won't see a lot of you guys after this, though." He lifted his head and sat straighter in his chair, his attitude one of a brave man off to be executed. "Anybody got a pen? We'd better exchange numbers now."

~*~

The staff gave us about a half hour to say our goodbyes, take a bathroom break, or whatever we needed to do. While we were busy putting numbers in each other's phones, the back of the room filled up with people who chatted while they waited for us to finish.

Moros went to the front one last time, her rough voice louder than all the conversations going on in the room combined. "Time's up! Everybody move to the back and find the person holding the sign for your new department. Pleasure working with you and all that. Good luck, and try not to screw up." She stepped aside and waved her hand to indicate the back of the room.

The new people lined up, each holding a small sign with departments printed in neat letters. *Cupid. Courier Service. Human Resources. Furies.* On the very end of the long line, a man held up a sign that said *Underworld.* Several people had already joined him. Hal gave us each a quick hug and wandered over.

Jilly and Elmore joined their representatives and left the room with them. The Underworld guy was the only one who had multiples, I supposed because he represented an entire company, not the individual departments. They all left together in a pack.

No matter how many times I read the signs that were left, I couldn't find one that said *Muse.* Twice, I slid my letter out and double checked it. It still said the same thing.

Within minutes, everyone was gone except for Ben. He stood there looking at me and holding up his Human Resources sign. "You must be Wynter."

I nodded. "There's nobody from the Muse department?"

He gave me a reassuring smile. "My office wants to see you first. Didn't you see my sticky note?"

"I saw it. I just didn't think it meant *now.*" My stomach felt like I'd swallowed a rock.

Something about the expression on my face must have made him realize how worried I was. He lowered his sign and patted me on the shoulder. "Stop looking like you're being sent to the principal's office. My boss just wants to talk to you. Someone from Muse will come get you from HR and take you where you need to go."

I readjusted my purse on my shoulder. "But why me? What do they need to talk to me about?"

Ben sighed. "Honestly, nobody told me. But I promise." He crossed his heart. "Nobody's going to yell at you or anything. Will you just come with me?"

I clutched my paperwork against my chest. "Let's get it over with, then."

Ben led me out the door and through a maze of hallways and corridors. After a few turns, I suspected we were following a metallic blue line embedded in the marble floor. When we arrived at a door marked *Mortal Resources,* Ben guided me in, then turned left toward a second door that said

Human Resources. Across the hall, the frosted glass on the door said *Non-human Resources.*

We stepped out of the hallway as a woman came out the other door holding a pile of folders. Half a woman, anyway. The other half, from the waist down, was the back end of a bright orange snake with large, black diamond shapes in scaly rows.

I turned away, trying to keep my face neutral and not show how freaked out I was.

Snake hair. Snake bodies. I'm going to lose my shit if my new boss has a snake head. That's where I draw the line, folks.

Ben took me through a room where a few perfectly normal-looking people waited, then stopped in front of another door.

He gave a sharp knock, turned the knob, and stuck his head inside. "You busy? I brought Wynter Greene."

A woman's voice drifted out. "No, I've got a minute. Thanks, Ben. Send her in."

Ben turned and gave me an encouraging smile. "This is where I leave you. Ms. Eunomia will get you all sorted out." He patted my shoulder. "Good luck!"

My heart sank as I watched him march back the way we came. I was on my own.

I pushed the door open and peered into office.

A dark-haired woman with an olive complexion waved me forward. "Come in. Come in. Shut it behind you and have a seat, Wynter."

I slid into the chair across the desk from her and waited while her long, blue-polished nails clacked on a keyboard. After a moment, she stopped and gave me a long look.

I twitched in my seat. Her gaze felt like a prodding finger.

"So," she said. "You've made it through training and orientation. You got your assignment okay?" She glanced at the envelope I still clutched against my chest.

I nodded. "Yes. The Muse department." I hesitated, then sat up straighter. "Did I do something wrong?"

Again, she fixed me with a long, prodding look. "Wynter, why were you in the Lost orientation group?"

I frowned. "Lost?" Had I been in the wrong room all week? "They told me to follow the line to Thebes. Was that wrong?" My cheeks burned with embarrassment. "Why didn't Mrs. Moros kick me out?"

Ms. Eunomia opened a file in front of her, flipped through the pages, then folded her hands over them on her desk. She cleared her throat.

"Wynter, on your application, you left the field blank where it asks for your father's name. Can you tell me who that is?"

In any other HR office, I'd have pitched a fit over the question. Here, I was mortified at not having an answer. My throat tightened, which made my voice sound small. "I have no idea. My mother won't tell me the truth."

She took a deep breath. "Ah. That explains so much. Well then." She pressed and held a button on her telephone. "Milly, would you call and ask the Muse department to send an escort for Wynter, please?" She released the button.

A voice blasted out of the phone's speaker. "Yes, ma'am."

Ms. Eunomia tilted her head and gave me a smile that felt quite a bit like pity. "Let me explain what's going on."

I gave her a slow nod. "Okay."

"There are two ways to join us here at Mount Olympus. You can manage your life so poorly that you trigger the Welcome Package that's attached to even the smallest percentage of divine or heroic blood."

I sighed. "Like I did."

"Well, yes." She shrugged. "It happens. A lot. That's very common with human/god hybrids. God blood makes for volatile personalities, especially when the blood is diluted by generations of humanity." She paused and took a sip of her coffee. "The other way is to come in as a Legacy. A person who's a direct descendent of a god or hero within no more than three generations can and should be brought in by their divine or heroic parent or grandparent to participate in their heritage."

I loosened my grip on my envelope and leaned forward. "Okay. So, where do those people go?"

She set her coffee down. "Legacies go through a single day of orientation, receive their job assignments, and go to their new departments."

I leaned back in my seat, my aching muscles reminding me not to get too comfortable. "That must be nice."

"Yes," she said, blinking at me. "It would have been very nice for you, had your father been able to bring you directly here. We tested your DNA, as we do with each new hire. You're a first generation mortal, Wynter."

My eyes widened, and my mouth opened and closed like a gasping fish out of water. "I'm the daughter of a god?" My mother was in so much trouble. "Who is he? Do I have powers? Does that make me…" I paused, grasping for the word. "A demigod?"

Ms. Eunomia chuckled. "Demigods went out of style centuries ago, I'm afraid. You're a regular human. The test results didn't indicate anything out of the ordinary." Her expression sobered. "The results couldn't tell us who your father is, either. That's between you and your mother." She closed my file and gave me a sad look. "And until she does, I can't change the status on your file."

"Does it matter? I've already been through training hell." My left calf shot a twinge of pain up my leg as a reminder.

She fixed me with a serious stare. "Legacies are a higher pay grade, receive better benefits, and have access to the tower cafeteria." She paused. "I'm sure you'll do fine in your new department, so I probably shouldn't mention this, but Legacies who do poorly are simply transferred to a new department to try again."

My mouth went dry. "What about someone like me? What if I don't do well?"

"Without an identified god, you're subject to the same rules as the Lost. Job failure would result in being transferred to the Underworld."

I had no time to react to that bit of encouraging news before someone knocked on the door, then opened it without waiting for an answer. A girl with short, dark curls, sea-green eyes, and an infectious smile bounced into the office. "Are you done? Can we have her yet?"

Ms. Eunomia smiled. "Wynter, this is Trina. She'll take you to your department and help you get around for the next few days."

I rose, giving the new girl a shy smile. "Hi."

She grinned. "Yay!" She threaded her arm through mine. "You're going to love it with us." She waved over her shoulder and tugged me out the door. "Bye, Ms. Eunomia."

I waved, too. It seemed expected. "Um, thanks."

Ms. Eunomia didn't wave back. "Wynter?"

I paused in the doorway. "Yes?"

"Talk to your mother again." Her expression was serious. "The truth could make a world of difference."

Chapter 7

I'd thought Jilly was perky. Trina made her look sluggish and pessimistic in comparison.

The energy she expended pulling me down the hall was nothing compared to what she spent talking and waving her arms around.

"Chelsea, hey!" She didn't slow as we passed a woman with bat wings who was hunched over a drinking fountain with a large wrench. "Thanks for fixing that. It's been down all week." She craned her neck to look back over her shoulder after we'd gone by. "You're awesome!" She gave a little wave.

Chelsea appeared unimpressed.

We turned a corner, and the hall spit us out into the atrium that seemed to serve as the hub for getting from one place to another. Trina pointed out the highlights as we crossed to the elevator. I had trouble following half of what she said, since she spoke in a steady stream with few pauses for breath.

"...is the door you came in, and on the other side is the exit to the rest of Mount Olympus, where the gods and heroes and non-humans live and shop and play. I suppose you've already met Patrice. Hi Patrice!" She shot her arm up in a wild wave, which Patrice completely ignored. "The glass overhead is made from Egyptian sand struck by Zeus's lightening, and the fretwork around it was made by Hephaestus himself in his forge. The dome is indestructible." She pulled me toward a bank of elevators, pressed the up button and grinned at me. "We're on the fifth floor."

I blinked. Was it my turn to talk? I wasn't sure. I gave it a try. "How long have you worked here?" That seemed like a safe enough question.

"About six months. My mother used to bring me in on her days off when I was a kid, so I already knew a lot of the history and how to get around. You'll pick it up pretty fast, though. Once you get the hang of which colored line to follow, it's all—"

She stopped midsentence as the doors slid open. A tall guy with dark skin and a goatee stood with his hands folded in front of him, as if he were military and had been told to stand at ease.

He gave a quick nod of his head. "Trina."

Trina pressed her lips together in a tight line. "Ian."

We stepped inside and watched the doors slide shut.

"Still the fifth floor?" Ian pressed the button, not waiting for an answer.

"Thank you," I said. Well, somebody needed to say it.

Trina stood stiff and straight, staring at the crack between the elevator doors.

The elevator dinged at the fifth floor. Trina marched out, and I followed her. Her heels tapped on the marble floor in the silence until the elevator doors whooshed closed.

She stopped and leaned her back against the nearest wall. "Oh, gods, that was so awkward. I am so sorry you had to see that, Wynter."

I frowned. "See what, exactly? Who was that?"

She sighed. "That was my ex, Ian. Really ugly breakup. Did you *see* how he looked at me when the doors opened?" Her eyes grew large, and her shoulders slumped with exaggerated emotion. "So awkward."

He'd seemed polite and normal to me, but I wasn't always the best at reading people. Still, I suspected Trina read a lot more into the situation than what had really happened.

She took a few moments to gather herself together, then pushed away from the wall. "Okay." She smoothed her hands over her tight green skirt. "I'm better. Let's move on."

Two corners, a long, carpeted hallway, and a story about how Trina once helped the janitorial department to water all the plants on this floor for an entire week, and we found ourselves in front of a door with frosted glass painted in gold letters that said *Muse Department*.

My stomach knotted as we stepped inside to meet my future.

I nearly turned around and walked out once I saw my new office. I'd expected…oh, I don't know. Something different. Something lovely and spacious, filled with a magical aura fit for something as mystical as a room full of Muses.

What I found instead was a cubicle farm.

My lower lip quivered as Trina led me to a desk not far from the door. I relaxed my face to erase what was likely the petulant look of a disappointed child. Showing disappointment at this early stage wasn't going to win me any brownie points.

The truth of having signed a three-year contract slapped me in the face as I sat in my new gray swivel chair surrounded by half-walls to keep me separated from the rest of the room. I half-expected they'd hand me a headset and ask me to start taking calls.

I'd quit my call center job for no reason. I was right back where I'd started.

Trina patted me on the shoulder, her voice excited. "You stay here for a sec. I'll go tell the boss lady you're finally here."

She did a little bounce on the balls of her feet, then took off between the rows of cubicles.

I spun the chair to face my new desk. It was pretty sparse. A black phone with lots of buttons. A desktop computer, currently running a screensaver of a cartoon fish tank. A spinning office supply holder containing one blue pen, two yellow highlighters, and an eraser. A stack of trays for paperwork. I touched the surface of the desk, and my fingers came away sticky.

I sighed. So, this was going to be my new life. Not a lot different from my old one. Possibly worse, since the PC seemed to be running on decade-old software.

Behind me, a voice like tinkling bells laughed, then called out to me. "Wynter, I'm so glad you're finally here. We've been waiting anxiously all week for you."

I spun around and blinked. The voice didn't fit the person standing in front of me. The voice was melodious and sweet. It should've belonged to a graceful young woman in diaphanous clothing—a woman who did pirouettes for no reason, frolicked in the forest, and wore garlands of flowers that matched her violet eyes.

It seemed nothing in this office would turn out as expected.

The short, sturdy woman thrust a calloused hand toward me. "I'm Polly. Want to follow me to my office? We'll get your paperwork all sorted and get to know each other."

It wasn't that Polly was ugly or even unattractive. She simply didn't match her voice. She had thick, dark eyebrows and gray eyes, her mouth was a little asymmetrical, which gave her a lopsided smile, and her nose had a bump, like she'd recently taken off a tight pair of glasses.

She did not look like one who frolicked.

I shook her hand and matched her tight grip. Neither of us was a limp shaker.

As I followed Polly to her office through the maze of cubicles, three heads popped up above the barriers to watch us. Trina was one of them, and she waved her hand so hard I thought it might fly off. I smiled and waved back.

Polly closed her office door behind us. "Have a seat." Her lovely, lilting voice soothed my jangled nerves. The office smelled like lilacs and had a quiet, calming feel.

I relaxed into the plush seat opposite hers. "Thanks."

Her eyes turned up at the corners, making smile creases, and she handed me a thick folder. "Here. Your insurance, 401k, and benefits package are in there. We'll fill that out in here, and the rest of the package will give you an idea of what we're about here. When we're done chatting, I'll send you out with one of the girls for a ride-along so you can see how an inspiration is created. Sound good?"

I nodded, feeling the weight of the folder she'd given me. A lot of reading was ahead of me. "Sounds great." It didn't sound great. It sounded terrifying, and I wasn't sure why. Benefits and 401Ks and ride-alongs. I was beginning to suspect I'd landed in a real job.

I might be expected to care about my work.

I thumbed through the stack of papers and pulled out the top section, stuck together with a giant clip. Everything in it was paperwork for me to fill out. The rest—a much larger stack—looked like an unbound departmental handbook. Dress codes, rules, parking information.

A lot of info to take in.

Polly guided me through the paperwork, then deposited me back at my new desk to read for a bit. Honestly, I didn't understand a damn word of what I read. The dress code section didn't even touch on how an outfit should look. It rambled on for several paragraphs about which types of material were compatible with Transmutational Thought Transference Bubbles and didn't stain easily.

The parking rules talked about radiuses and angles of approach. That section also specified that I wasn't allowed to have personalized plates on my car, and blue or brown were the preferred vehicle colors this year. I shrugged that one off. If they wanted my silver Honda to change color, they'd have to pay for it themselves. Too bad about the vanity plate though. "I MUZ U" would have been hilarious, even if I were the only one who got it.

An hour and a half later, I realized I was still sitting there reading. I scrounged a box of raisins and a protein bar from the bottom of my purse, since no one had said anything about lunch. It wasn't ideal, but it was probably better than whatever the snake lady was serving in the cafeteria.

Plus, it gave me a chance to reread the section on pet management. In fact, I read it three times and still didn't understand what Beastie Discombobulator Dust did, exactly.

The more I read, the more I suspected my initial assessment that I'd landed a desk position was wrong. What little I understood from the handbook indicated I was in for a field job. I supposed that made sense, since I was supposed to be a Muse, but I still wasn't clear on where the clients came from or how the job was done.

I sighed and closed the folder, then tapped it against the desk to tidy the papers. I had a lot of learning ahead of me. I wouldn't be able to half-ass this the way I'd done at the call center. Or the bank. Or the dry cleaner.

A hand dropped to my shoulder, and I jumped. Spinning around, I found Polly standing behind me.

"Ready?"

I nodded, though I wasn't entirely sure if I was ready for anything. "Sure."

She gave me a lopsided smile. "You look terrified, Wynter. This will be fun. Trust me."

A gangly redhead in outrageously tall high heels appeared behind Polly. She eyed me up and down as if I were last year's coat hanging from a clearance rack. A brief look of distaste crossed her face before she settled on a polite smile. "Hey."

Oh, she was going to be an absolute freaking delight. I could already tell.

Polly stepped aside and held her hand out to indicate the new woman. "Wynter, this is Audrey. She's going to take you out and show you the ropes." She gave me a reassuring smile and pat on the arm. "I'm not in the office a lot, but Audrey's been here a long time. If you have any questions at all, she'll be happy to help. Right Audrey?"

The redhead folded her arms across her chest and leaned against the wall. "Of course. I'll take good care of her."

Polly patted me again as if I were a flight risk. "Okay, then. I've got work to finish up before my next meeting. Good luck!" She darted away and disappeared into her office.

Audrey sighed and rolled a chair over to me. She dropped into the seat and held out her hand. "Give me your folder, first of all."

I handed it over. "I've been reading it for nearly two hours. I don't understand a damn thing."

She licked her index finger and rifled through the papers, then pulled a chunk of them out. "These are totally bogus. You don't need to waste your time on them." She dropped them in a recycling bin next to her. "And this whole section on dress code is so outdated it's ridiculous." She dropped it into the bin with the rest.

"What should I wear, then?" I tried to keep my gaze on her face and away from her skyscraper heels. I couldn't possibly walk in those things. And Trina's skirt had been so tight, I'd never be able to sit down without ripping it if I wore one like it. I was doomed.

Audrey snorted. "Whatever the hell you want to wear. You'll be invisible. Nobody cares." She closed the folder and handed it back to me. It weighed considerably less.

A woman with tanned skin, braids, and almond eyes walked past, then stopped and backed up. "This her?" She gave me the same once-over Audrey had given me.

Audrey nodded. "I was just giving Wynter the lowdown on the dress code." She waved her hand. "This is Kayla."

Kayla didn't smile. "Welcome." She folded her arms and leaned against the same spot Audrey had.

"Thanks." I swallowed. For people whose job it was to be inspirational, they didn't seem very friendly. "Have you been here very long?"

She shrugged. "About six years. Most of us have been here awhile. The rest…" She shrugged again. "The rest of the slots have a higher turnover rate."

I frowned. "Slots?"

Audrey and Kayla exchanged an amused look, then Audrey cleared her throat and returned her attention to me. "Nine muses, right? You know that much?"

I shifted in my seat, and a stab of pain throbbed up my leg, reminding me that I'd been through worse things than a couple of condescending coworkers in the last week. "Sure. Nine Greek Muses. I just didn't know the department kept with that tradition."

"Well, we're mortals, not gods, so there are three slots per original Muse. So, twenty-seven Muses per region." Audrey rose and pushed her chair away. "Grab your stuff, Snow White. I'll take you to the supply room and get you set up, then we'll take a ride."

Kayla smirked. "Have fun, Snow."

It was like being in high school again. Except, I hadn't put up with it in high school. I'd have to deal with it, here, though. No more walking away from things when they got tough. I'd signed a contract. I was stuck.

I followed her to another room where she pointed at a wall of gold belts in various sizes hanging from hooks. Most of the hooks had names written on small wipe-off boards above them. One of the boards was had a black smear across it, the name no longer legible. Audrey snatched a cloth hanging from a hook and wiped the board clean, her face scrunched into a frown.

She turned away from the board and eyed my figure for a moment, then chose a belt and handed it to me. "Try this one."

The gold was warm and lighter than I expected, as if it were woven of spun-gold thread rather than crafted of solid metal. I wrapped it around my waist and clicked it in place. It settled over my hips like it was made for me. "Perfect."

She nodded. "Thought so." She wrote my name above the empty slot. "From now on, you're responsible for that belt. Make sure you always hang it up before you leave every day."

I ran my fingers over it. "It's beautiful. What does it do?"

She led me to a storage closet on the other side of the room. "Your belt holds your supplies, renders you invisible, and modifies your voice. It's what makes a human into a Muse."

This was going to be the craziest job ever.

Audrey pulled out a large plastic bottle and a silver can, then showed me how to hook them to my belt. I was a little disappointed. The belt went from a stylish accessory to a piece of utilitarian equipment. The containers weren't too big, though, so the belt didn't drag much.

"There's more of everything in this closet. When you return your supplies, refill them for the next person. Nobody likes to get to an assignment and find out they're out of juice." She grabbed her own belt and loaded it, then led me out of the supply room.

Back in the main office, we found our way blocked by two men standing in the middle of the hallway, talking to each other and oblivious to our attempts to get past.

Audrey tapped their shoulders. "Step aside, boys. I have new meat to tenderize."

They turned slowly to face us, apparently in no rush to comply. The one on the left was taller with a round face, thick lips, and squinty brown eyes. The shorter man on the right had blue eyes that were a little too wide apart on his face, flat cheekbones, and a sparse attempt at a soul patch on his cleft chin. Neither was terribly attractive, but the shorter one seemed to think he was.

"Well, hello." He scanned me up and down and licked his lips. "New meat is always welcome in this place. I'm Dave." He tipped his head at the other guy. "And that's Jeremy. We're the only foxes in this henhouse. What's your name, chicky?"

My skin felt like it was physically drawing away from him. The guy next to this waste of air didn't seem the least bit embarrassed by his friend, either. In fact, Jeremy looked as if he wanted me to answer and move on so they could resume their conversation.

While I tried to decide on a pithy comment that would smack this guy down, Audrey groaned and pushed him out of the way.

"Her name's Wynter. And we've warned you about that henhouse shit before, Dave. Don't make me call HR again. They're running out of sexual harassment videos for you to watch." She grabbed my arm and dragged me past the two guys and out into the lobby. "I have no idea why those guys are still here. Dave's an ass and Jeremy's just plain creepy. Ignore them."

I shivered. "Hard to believe they're out there inspiring people."

She shook her head in disgust as she hit the down button for the elevator. "They get the job done, apparently. I don't know how."

We stepped into the elevator and she pressed the L button. A moment later, we were back in the atrium where I'd started.

Audrey led me through the busy lobby, past a man with a bull head, two arguing satyrs, and dozens of humans traveling to and from other parts of the building. I didn't see Phyllis anywhere, but couldn't stop to look for her. Audrey kept moving toward the front door where I'd come in that morning. She grabbed my sleeve and pulled me through. I blinked in the bright sunlight.

We were not in Topeka, Kansas.

Chapter 8

I frowned and looked back at the door. The building behind us was now an abandoned McDonalds. "What just happened?"

Audrey rolled her eyes. "I touched the door first. Didn't they explain it to you in orientation?"

I shook my head. "If they did, I missed it. We're not in Topeka?"

"No, we're in Charlotte, North Carolina." She waved her arm. "This is the town I'm connected to, right now."

"So, I live in Topeka, but I work in Charlotte, halfway across the country?" My head felt like it was full of bees. "What if I went out the door first?"

"Then we'd be in Topeka. Your base." She pointed at a single car in the parking lot as she walked. "Your assignments will be in Topeka when you're on your own."

It made sense, if I didn't think about it too hard. All week I'd been parking on the street in the worst part of town outside an abandoned building. No other cars were parked around me, and the only person I saw was that homeless dude who hung out near the entrance.

I glanced back at the empty restaurant as I slid into Audrey's car. A scruffy man walking a pair of corgis appeared around the corner. He raised his arm and waved at Audrey, and she waved back.

Interesting. Next time I saw the homeless dude in Topeka, I'd have to take a closer look.

Unless he was peeing on the wall again. I did not want a closer look at that.

Audrey drove us across town with the radio up loud enough to discourage conversation. I hoped she'd warm up to me eventually, but so far, I was still feeling a chill from her. Maybe that was her personality, or maybe she disliked training new people. Who knew? For now, though, I tried not to rub her the wrong way. I already felt like I was off to a rocky start at this new job.

We parked and left the car at the curb in an average-looking suburban neighborhood filled with older trees, two-story houses, and family cars in the driveway.

"The first thing you need to know is about parking." Audrey pressed the auto-lock button on her keys and the nondescript, blue four door's lights flashed. "One block up, one block over. That's the rule of thumb. Of course, you can't always do it that way, but that's the ideal we strive for. The most important thing is not to park right out front. Especially since you could end up going to the same place every day for weeks. Don't look like a stalker. Neighborhood watches are filled with assholes."

She handed me a sheet of paper with a name, address, and description of a person living at that location. The address was 1311 Oak Street. We currently stood in front of 1214 Elm Lane. I glanced at my high heels and made a face. Then again, hers were three times higher than mine. She must've built up some stamina to wear the damn things every day.

We walked one block up, then turned the corner and walked half a block before Audrey stopped me.

She glanced around. "Okay. This is where it gets tricky. Give a little look around to be sure no one's watching. It's okay if they see you. They'll forget. But if they're actually watching you, they might remember." She looked around again, then pointed to a spot on my belt buckle. "Now, press that." She did the same.

Absolutely nothing happened.

"What did we do?" I held my hand out and examined it. No difference. Not even a fancy shimmer effect.

She took off again, talking over her shoulder. "We're invisible."

"I can *see* you, you know."

She flapped her arm at me but didn't slow. "Of course we can see each other. We both have belts on."

"Oh. Of course." I directed a scathing look at the back of her bobbing head.

We turned again at the corner, walked past two houses, and stopped at a brown and blue house with a detached garage. Audrey held up the paper and squinted at the numbers above the front door. "This is it." She marched up the front steps and took my arm. "Hold your breath."

I didn't have time to do anything. She yanked me through the front door before I had a chance to inhale. I couldn't have breathed if I'd wanted to.

My head spun and my stomach lurched. I'd walked *through* a door. A *door*.

Of course, I hadn't thought it through first. Walking through walls and doors was how it would have to happen. We couldn't exactly ring the doorbell and wait to be let in.

A soft scuffling came from another room, and we followed the sound. A woman not much older than I was sat on the floor in front of a small wooden table. Paints, brushes, and newspaper lay scattered around her, untouched.

The look of despondency on her face didn't alter when we entered the room. Up until that point, despite having been pulled through a solid door, I hadn't really believed people couldn't see me. Being invisible isn't exactly something a person should take on faith.

"Okay. Let's get to work." Audrey unhooked a bottle from her belt and unscrewed the top. "This is your most important tool. Everything else is meant to make things easier for you. But if you don't have this, you can't do your job." The cap came off with a plastic stick attached inside. At the bottom of the stick was a loop.

My eyes widened. "Are those soap bubbles?"

"These are Transmutational Thought Transference Bubbles. We just call them Thought Bubbles." She dunked the wand in the solution, pursed her lips, then blew a stream of bubbles in the direction of our would-be artist.

Some of the bubbles went wild and floated away. Others popped before they reached her. One bounced off her shoulder, and another smacked her right between the eyes before it splattered in a rainbow. I winced, but she didn't react.

Audrey drew closer to her target, and her voice was soft and musical. "Relax, Sophie. Let the colors and shapes guide you. Creativity flows through you, and you have so many new ideas. You can do this."

Sophie tilted her head as if she could almost hear Audrey's words. Her lips turned up in a dreamy smile, and she chose a paintbrush from the selection scattered across the floor. Dipping the tip of her brush in crimson paint, she hummed to herself and made a spiral in the center of the table.

Audrey cleared her throat and screwed the cap on her bottle, though she continued to hold it loosely in her hand. "That is what we call *creating an inspiration*. Done right, the client should mostly continue on her own momentum with only a few minor stalls."

We watched as Sophie alternated her brushes and paint colors, dabbing dots and squiggles in elaborate patterns. Each time she paused for more than a minute or two, Audrey whipped out her bubbles and sing-songed words of encouragement. We stayed for over an hour. I was gratified and amazed to watch the project blossom from a plain wooden surface to a fantastical work of folk art.

Audrey clipped her bubbles to her belt. "I think she's got it. She doesn't need any more help. Time to bug out. We've got more work to do."

I didn't say anything as we walked back to the car. I'd been touched by what I'd seen, and I was still mulling it over. Sophie had looked so sad and frustrated. With a few words of encouragement—and some magic bubbles—everything about her had changed. Her entire demeanor had opened up, her body language becoming more positive and self-confident. And the work she did was beautiful. She'd been a whirlwind of creative passion.

Could I possibly do a job like this? Could I inspire people? Help them achieve great things? Make them happier with their lives?

I didn't notice when we arrived at the car.

Audrey snapped me out of my thoughts. "Hit the button. You don't want the car doors to swing open when you're invisible. People will notice that, and it's weird enough that they won't forget, no matter how powerful the spell is."

I touched my belt buckle and climbed into the car, frowning. "Why don't we fall through the car door? How could I affect it when I'm invisible if I'm also able to walk through front doors?"

Audrey pulled out a tube of lipstick and used the rearview mirror to apply it. "It's all about intent. You can affect things if you expect to, and they can affect you. Otherwise, you wouldn't have been able to sit down while were in there. You'd have fallen through the chair. In fact, it's easier to affect things in a normal way than it is to walk through it. That's why you had to hold your breath when went inside. It helps. If you're concentrating too hard to make something happen, it actually gets more difficult."

"What about people, though? Can we affect them?"

Audrey blotted her lipstick on a tissue and turned to face me, scowling. "Do not touch the clients, Wynter. Ever." She put the car in gear and pulled away from the curb, muttering under her breath.

"But what if they move too fast and you bump into them? How do I keep that from happening?" The good feelings I'd come away with now felt closer to panic.

"Simple instructions. Don't make them complicated. Just don't touch anyone. Got it?" She didn't wait for an answer before she turned the radio back on and cranked it too loud for us to speak.

Twenty minutes of very loud country music later, Audrey stopped at an office building. "This is it. Keep up." She took off toward the revolving glass door situated between two columns of brick.

I followed behind and stepped into the elevator with her. She pressed the button for the third floor, then touched her belt buckle to render herself invisible. I did the same. When the doors opened, we stepped out and turned left, then stepped through a door marked *Southern Puppy Love Magazine*.

The receptionist never looked up from her book as we waltzed past. One of the advantages of being invisible was not requiring an appointment. Audrey took us to the last office on the right and disappeared through the door. I stepped through behind her.

The office was actually a conference room. One long table filled the space, and padded, wheeled chairs ringed the edges. Though the room could seat at least a dozen people, only one man occupied the space with us. His dark blue eyes were narrowed in concentration as he paced the table, stopping occasionally to shuffle the photos, articles, and ads spread across the dark wood.

The man's suit jacket lay crumpled over a chair, and his shirtsleeves were rolled up. He frowned, swapped out a photo of a shih tzu with a black lab, then switched them back. He groaned and plopped into a chair, scowling.

"What the hell is he doing?" I walked the length of the table, looking at the mess of papers and photos.

Audrey snorted. "He's planning the layout for the summer issue. What do you think he's doing?" She gave me a look like she thought I was an imbecile.

I gave the look right back at her. "Yes, but why is he doing it *this* way instead of on a computer?" I gestured at the chaos on the table. "I could name ten different kinds of software that could do this, and half of them are free."

Audrey shrugged. "Some people like to do things old school." She rested one butt cheek on the edge of the table. "And what makes you such an expert?"

"I'm not. I've just…spent some time working in various offices." I looked away, not wanting to discuss my past work history.

She unclipped her bubbles and unscrewed the lid, smirking. "Yeah. I forgot you're a Lost, not a Legacy. I suppose you've had a lot of jobs. I shouldn't be surprised."

There was something incredibly insulting about how she said those words. I decided I didn't like Audrey any more than she liked me. I said nothing, though. All I had to do was learn the job, then I could ignore her. At least, that was my hope.

"Carl, you need to relax. Take a deep breath and let the doggies speak to you." Audrey blew a stream of bubbles directly at the man's forehead.

The bubbles popped on his face, and my eyes watered in sympathy. Carl didn't flinch.

In fact, Carl didn't move. He continued to stare at the layout, his expression glassy and far away.

Audrey made a sound of disgust. "Oh, come on, Carl. I've still got one more client to see today." She cracked her neck, shook out her arms, and took a deep breath. "Carl, you're brilliant at this. Every issue, you pull it together at the last minute. This is the last minute." She blew slower this time, creating one big bubble instead of a series of small ones. "Close your eyes and see the layout. See the finished magazine in all its glossy, furry glory. You know how it should look. *See it* in your mind, Carl. See it."

The bubble wobbled toward his wide-open eyes, bumped into his chin and splattered. Carl closed his eyes and rubbed his face, then sat still for a moment with his face covered. When he opened his eyes, he leaped from his chair and spread his arms across the table, gathering all the papers together in a massive pile.

Audrey snickered. "Every freaking quarter. He falls apart, I loosen him up, and he slaps together the perfect layout. Whatever that is. Let's go."

"Wait—we're just going to leave?" I watched him slap the table with a series of photos of beagle puppies in birthday hats playing in a kiddie pool. "What if he still doesn't have it right?"

"He'll have it right. Like I said—happens like this every quarter." She slipped through the door.

Carl's eyes were wide and crazed, and he muttered to himself as he placed everything as he wanted it. She was right. He had this. I backed my way out the door and followed her all the way to the car.

Once we were visible and on our way again, I turned off the radio and wiggled sideways under the seatbelt to see her better. "I have questions."

She scowled. "I was listening to that."

"Answer a few questions, and I'll turn it back on."

"Fine." She tilted her head in my direction but didn't look at me. "Ask."

"How do they determine who gets a Muse? Where does the bubble juice come from? If there are only so many of us, and we're each bound to a city, how is the rest of the country getting inspired? Why does—"

"Whoa, there." She held up her hand as if to block the stream of questions. "That's a lot of questions. And they're all pretty stupid."

I sat up straighter. "Excuse me?" This chick in her skyscraper heels had to be the worst trainer I'd ever had in any of my bazillion jobs.

"Don't get your panties in a bunch." She pulled the car to the side of the road and turned to give me a scathing look. "Seriously. Think about it. Where do we work?"

"The Muse department." Where the hell was she going with this?

She rolled her eyes. "What company?"

"The Mount Olympus Employment Agency."

"So, who do you think is running the show?"

"I don't know. Management."

Audrey didn't say anything. She sat there, staring at me, waiting for something. Waiting for me.

I thought over her last question and realized what she was getting at. "Oh." My eyes grew wider. "Oh!"

She nodded and put the car in gear. "At last. A tiny bit of intelligence peeks through."

Gods. The whole place was run by gods. Of course it was. As much as I wanted to yank this chick's hair out for being so smarmy, she was right. I hadn't been thinking, despite all the crazy things I'd seen.

"So, gods determine who the client is?"

She signaled, then pulled away from the curb. "Yes. Well, no. We get our orders from the Fates, actually." She changed lanes abruptly, and a car honked. "Back off, you moron!"

The other car went around us, and a lady with two kids in car seats in the back gave us the finger.

I twisted around and fixed my seatbelt. "And the bubbles come from— what? Or rather, who?"

"Muses bring it in and refill the dispensers. Usually it's Polly. She hangs around more than the rest do."

It took another minute for me to process what she'd said. "Muses. You mean real ones, not just people doing the job? And Polly's one of them?"

"Polyhymnia. Muse of sacred poetry."

For some odd reason, this information made my head spin far more than walking through a door had. Or seeing mythical creatures in my workplace.

Seriously. Real gods. And I'd talked to one of the nine Muses that morning. I felt a little giddy, as if I'd met a celebrity. How many other gods or demigods had I come into contact with over the last week? Was Mrs. Moros a god? Ben from human resources? Trina's ex, Ian, from the elevator?

I opened my mouth to ask, but I was too late. Audrey hit the button and blared the radio to shut me up.

Fine. I'd ask Phyllis later. And this time, she damn well better answer my questions.

As we pulled into the parking lot of a burger joint, I decided to try not to ask Audrey any more questions. I'd be better off asking someone else. Let her teach me what she had to teach me, and I'd find a better mentor on my own later.

We crossed the parking lot, stepped over a curb, and walked diagonally through a small field. I wondered again at Audrey's ridiculous shoes, but she didn't seem to be bothered. She strode through the weeds with purpose and out the other side to a paved lot with a small Baptist church in the corner.

"Here?" I bit my lip. I'd already broken my vow not to ask her any questions.

"Here."

We hit our belts and went up the steps through the door.

I wasn't raised in any particular religion. I certainly hadn't seen the inside of many churches when I was growing up. But I read things. I had a pretty good understanding of the various religions available to choose from.

The irony of a Greek Muse creating an inspiration for a Southern Baptist preacher's Sunday sermon on idolatry was almost more than I could bear. I had a lot less trouble staying quiet while Audrey blew her bubbles at him than I'd thought I would.

In fact, I spent the entire ten minutes we were there with my back against the wall, pressing my lips together.

The reason we were there for so short a time was Pastor Roy Roberts was incredibly open to suggestion. Carl had only needed a nudge because he knew how to do a layout for his magazine. He just got stage fright before every issue. Pastor Roberts needed every bubble Audrey blew at him, but he sucked them in pretty quick.

When we arrived, he was sitting at his desk in front of his computer, scratching his chin. "Idolatry. Idolatry. When we…no, that's not it. If you give a man…" He deleted several lines and began again. "After the fall, Adam…" He groaned and pounded the delete key repeatedly.

It amused me that he read everything out loud as he wrote it.

Then Audrey stepped forward with her Transmutational Thought Transference Bubbles, murmuring words of encouragement.

From the moment the first bubble burst against the side of his bald head, Pastor Roberts stopped speaking out loud and started typing in earnest. And could he type fast. His fingers flew over the keys at a rate that spoke of countless hours spent typing "the quick brown fox jumped over the lazy dog" in Miss Panganini's typing class. For ten straight minutes he never paused until, with a flourish, he hit a last key and leaned back in his chair with a satisfied smile.

Audrey peered over his shoulder and read what he'd written. She grunted. "Nice. He totally switched gears on that idolatry thing and wrote about stealing from your neighbors." She shook her head. "Pretty big words for a man who cheats on his taxes." She patted the top of his desk. "See you next week, Roy."

She strode out without looking back, and I trotted behind her. The woman could really work those damn shoes.

On the way back to the office, I stared out the window, lost in thought. A sense of unease worried at my gut the more I went over everything I'd seen that day.

I'd never finished anything in my life. I was a joke. How was I supposed to be responsible for helping other people finish what they needed to do? There was no way I could do this.

I was doomed to fail before I'd even begun.

~*~

It took most of the weekend for Phyllis to talk me down from my doom cloud.

"You'll do fine," she said for the fifth time. "But you'll have to buy a whole new wardrobe if you don't put down the ice cream."

I sat curled on the sofa eating mint chocolate chip straight from the carton. With a really big spoon.

"So what? The dress code didn't say anything about the size of my ass." I waved my spoon in her general direction. "Besides, I might as well eat all the ice cream I can before I get sent to the Underworld. I bet it's super hot down there."

Phyllis let out an exasperated sigh. "That's Hell, darling, not the Underworld. And I can't believe you're throwing in the towel before you've even started. You don't even have your first client, and you're already resigned to failure." She clucked a non-existent tongue. "I thought with everything that's happened in the last week, you'd have given up on giving up by now."

I grumbled vague noises into the carton cradled in the crook of my arm. "Oh, sure. I should embrace my deity heritage. Throw off my pathetic past as a loser and become a demigod, capable of changing the lives of the regular mortals around me." I swirled the melting ice cream so it resembled a thick milk shake. "Maybe if I knew who my father was, I might be able to do that. But I don't even know who I am, Phyllis. And until I do, I can't even eat in the big kids' cafeteria. How sad is that?"

Usually, smooshing the softened ice cream made it more appealing. This time it looked like unappetizing goop. I dropped the spoon into the carton and contemplated how much effort it would take to go into the kitchen and put it away.

"Wynter." Phyllis' voice was gentle.

"What?" Mine was more on the petulant side.

"I know this whole thing is frightening. And I know how hard it's been for you, always moving around, never fully committing to anything or anyone. But I need you to trust me on this. You're going to be fine. This is your fate. Fate will never steer you wrong."

I sighed and pulled myself from the couch to head into the kitchen. "I know you believe I can do this." The spoon made a jarring clang when I dropped it into the sink. "I just wish I could."

"It's okay, sweetheart. I believe in you enough for both of us."

Chapter 9

To my utter dismay, one day of training was all they gave me.

I came in Monday morning, fully expecting to go on another ride-along with Audrey, only to find an assignment in my inbox and Audrey nowhere to be found. I grabbed the paperwork out of the tray and took it to Polly's office.

Her door was open, and she looked up when I knocked. "Did you get your assignment?"

For a moment, I stood there like an idiot, unable to speak. I'd forgotten until that moment what Audrey had told me. Polly was a real Greek Muse. Daughter of the gods. Possibly responsible for the words of Homer and Shakespeare. I swallowed hard and held up the papers I'd brought with me. "Now what do I do?"

She drew her thick eyebrows together in a quizzical look. "You go to the address and create an inspiration. There isn't much to it. Audrey showed you how and when to use your tools on Friday, right?"

I was too flustered to form a sentence to object at first. One day of training seemed ridiculous. I had zero confidence in my own abilities. "What if I do it wrong?"

She shrugged. "As long as you remember to go invisible, no harm done. Try again tomorrow." She frowned when I didn't move. "You'll be fine. Go." She shooed me away. "Motivate. Inspire. Provoke art. And close the door, please."

Scowling, I made my way back to my desk. I sat for a few minutes thinking about how hard I was going to suck at all this. Then I pulled myself together and used the outdated computer in front of me to map the address on my assignment.

At least I could figure out where I was going.

My client was a guy named Alex. He lived in Topeka, a short distance from my apartment. I punched the address into my phone's GPS so I wouldn't get lost, then scanned the sheet to find out what Alex's project was. My mouth opened in disbelief.

"Toothpick art? Seriously?" I leaned back in my chair and threw my hands in the air. "Whatever happened to poetry and ballet? This isn't even a thing."

Kayla walked past, reading an assignment of her own, and stopped to glare at me over the half-wall of my cubicle. "What's got your knickers in a twist?"

My voice sounded whiny, even to myself. "They gave me toothpick art. That's not even real."

She gave me a disgusted look. "Did you think you were going to start off helping someone write the Great American Novel or something? You have to begin at the bottom. My first assignment was for a graffiti artist." She started to walk away, then stopped again to look back at me. "It's not like you ever finish anything yourself, anyway."

What the hell was that supposed to mean? I would have asked her, but she was already gone. She wasn't wrong, but she wouldn't know that. She'd just met me.

Muttering, I did a quick search on the computer. To my surprise, toothpick art *was* a thing. An impressive thing, in fact. I clicked through pages filled with incredible works of architectural art.

"Ha. Fooled you, you cow. This is a great assignment." I really wanted to believe that.

After a few minutes, I logged off and went to the prop room for my gear. I clipped the belt around my waist and loaded it with a fresh bottle of bubbles and the Beastie stuff Audrey had failed to demonstrate or explain. As I turned to leave the room, I found my way blocked by Dave and Jeremy.

Seriously. For an office full of people who were supposed to be inspirational, the employees in the Muse department mostly seemed to be a pack of crap-weasels. They were worse than the folks I'd worked with for two weeks at the DMV.

I really needed to rethink my life choices.

Dave stuck his hands in his pockets and grinned. "Hey, chicky. Ready for your first solo?"

I took a deep breath, counted to three, and let it out. "I am, yes."

Jeremy snickered, and it was every bit as creepy as I'd expected it to be. "Can we watch?"

I narrowed my eyes. "Watch what?"

"You," Dave said. "Solo." He turned to Jeremy, and they high-fived each other.

It occurred to me that I should say something to my boss. Or maybe march down to Human Resources and file a complaint. I'd never been very good at following rules like that. I knew if guys like that weren't reported, they'd continue their bad behavior, and girls who were easier to shake up would end up targets.

But it might also be the case that this was some sort of hazing ritual. Everybody but Trina seemed to hate me already for some reason, and frankly, it was my first real day on the job.

I shoved past them, elbowing my way through. "Not till you have notes from your mommies. You're not grown up enough to even talk to me right now."

Whatever reaction they were expecting from me, that wasn't it. I left the office without hearing another word out of them. Tomorrow I'd probably have another problem from them, but for now, at least I was away from them.

"Crap-weasels."

Halfway down the hallway, I'd cooled off enough to realize I had no minder. Nobody was watching over my shoulder or tracking my hours. And Polly didn't seem at all concerned about how long it took to inspire this guy Alex to get his work done. If I didn't get him motivated today, I could do it tomorrow. The sudden freedom felt like an elephant had stepped off of my chest and let me breathe.

That didn't mean I meant to totally slack off or anything. But at least I could stop somewhere and get coffee on the way. I was, for all intents and purposes, my own boss during the day.

I stepped into the half-full elevator, golden tool belt jingling on my hips, and pressed the button for the lobby. One floor down, a few people left, and a few more got on. The doors closed, the elevator moved, and the doors opened. I marched out, confident and full of myself.

A split second later, I realized I was on the second floor, not the lobby. I groaned. I could spin around and hit the button. The doors had only begun to slide shut. If I were super quick, they'd open again and let me in.

Of course, then everyone inside would know I'd prematurely jumped out of the elevator.

Opting out of the embarrassment scenario, I moved forward with purpose so the last thing the folks in the elevator would see was me getting on with my business. Or pretending to, anyway. Once the doors closed, I stopped and looked around.

The second floor was neither wide open like the lobby, nor a maze of hallways like the fifth floor where I worked. The main hallway was wider and led to a central waiting area that branched off in several directions. Also, I smelled coffee.

I followed the big hallway to the center and peered up at the directory on the wall. Arrows pointed in different directions to the Medical Clinic, Library, Chapel, and Midlevel Cafeteria.

Midlevel cafeteria? That sounded intriguing. No one had told me about any of these places, and I wasn't certain if I was allowed to use them. But if I had a better cafeteria option than the one with the snake lady serving slop, I'd take it.

I followed the arrow in the same direction my nose told me there was coffee. I stopped outside the doors, hesitant to go in without knowing first if I'd be humiliated and tossed out. The view through the windows showed me a much more comfortable eating area than the one downstairs. People sipped coffee and typed on laptops or phone displays while a young girl helped people from behind the counter.

It looked perfectly normal. There had to be a catch.

The back of my neck itched, as if a bug had landed there. I swatted at it and felt warm air brush my fingers.

"This isn't a Dickens novel, you know." The voice behind me was deep and rumbled with amusement. "You don't have to stand outside and watch people eat."

I whirled and faced the guy breathing on my neck. He stood several inches taller than me, had broad shoulders, blue eyes, and soft blond hair. Perfect. Or nearly so. For some strange reason, he was wearing a cowboy costume, complete with chaps and gun holster. He clutched the brim of a black cowboy hat with one hand.

Swap all that out for a nice suit, and he'd have been perfection. Though the chaps weren't at all off-putting.

I cleared my throat in an effort not to stutter with a sudden bout of nerves. "Howdy, partner. Did I miss the rodeo?"

He grinned and reached around me to open the door. "Work clothes. I don't look like this all the time. Honest." He held the door and waited for me to walk through.

I frowned "Thanks. But am I supposed to be in there? Nobody told me. I'm new."

He rested his hand on the small of my back and ushered me in. "Anybody who's out of orientation can be in here. You hungry?"

I shook my head. "I was just hoping for some coffee before heading out to my assignment."

He winked. "Allow me, New Girl." He strode to the counter. "Hey, Gretchen. Could I get two large cinnamon lattes?" He turned his head toward me. "You like cinnamon, New Girl?"

I nodded, surprised. "I love it." On my own, I probably would have ordered something simple, since it was my first time in there. But he'd managed to pick out something I would really enjoy, instead. Who *was* this beautiful man?

He paid for the drinks and carried them both to a table in the corner with the hat clenched in his teeth. I followed like a little lamb, feeling awkward and a little like I'd swallowed a nest of baby hummingbirds.

"So," he said, handing me my drink. "I'm Rick. Welcome to Mount Olympus."

I grabbed my cup with both hands to have something to hold on to. "Thanks. I'm Wynter."

"Pretty." He patted the sheriff's badge pinned to his tasseled, suede vest. "I'm with the Dreams and Nightmares department. Last night I had to be a cowboy for some kid."

"Ah." I nodded, as if I knew what he was talking about. "I'm a Muse." I bit my tongue and felt my face flush. "I didn't mean I'm 'amused.' I mean I work as a Muse."

He took a sip of his coffee, eyes sparkling with suppressed laughter. "I knew what you meant. The belt is kind of a giveaway."

"Oh." I glanced at the clock on the wall over the counter. Freedom or not, if someone from my office saw me sitting there when I was supposed to be out working, it wouldn't look very good. "It's late. It's my first solo mission today. I should probably get going." I scooted out of my seat and thrust my hand out at him. "So, it was nice meeting you. Thanks again for the coffee."

He shook my hand slowly and nodded toward the cup in my hand. "You haven't even tasted it yet."

I took a gulp, burning my mouth. Probably would have been smarter to take a smaller sip. Still, it was heavenly. I sighed. "Oh, that's good. Really good."

"I wouldn't steer you wrong." He let go of my hand and raised his paper cup in a toast. "Good luck on your first solo, Wynter. See you around."

I gave an awkward wave and darted out the door. He may have watched me go, or he may have forgotten me the minute I walked away. Either way, it felt like his gaze was a laser between my shoulder blades the whole way out.

He was way too pretty for my current lack of self-confidence. I'd have to work on that if I ever ran into him again.

~*~

I sat in my car holding my assignment and staring at the garish house I was supposed to enter. Dozens of moving, spinning, reflective ornaments decorated the sparse lawn. The front door was painted a pristine white, but the house itself was an eye-bleeding yellow trimmed in lime green.

I checked my tool belt to be sure I had my can of Beastie Discombobulator Dust. A house this showy no doubt housed an array of pink and blue poodles wearing hats and tutus.

Once I had the car parked the required block and a half away, I returned on foot. At the mailbox, I touched the button on my belt when I was sure no one was looking, then made my way to the front door.

The invisibility thing seemed flawed to me. What if it didn't work? I'd have no way of knowing unless someone started talking to me. Or, you know, screaming, if I were in their house. I supposed if I could walk through doors, I should assume I was also invisible.

I took a deep breath and pushed my hand against the front door, then stepped through into the house.

The inside was every bit as disturbing as I'd expected. Rows and rows of porcelain dolls sat on shelves around the pink and white living room. Doilies decorated the arms of two chairs and a rose-silk sofa, and the painted coffee table was covered in carefully posed panda figurines.

Everything smelled like lemons.

I shuddered and stepped onto the clear plastic floor runner to search for my target. A display of photos led me down the hallway, telling the story of a happy family of four—Mom, Dad, Sister, and Brother. Judging by the pointed collars, Dad's groovy sideburns, and the blue VW bus, I placed them in the late 1960s. As I moved down the hall, the kids grew taller, clothing styles changed, Mom's hair got shorter, and Dad stopped appearing.

I ran a fingertip over a department-store-posed shot of the three remaining family members. Both kids were in their teens by then, and Mom's smile looked a little forced.

It was the last photo on the wall.

At the end of the hall, I found a bathroom and three closed doors. I tried to grab a doorknob and turn, but my hand went through it.

"Woops." The sound of my voice startled me in the silent house.

Holding my breath, I stuck my head through the first door. The room contained a white and gold dresser, a neatly made bed with a pink chenille bedspread, and an army of Precious Moments figures.

The next room had posters of '70s heartthrobs on the walls. The tape holding them up was aged and brittle looking. A twin bed was shoved into the corner with several boxes piled on top of it, and a sewing machine held court in the center of the room.

The third room smelled like muscle cream and dirty socks. The bed was unmade, muddy shoes lay forgotten in the corner next to a discarded pair of pants, and the dresser was covered in loose change and receipts.

I had to assume my client lived in that room. I wrinkled my nose at the odor and withdrew my head.

So, Alex wasn't at that end of the house. Back the way I came, the picture wall became the weird story of a family of three who took anti-aging drugs and found a badly dressed hippy to join their band.

I passed the living room and entered the kitchen. Everything in there was covered in daisies. Even the toaster hid beneath a quilted daisy cover. Pot holders, salt and pepper shakers, dishtowels, soap dispenser, fridge magnets, table cloth, placemats—everything everywhere was done up in daisies. A giant daisy clock hung on the wall with a trailing stem swinging back and forth like the tail on those old-fashioned, kitschy cat clocks.

I cringed and headed for a door across the room I hoped led to the basement.

A peek on the other side confirmed my suspicion. And the light was on. I stepped through the door and headed down the stairs.

A stout man—I assumed he was Alex—with greying hair, three days' worth of stubble, and the droopy expression of the defeated sat at a long table fashioned out of a sheet of particleboard and two plastic trash bins. A desk lamp sat on the edge of the table, lighting what it could of the area. Multiple types of glue, pieces of wax paper, scissors, razor blades, chunks of wood in various sizes, and boxes and boxes of toothpicks were stacked around the table.

Alex huddled over a pad of graph paper, drawing and erasing lines, muttering to himself, then ripping off the top page and tossing it away in a crumpled ball. The concrete floor was strewn with similar discarded failures.

Dude really needed a Muse pronto.

I ran my hands over my belt to find my Thought Bubbles. Something near my foot yipped, startling me.

I'd been wrong about the poodles in hats and tutus. It was a wiener dog in a sweater—a pink sweater with a daisy on it, of course—and she was looking straight at me.

That was definitely not supposed to happen.

"Oscar, what are you doing over there? Come lay down." Alex peered into the gloom and patted his leg.

Okay. So, first of all, yay, I really was invisible. And second, the dog in the girly sweater was a boy. Very progressive. Good for him.

"Hey, Oscar. That's a great look on you. Dapper as hell." I unhooked my can of Beastie Discombobulator Dust and twisted the top to open the shaker holes. No one had trained me with the stuff, so I hoped I could figure it out. "How about you forget you saw me, little guy? How would that be?" I flung the contents at him, clutching the bottle in a vice grip so it wouldn't go flying.

Oscar blinked and sneezed. Dust coated his fur like baby powder. He shook himself, ears flinging in the air, then turned away, bumped into Alex's leg, and flopped into a padded basket to sleep.

Alex glanced at the snoring pooch. "Damn, that was fast." He jotted something down, tried to erase, then moaned. "I can't do this."

I reattached the powder to my belt, then freed my Thought Bubbles. "Dude, you need to chill. Try this." I dipped my wand into the solution, pursed my lips like Audrey had shown me, and blew.

The solution splattered on my face.

I tried again. Dip. Purse. Blow.

One big bubble wobbled out and moved in the direction of Alex's head. It was close enough to brush his cheek, then he bent over and scratched Oscar's head.

The bubble drifted away without making contact.

"Oh, for Hades' sake, dude. Hold still." I blew again, this time a stream of smaller bubbles. Several went wild and popped on the table, the ceiling, or the floor. But several more hit the target in quick succession. Pop. Pop. Pop.

Alex froze for a moment, leaving me to worry he'd felt the bubbles and would turn around any second to look at me.

"Yes!" He punched the air, then bent and resumed sketching, mumbling as he drew. "Everybody always does a manmade structure. The judges won't expect something from nature."

Judges? I scanned the table and found an application for entry into the Mid-American Toothpick Championship in Akron, Ohio. I raised my eyebrows in surprise. Seriously? This was for a competition? I peeked over Alex's shoulder to see what he was drawing.

A series of intersecting lines formed a big, shapeless blob on the page. From this close, I could see the sweat beads forming on Alex's upper lip.

"Here and here," he said, adding lines. "And when I get the cliff face done, I can add trees over here and a river running down the center." As he spoke, his pencil flew back and forth adding lines until I realized what it was he was trying to do.

"Oh, hells, no. Is that supposed to be the Grand Canyon?"

It was terrible.

He paused and tilted his head, almost as if he could hear me. "I'm going to need more toothpicks."

I ran my fingers through my short hair in frustration. This was not going work. "Dude. Nature doesn't have straight lines. That's why they recreate architectural works of art. Don't you want to win?"

He chuckled to himself. "I'm totally going to win this year."

I groaned. "No. You're my first project. This is not going down like this." I dipped my wand in the bottle and blew bubbles at him, dipped, blew, dipped, blew. The room was filled with bubbles bouncing and popping everywhere.

Including Alex's head.

"Tiny donkeys carrying tourists down the path," he said, pounding his fist on the table. "This is going to be fantastic."

"No!" I paced behind him, shouting in his ear, hoping something would get through to him. "Choose another idea, you idiot. I just bombarded you with a dozen other choices. What the hell is wrong with you?"

He continued to draw and mutter, pausing occasionally to erase a line, then add another. After about ten minutes, his momentum slowed until he stalled completely.

Alex stared at his graph paper drawing. "This is the stupidest idea I've ever had." He dropped his pencil, then rubbed his face with both hands. "I suck."

I leaned closer to him. "You don't suck. It was one bad idea. Come on. Work with me."

He rose from his stool, stretched, then bent to pick up the limp, unconscious dachshund. "Let's go upstairs, Oscar. I'm not getting anywhere down here."

"No. Don't go." I tried to stand in his way, but he walked right through me.

Alex trudged up the stairs carrying the little dog while I stood below, watching him go. At the top of the stairs, he flipped a switch and closed the door, leaving me alone in darkness.

My first day on my own, and I was an absolute failure as a Muse.

Chapter 10

One of the problems with working in a field-agent type of department is the lack of people in the actual office. By the time I got back, nobody was there. Polly wasn't in her office, and Audrey's belt wasn't on the wall. Neither was Trina's. I didn't know enough people in the department to tell how many of the belts on the wall were from people who'd already come back for the day, but several of the belts were still out.

On the bright side, I didn't see Dave or Jeremy's belts, either.

I unlatched my supplies, refilled the bubbles and the dust, and put them away in the closet. My belt hung neatly beneath my name. Everything was in its place. Back at my desk, I dropped my paperwork in the inbox, then changed my mind and stuffed it in my bag. I wanted to do a little research on Alex. And maybe tomorrow I would come in early to talk to Polly about what to do when the client didn't cooperate.

In the meantime, I was going home to open a bottle of wine, eat an entire pizza, watch television in my pajamas, and maybe bitch at my houseplant for getting me into all this.

On my way out the door, Trina burst in, nearly knocking me into the wall.

"Oh! Hey, Wynter. How was your first solo?" She grinned at me and bounced from foot to foot almost as if she had to pee.

I gave her a pained expression. "It could have been better."

Her smile wavered and she nodded. "Yeah. That happens." She sighed. "A lot."

"What do I do?"

She patted my shoulder. "Go back tomorrow and keep trying until you get through."

I frowned. "Then what?"

"You go every day until they get it." She bounced past me down the hall. "You'll break through eventually. Don't worry." She disappeared into the prop room.

I shrugged. "Okay, then. I guess I'll stop worrying."

A little less stressed, I went home to discuss it with Phyllis.

Phyllis was not amused. "So, what? You're just going to be all casual about it? It'll take as long as it takes?"

"I guess. Trina said—"

Phyllis sputtered at me, and three leaves drifted to the floor. "Trina said? That girl has been through two transfers already. Her status as a Legacy is the only thing that's kept her from being reassigned to the Underworld. Do *not* follow her lead."

I scowled. "Well, at least she's giving me advice. I can't get anybody to teach me anything in there. I might as well take my time if I've got to figure it all out myself."

All of Phyllis's branches stood up straight. "Take your time?" She waved a few leaves at me, as if waggling a finger. "Take your time? Did you even *check* the deadline on your assignment?"

I blinked. "Deadline?" I rummaged in my bag and took out the paperwork.

Phyllis let out a heavy, dramatic sigh. "What? Did you think you could just go there every day for a few years, watching him, hoping eventually he'd figure it out himself?"

I scanned the categories on the page. Name. Address. Art. Terms. And there it was at the very bottom. Deadline. Each of the fields had been filled in the old-fashioned way—by hand in black pen.

I really needed to pay attention to the paperwork these people gave me. The print was small, but it was there. I had twenty-eight days. Worse— according to the terms I'd also failed to do more than skim—my mission wasn't fulfilled until Alex was entirely finished with his project. It wasn't enough for me to help him figure out the perfect idea. He had to bring that idea into concrete form. And he had to get his ass to Akron, Ohio with his finished project to compete in the Mid-America Toothpick Contest.

I slapped the paper on my kitchen table. "Why didn't anybody tell me about this?"

Phyllis was gracious enough not to yell. "Wynter, it was on the assignment. They did tell you."

"If I fail, I go to the Underworld, don't I?" I dropped into a kitchen chair and held my head in my hands.

"It takes more than one failure, sweetheart. And you've got—what— twenty-seven days left on this one? You'll be fine."

I shook my head. "I'm not good at anything, Phyllis. Don't you remember? That's how I got into this mess in the first place."

~*~

I didn't talk to Polly the next day like I'd planned, though I did get in early. After a long night of soul searching, I'd decided to make this work. One way or another, Alex Meyer would finish his damn toothpick sculpture thing.

Since I was early, most of the belts still hung on the wall, though a few were already checked out. I grabbed mine, attached my gear, and took off through the door without seeing anyone. On the way down to the lobby, I stopped on the second floor to grab a cup of coffee.

Okay, let's be honest. I also stopped to see if that guy Rick was around. I tried to look casual, like I wasn't looking for anyone in particular, while Gretchen made my latte. I didn't fool her a bit.

She smiled as she handed me my change. "He's got a weird schedule. He doesn't come in every day."

I thought about trying to look innocent and pretend I had no idea who she was talking about, but I didn't want to be that person. I'd been caught. I might as well go with it. "Thanks. Maybe I'll see both of you tomorrow." I dropped a tip in the jar next to the register, then tried my best to exit with my head up rather than slink out in embarrassment. Sometimes it was necessary to suck it up and be a grownup.

Still, I kept my eyes open for him in the hallway, the elevator, and all through the crowded lobby. I did slam right into a teenaged girl with three heads, though. Two of her heads were pretty brunettes with big eyes and long eyelashes. The head in the middle, however, was pale and sickly-looking with lank blonde hair and puffy eyes. When I walked into the girl—girls?—she dropped her purse, and I helped her pick it up.

"I'm so sorry," I said.

The girl snatched the purse from me, and one of the brunette heads sneered. "Watch it."

"Thank you!" The other brunette head grinned at me.

The third head said nothing, but the look of annoyance on her face made me think the happy head was the odd woman out. I apologized again and walked around her.

I didn't quite give up looking for Rick until I left the building. Once I did that, of course, there wasn't any chance of seeing anyone from Mt. Olympus. I doubted very many people were exiting for Topeka, Kansas.

I nodded at the homeless guy as I walked to my car. He smiled and waved. I'd have to remember to ask somebody about that. I would've bet hard cash the guy was there to watch the door and not because he was actually homeless.

Good disguise, though.

I climbed into my car and fastened my seatbelt. My work belt was a clever contraption. It never seemed to get caught on anything or get in the way, despite all the dangling bits and bottles. People didn't stare at it when I walked down the street, either. It was as if their eyes rolled away from it.

Tools of the gods.

On the way to Alex's house—or rather, Alex's mother's house—I worked on my game plan. If Alex wasn't working in the basement, I'd follow him around and blow bubbles at him until he felt compelled to get to work. If he *was* working, I'd stand over him and try my hardest to get him to think of a *good* idea this time.

I wasn't sure how long it would take to build a sculpture out of toothpicks, but I had a feeling we'd need the better part of the month to complete it. Having lived a life of procrastination and not finishing things, I knew how inviting it sometimes was to get caught in the vortex of Idea Land. It was tempting to stay there, fantasizing about all the possibilities. And each new idea would be bigger, flashier, and less likely to actually be possible to finish. Alex needed to get started fast, or he'd never get started at all. And it needed to be a scaled-down idea he could complete in such a short time.

I parked on a different street than the day before—I wouldn't want the neighborhood watch to get suspicious—hit the button on my belt, and marched to Alex's front door. I held my breath and stepped inside.

Today, the pink living room smelled like bacon. When I entered the kitchen, Mrs. Alex's Mom was there, daisy oven mitts on her hands, pulling a pan of cinnamon rolls from the oven. I inhaled with a sad sigh. Bacon and cinnamon rolls. How crappy was that? I couldn't even touch them, let alone eat them.

Mrs. Meyer set the pan on the stove to cool, then tore off a bit of bacon from a huge pile and dropped it to the floor, clucking and cooing. I peeked around the counter and found Oscar crunching away. He swallowed, then caught sight of me and yipped.

Mrs. Meyer squatted down, her chenille bathrobe pooling around her on the linoleum. "What's the matter, my darling? Did it go down wrong?"

Oscar shivered and buried his nose in her hand.

I hadn't meant to make him afraid of me. Did the Beastie Dust give him a headache? Did I use too much yesterday? If I left him alone, maybe he'd get used to having me around. It wasn't as if I'd been given real training on what to do about pets.

Or on anything else, for that matter.

Mrs. Meyer gave Oscar a pat on his head and straightened up. She took in a lungful of air and shouted down the half-open basement door. "Alex! Breakfast!"

I cringed. The woman was loud.

Alex appeared a moment later, and I hopped up on the counter to watch him eat with his mom.

Watching them interact gave me a better feel for who my client was. And if I hadn't felt bad for him the day before, I certainly did today.

"I don't know why you spend so much time down there." Mrs. Meyer crunched a piece of bacon. "It's not like you've got a chance of winning anyway. What's the point?"

Alex licked icing off his finger. His voice was quiet. "I have as much chance as anyone, Mother."

"About as much chance as finding a job." She leaned over and fed a chunk of cinnamon roll to Oscar. "Isn't that right, sweetums?"

Alex said nothing in response. In fact, he didn't say another word until he was finished, despite his mother's continued insults and prodding. When he was finished, he took his plate to the sink, rinsed it, and put it in the dishwasher. "Thank you for breakfast, Mother. I'll be in the basement. Working." He turned away without looking at her and clomped down the stairs.

I hopped off the counter and gave her a dirty look. "Yeah. We'll be working." I glared at Oscar. "Don't follow us. I don't want to have to dust you."

He yipped and hid under Mrs. Meyer's bathrobe.

Down in the basement, Alex paced and muttered. He pulled at his thinning hair and made it stand out on the sides of his head.

I leaned against a wall and crossed my arms. "Dude. That's not a good look. Stop doing that."

He mumbled louder and waved a fisted hand in the air. "…determined to undermine me every chance she gets."

I unhooked the bottle of bubbles from my belt. "Let it go. Stress doesn't get you anywhere. Let's just prove her wrong, shall we?" I blew a series of smallish bubbles at him in a stream. Most of them exploded around his head. I was getting better at aiming, anyway.

Alex stopped and pressed his index finger against his lips. "I'll prove her wrong. That's what I'll do." He pulled out his stool and took a seat at his worktable.

"Whoa. That's exactly what I said." I moved closer to him. "You can't hear me, can you?"

He didn't react. Nope. He couldn't hear me.

I blew bubbles at him again. "Today you'll come up with the perfect idea."

He stretched and cracked his knuckles. "Today I'll get the perfect idea."

"Whoa," I said again. "So, that's how these babies work." I held up the bottle of Thought Bubbles in the dim light. Nope. No directions I'd missed.

Audrey was the shittiest trainer ever.

"How about a building instead of a natural structure, Alex? Something with straight lines." I encased his head in bubbles.

Alex crumpled up the top page on his notepad and discarded it. "No more nature. Nature is irregular and rounded. I need a manmade structure. Let's see." He stared at the paper, holding his chin in his fingertips. "A bridge?"

I rolled my eyes. "Everybody does bridges."

His hand moved quickly as he drew the outline of a bridge, despite my words.

"Dude. I said no bridges."

"The Golden Gate Bridge is a classic." His pencil flew over the page.

"Why aren't you listening to me?" My arm hung at my side, and the bubble wand I held dripped on my leg, getting my attention. "Oh. Yeah. Okay." I dipped and blew. "Bridges are overdone."

Alex stopped. "Everybody does bridges. What am I thinking? I can't win with a bridge." He crumpled up the paper and started over. "The Taj Mahal, maybe?" His voice wavered.

Dip. Blow. Pop. "How about something more personal? Something you love?"

"I should do something I love." He scratched his head. "Or something *she* loves."

It was as if someone had lit a bonfire under his stool. He drew again, but this time with a purpose I hadn't seen before. He paused occasionally, tapped the pencil against his teeth in thought, then redoubled his efforts.

"What are you making?" I peered over his shoulder. "A house?" The longer I looked at the two-dimensional image, the more familiar it looked. Then it hit me. "You're building a replica of *this* house." I patted him on the back, but my hand slid through. "That's a fantastic idea. And you're right. Your mom will love it."

I watched him for hours. Once he finished drawing out the basic structure, he pulled out several boxes of toothpicks and a bottle of glue. One toothpick at a time, he glued them together on wax paper so they wouldn't stick to anything but each other.

It was slow going, but by lunchtime, he'd done half of one wall.

I rose from the pile of milk crates I'd been sitting on and stretched. "Well, Alex. I think you've got this. I'll be back to check on your progress."

Surely, I figured, they didn't expect me to be here every second he was working on the project. It wasn't as if he was going to get stuck again any time soon. Judging by the look of concentration on his face, I doubted he'd come up for air before dinner.

"See you later, Alex." I climbed the stairs and blinked in the bright kitchen. Mrs. Meyer wasn't around, but Oscar eyed me from the corner with distrust.

He sneezed and ran from the room. I laughed and left through the front door feeling especially full of myself.

~*~

When I got back to the office, I found another assignment in my inbox. I nearly vomited. So much for that wave of pride I'd been riding. I had to start all over with another client.

Missy Franklin was a scrapbooker. My heart sank. I knew nothing about scrapbooking. And while I didn't know anything about toothpick art either, at least I understood the basics. Toothpicks, glue, and some engineering skills could carry a person a long way.

Scrapbookers were a different story. I'd known one, once. She'd had crazy tools like hole punches shaped like ducks and scissors that cut scallops on the edges of thick, patterned paper. I honestly wasn't clear on what the end result was supposed to be.

I'd tried—and abandoned—a lot of projects in my life, but the scrapbooking aisle at the craft store was too intimidating even for me.

Rather than get myself into the same trouble I nearly did with Alex, I took the time to read Missy's entire profile. Apparently, Missy did have an end goal. She was working on a scrapbook to give to her parents for their golden anniversary. The deadline, of course, was twenty-eight days away. That meant I now had two clients with deadlines a month away, one day apart.

Somewhere from the other side of the cubicle farm, several women squealed and laughed. I popped my head up in time to see someone I didn't know light candles on a cake, and three more women I didn't know sang "Happy Birthday" to someone I couldn't see.

Polly's office door swung open, and she popped her head out to join in the singing with her ridiculously melodious voice. When the song was over, she noticed me standing at my desk. "Oh. Wynter. Welcome back. Did you get the new assignment I left for you?"

"I…yes. I got it." I held it up. "Can I talk to you for a—"

She cut me off. "Well, great. Good luck with it. Hope you're enjoying the job." She pointed over her shoulder. "I have to get back to a phone call. Have a fantastic rest of the day." She disappeared into her office and shut the door.

What the hell? The gaggle of women laughed in the distance, oblivious of the new girl who'd been cut out of everything. Other than Trina, the few coworkers I'd met were horrible people. My boss was decidedly hands-off. And my desk was about as far from everybody else's as possible. Not that I spent much time at it.

I sighed and pushed my chair in. Might as well quit feeling sorry for myself and get back to work. Those scraps weren't going to book themselves.

The trip up and down the elevator yielded no good-looking guy dressed as a cowboy, but I did share the ride with a surprisingly short cyclops woman. She smiled. I smiled. We both minded our own business and got off in the lobby. I did not see the three-headed girl.

Missy lived in an apartment on the third floor of a sprawling complex. Audrey hadn't told me the rules for parking in a parking lot, so I opted for a spot as far from the buildings as possible. At the top of the stairs, I turned left, found Missy's apartment, and walked through the door.

I'd kind of expected she wouldn't be home. After all, people had to go out to work, right? Nope. Missy was a stay-at-home mom. I could tell from the empty baby swing in the living room and the tired face of my client. She was pretty in a washed-out, I-used-to-have-time-for-myself way. Her golden hair was pulled up in a messy bun that poked out one side, and her oversized T-shirt looked like it had spit up on one shoulder.

She sat on the living room floor staring at a pile of plastic shopping bags filled with paper, string, stickers, and other things I couldn't see.

Missy appeared to have raided the craft store of every scrapbooking item they had, and she didn't know where to start. I recognized the overwhelmed expression. She'd overdone it before she'd even begun.

I'd done that so many times, I'd lost count.

Glancing around for a good spot, I settled on a love seat covered in what I hoped was clean laundry. Hard to tell, since it wasn't folded. It didn't smell, though.

Missy folded her arms across her chest and glared at the bags as if daring them to make her unpack them.

I blew a medium-sized Thought Bubble at her. "First step is to get organized, honey. You have to lay it all out." I blew a few more bubbles. "You can do this. Little bites."

She gave a weary sigh and opened the first bag. Out came package after package of colored and printed paper. She stacked them together on the coffee table and went for another bag. Next came piles of stickers and alphabet letters. Puffy cutouts and lacy decals. The third bag held four different hole punches in different shapes, three pairs of fancy scissors, and a straight-edged paper trimmer. The last bag was filled with several types of glue, six colors of twine, and a variety of double-sided tapes and dispensers.

I was appalled. No wonder she was overwhelmed. She'd spent hundreds of dollars on supplies for a craft she'd never tried before. She was destined to fail.

This crazy woman was my soul mate.

Once Missy had everything lined up on the table, she lost her momentum again. I hated to pressure her into opening everything. She wouldn't be able to take it back if she did. But until she had a sense of order, she wouldn't be able to get going on the craft itself. I knew this from experience. Also, I couldn't let her return it. My career success depended on her crafting success.

I chuckled at the irony. I'd thought I'd be the worst possible choice to be a Muse, but I had life experience an organized, type-A personality could never understand. I understood failure and how a person got herself there.

The next bubble was accompanied by the strong thought that she should open all her tools and lay them out. Get rid of the packaging and maybe check out some of the paper.

She tore through the plastic and cardboard for the various cutting and sticking items, threw away the trash, then sat down in front of her workspace. She still didn't appear ready to start cutting and pasting stuff—and I honestly didn't know how to do any of that—but she didn't have that defeated look to her anymore. Without my prompting, she opened a package of thick paper and fanned the pages across the table. The colors and patterns all complemented each other, and she chose a few to hold up next to each other and compare.

91

She nodded to herself. "This looks good." She reached under the table and pulled a photo from a box filled with them. A smiling bride and groom looked back at her. "What do you think? Will you look good against these colors?" She glanced at the clock and shrugged. "But not now. Cassie will be up any minute."

She returned the photo, then stacked her new supplies neatly together inside the photo box. I didn't think it would all fit, but she got it. As if on command, the second she closed the box, a baby cried from the next room.

"Well. I guess we're done for today." I rose from the loveseat and stretched. "Wish we could've gotten more done, but I feel good about it. How about you?"

Missy didn't answer. She left the room and came back with a tiny person with blue eyes and wispy blonde hair. They disappeared into the kitchen.

"I'll let myself out," I yelled over my shoulder. I went through the door and back to my car, wondering if talking to myself was going to be my only source of companionship in the future.

And also wondering if maybe it was what I deserved.

Chapter 11

A week had gone by since the last time I'd tried to pry my identity out of my mother. It seemed like a good idea to give it another try. Especially after the Human Resources lady made it seem so important.

For one thing, what was the *upstairs cafeteria* if the new one I was using wasn't it? If I found out who my father was, would my coffee come in ceramic cups instead of paper? Whatever the difference was between Legacy and Lost, I could use the higher pay and better benefits.

Still. She kind of made it seem ominous. Like being a Legacy was a protection I'd regret not having. Certainly, it would be nice if I didn't have to fear being sent to the Underworld if I failed at my job.

But maybe I was reading too much into it. More money would be welcome, regardless.

I knocked on Mom's door, then went inside without waiting. She wasn't in the living room, so I searched the rest of the house, finally ending at the back door to the kitchen. From my vantage point on the wooden deck, I could see her shadow moving around inside the greenhouse.

Before I had a chance to walk out there, the greenhouse door slammed open and she ran out, barefoot, waving her arms in the air. If it had been anyone else, I'd have been alarmed.

But no. It was my mom. Cora Greene. Even before her mind had started slipping a little, she'd been weird.

So, I waited and watched. She came around the corner of the greenhouse, flapping her arms, whirling around a few times, then running full tilt to the other side of the building. I watched her do it three times before she slowed.

I walked down the steps and waited for her to return on her fourth circuit.

She saw me and stopped, her chest heaving from exertion. "Wynter. Hello. I'm so glad you're here." She bent over with her hands on her knees while she caught her breath.

I lowered my head to look her in the eye. "Are you okay?"

She waved her hand at me. "I'm fine. Fine. Just got a little winded." After a moment her breathing returned to normal and she straightened. "That's better. I didn't realize I was so out of shape."

I touched her sleeve. "What were you doing, exactly?"

She held her arms out. "I accidentally sprayed myself with the hose. I was trying to dry my clothes out."

I stared at her without blinking. I had no words. Nothing I could say seemed appropriate.

She didn't wait for a response and linked her arm through mine. "Come inside. I'll make you some lemonade, and we'll talk about that new boyfriend of yours. Have you had dinner?"

I sighed. She'd keep asking if I didn't answer. "No boyfriend, Mom. We broke up."

She patted my hand. "He'll come crawling back, honey. You'll see. Men like that can't stay away from women like us. How about the bank? Did you get the promotion, yet?"

Most of the time I spent visiting my mother, she aggravated me with her weird behavior and her lack of truthful answers about where I came from. But more and more, I was worried. Her short-term memory lapses were less eccentricity and more a potential medical problem. Getting Mom to go to a doctor was nearly impossible though. She preferred her unguents and tonics to Western medicine. She didn't trust doctors.

I'd have to keep a closer eye on her.

We drank lemonade, ate leftovers of a vegetable and quinoa casserole she had in the fridge, and talked about my new job. I had to be careful not to mention my job title or the name of the company I worked for, but she didn't ask. I described my clients and told her about how I was helping to motivate them.

She chuckled. "That's perfect for you. You've always been good at telling other people how to do stuff." She graciously didn't mention how I lacked that ability with myself. "Are you meeting lots of new friends?"

I shrugged and chased a mung bean around my plate with my fork. "I don't interact with a lot of work people. Mostly, I'm out in the field."

"But surely you've met a few people." She reached over, picked up the slippery bean between her fingers, and stuck it on my fork. "You're not being yourself, are you?"

I shrugged and ate the bean. "I'm trying, Mom."

She smiled, as if I'd told her I'd won Miss Congeniality at the prom. "Well, then. You'll succeed." She stacked our plates. "I think I've got some appleberry pie in there. Let me check."

While she busied herself cutting perfect triangles of apple-raspberry pie, I considered what she'd said. I did need to be less…me. I could have walked the length of the office and met all those people having birthday cake. I had phone numbers for three really nice people I'd met in training. But I'd made no effort. I needed to be less like myself.

But not knowing exactly who I was had become part of the problem.

"Mom?"

"Mmm?" She dropped a generous dollop of homemade whipped cream on top of the pie.

I paused, saying a silent prayer to whatever god ruled truth. "Will you tell me about my dad?"

She stood for a minute, wiggling the whipped cream into a decorative swirl, then quietly put down the spoon she was using and brought the plates to the table. "Why is it so important, Wynter? Aren't I enough?"

My heart squeezed in my chest. "It's not that, Mom. You've been a great parent. You raised me by yourself, and I've never needed anything. I just wish…" I stopped, wondering what exactly I wanted from this conversation. If I were being honest with myself, I'd have to admit it had nothing to do with pay grades and better cafeterias. "I just want to know who I am."

She sighed and looked me in the eye. "The truth is, my darling, I didn't really know your father very well. I didn't want you to know the truth because I didn't want you to think less of me."

I frowned and placed my hand over hers. "Nothing in your past could make me think badly of you, Mom. I don't expect you to be perfect. I've made too many of my own mistakes to judge."

She flipped her hand over to hold mine. Her eyes were filled with sadness. "I used to be married, a long time ago."

My eyebrows rose, and I started to speak, but she stopped me.

"No. He wasn't your father. I cheated on him with a man I barely knew. And when I found out I was pregnant, I ran away rather than face my husband." She dropped her voice to a whisper. "He had a terrible temper."

"That's why we moved around so much when I was a kid?"

She nodded. "I ran away, and we've been running ever since."

I put my arms around her and hugged her. "I'm so sorry, Mom."

She hugged me back, then pulled away, her expression confused. "Why on earth is my shirt wet?"

~*~

95

By the time I got home, it was well after dark. I trudged into the apartment through the front door, dropped my keys and purse on the table, and went to the kitchen for a glass of water. Phyllis was on the window ledge, basking in the moonlight.

"How was your day, dear? Get a lot done? Make new friends? What'd you have for lunch?" She sounded genuinely interested, as if staying home alone all day wasn't much fun. I guessed it probably wasn't.

I shrugged. "The day had its ups and downs. I have two clients now."

"Already?" Her leaves shivered in excitement. "They must think you're doing a good job to already give you more responsibility."

My voice was thick with sarcasm. "Yeah. I'm sure that's it."

"Don't you think you're doing a good job?" One of her leaves dropped in the sink.

I sighed. "I think I'm doing the best I can." I touched the dirt in her pot. "You feel a little thirsty." I ran water in a glass and poured some into her soil, then drank the rest. "I had dinner with Mom tonight."

"Wonderful! How was she?"

"Troubling." I refilled my glass while I thought about how to tell my houseplant what was bothering me. "Phyllis, you saw Mom last week. You saw how…absent-minded she is, right?"

"I did, yes."

"Do you think I should worry? Do I need to intervene?"

"What do you mean, dear? Like put her away or something?" Her leaves went still.

"No. Yeah. I don't know. She's getting worse. I'm worried that I should do something. Should she be living alone?"

"Oh, I don't think you have anything to worry about just yet. She's fine."

"Are you sure?"

"I am."

She sounded so sure of herself. But I still wasn't convinced. Who makes health decisions for their parents based on the advice of their houseplants? Maybe I should ask a ficus for a second opinion.

My lip twitched, but I stopped myself from laughing.

Phyllis wasn't fooled. "What's so funny?"

"Nothing." I glanced out the window. "Did the neighbor come out naked again today? What did I miss?"

The silver-painted tires were gone from the courtyard. Instead, a pile of wooden planks sat off to the side with a half-finished wooden box next to it. It looked as if he had a new project, and it wasn't finished yet.

Phyllis brushed the back of my hand with a branch. "I don't know what that boy is building, but he's been at it for days. I think the smaller projects are part of one big thing."

"But what is it?" I looked away and put my glass in the sink.

"Who knows? But he certainly likes to walk around without his shirt." She snickered.

I groaned. "Tease. I'm going to bed. Say a prayer to the gods that tomorrow is easier on me."

As I walked down the hall, I heard her answer me in a soft voice. "If I did that, how would you learn anything?"

~*~

On Wednesday, I popped in on Alex and watched him finish a toothpick section of garage on his house model. The work was smooth, and he didn't need anything from me. In fact, he hummed to himself while he worked and ignored Oscar when the dog whined at me.

After a half hour or so, I was satisfied with his progress and left.

When I walked into Missy's apartment, I found her in the same place she'd been sitting the day before, but this time the baby was in the swing, cooing and chewing on a rubber ring shaped like a bunny.

Missy thumbed through a pile of gold, blue, and maroon paper, each page with a different pattern on it. She tapped the stack against the table and started over.

Halfway through her third try, she groaned and dropped the pages. "Cassie, I don't even know where to start."

Cassie burped and dropped her bunny ring on the floor.

Missy crawled over to the swing, retrieved the teething ring, and placed it in the tiny, chubby hand. "Mommy sucks." She spoke in a cutesy, cooing voice that made the baby giggle. "Mommy needs a wine break. Yes she does!"

I glanced at the clock on the cable box. It was quarter to eleven. I really hoped she wasn't going to open a bottle of wine. There was no telling how the Thought Bubbles would interact with alcohol, especially this early in the morning.

But Missy didn't go to the kitchen. She crawled back to the coffee table and opened a second package of brightly colored paper—this one in greens and purples and yellows.

I unlatched my bottle and blew like a tornado. The entire room was filled with bubbles.

"Don't pick a pattern, yet. Remember what we said yesterday? Little bites. Pick a photo, first. Start from there." I blew another stream of bubbles.

She frowned and put the papers down, then fanned out a pile of old photographs. After a moment of fierce concentration, she placed her finger on a shot of two women and two men on a picnic, hamming it up for the camera. "What do you think, Cassie? Shall we start with their first date?"

And just like that, the pieces for the first page fell into place. She chose a solid light brown sheet of paper for the background, then added several different green and darker brown patterns to it. Before long, she was cutting and stamping and trimming like a pro, and the page was on its way.

After watching what she was doing for a time, I finally figured out what the point was. She was telling a story. This was a photo of her parents on their first date, and she created objects around the photo that both drew out the story—stickers of sandwiches and wine bottles—and made the photo pop by decorating around it in ways that simply made it more attractive.

It was a photo album in which each page celebrated and expanded on an individual picture.

Once she'd chosen the layout and cut all the parts to fit her vision, she grabbed a gun that held double-sided tape and put the first piece on permanently.

"Well, that's actually kind of nifty," I said. My stomach rumbled. "I need food. Think you can handle it from here?"

Missy sang to Cassie while she dragged the gun across a dark green and gold plaid strip. The baby dozed in her swing and hiccupped in her sleep.

"Okay, then." I waved. "Great work, Missy. I'll see you tomorrow." I held my breath and backed through the wood of the door. No one noticed me go. It was a little disheartening.

Being invisible kind of sucked. When things went well, there was nobody to high five me.

Still, I was so pleased with myself and the progress both my clients were making, I was halfway down the road before I realized I hadn't hit the button on my belt to become visible again. Fortunately, nobody seemed to have been watching my car pull out and drive down the street by itself.

Of course, my self-congratulations were short lived. After a quick burger, I went back to the office.

A third client order sat in my inbox.

I stared at it, rage replacing my earlier cheer. "Son of a bitch."

Polly's office door was closed and the lights were off. I toured the entire room, hoping to find someone. Anyone.

Nope. The office was empty.

I returned to my desk and smoothed the paper I'd crumpled in my fist. Mark Willoughby. And he lived in my apartment complex.

My next client was the weird, shirtless guy across the courtyard.

Chapter 12

Having my neighbor as a client brought a dilemma I hadn't expected. Should I go all the way out there, get him started on his project, then go all the way back to work to hang up my belt? Or should I hang on to the belt and stay home afterward?

It seemed like a waste of time, gas, and energy to drive across town when I would be there again in the morning.

I debated with myself all the way home. By the time I pulled into my regular parking space, I'd decided it came down to one thing: no one had specifically told me not to keep the belt overnight.

After all, if I were a mechanic, they wouldn't expect me to drive back to return the tools, would they? Of course not. If they weren't going to lay down any rules, I would make my own.

I went into my own apartment first and dropped off my purse and keys. Glancing out the window, I found Mark—now I had confirmation of his correct name—standing in the courtyard again, staring at the unfinished boxy thing I'd seen the night before.

"He's been out there for an hour staring at that thing," Phyllis said in a hushed voice.

"Well, guess whose job it is to help him?" I did a twirl for my houseplant to show off my well-appointed, fancy belt.

"You're joking." She sounded appalled.

"Nope. I'm not off the clock yet. See you in a bit." I touched the button on my belt and went invisible.

Before I stepped through my closed back door, I reached out to touch Phyllis, hoping to startle her.

"I can still see you, Wynter." She waved a branch at me.

"Well, that sucks. It didn't malfunction, did it?" I adjusted the belt and looked to see if anything was wrong—not that I'd be able to tell.

"It works. It just doesn't work on me. Move me to the left a bit before you go, would you? I can't see the entire courtyard. I don't want to miss this."

I was tempted to move her to the bathroom where she wouldn't be able to see anything, but I adjusted her until she was happy. "I'll be back in a bit." I drifted through the door into the sunlight.

The work order had said *urban renewal* on it, nothing more. It did have the deadline on it—no surprise, it was twenty-eight days. But the explanation and requirements field had been left blank. Whatever the hell Mark was working on, nobody knew how to describe it.

That didn't help me one bit.

He stood over the half-built, boxy structure with his hands on his hips. After eyeing it for a long moment, he moved to the other side and did it again.

Finally, he shook his head and grabbed a hammer from the tool belt slung low over his hips. "It's too small. And the wrong shape." He pulled a board off the side using the claw side of the hammer. "It's all wrong."

I had no idea how long it had taken him to build the frame for whatever this was supposed to be, but it came apart faster than I expected.

"Talk to me, Mark. What are we making here?" I paced around him, squinting and trying to imagine what the intent had been. "Urban renewal. Is it a garden plot? A compost bin? What?"

He pounded the nails out of the planks, then dropped the planks in the pile they'd come from. "Back to the drawing board."

"Come on, buddy. Give me something. Tell me about the silver tires you painted over the weekend, at least."

Mark appeared to be a lot more Zen about the situation than I was. I was ready to tear my hair out. He stood there with his arms folded and his face tilted to the sun while he thought mysterious thoughts about whatever he was making.

The angle of his chin highlighted the stubble on his jaw. I'd never seen him up close before, and with the sunlight reflecting the reddish highlights in his dark hair, I wanted to reach out and touch that stubble to see if it was soft or scratchy.

But I didn't. For one thing, my hand would have gone right through him. For another, Phyllis was watching through the kitchen window.

I cleared my throat. "Okay. I don't know what you're trying for, so I don't know if this will work or not, but let's give it a try." I unhooked my bubbles and pulled out the wand. "You can make it work, Mark. You already know what you want to make. You just have to trust the idea is a good one." I blew a stream of bubbles.

The wind picked up, and every last one of them flew over his left shoulder.

"Crap." I jogged around to the other side of him and tried again. "Trust in yourself. You can do this." I blew another stream of small bubbles, hoping my aim would be better and that my vague thoughts of encouragement would help.

Neither of those things happened, since the bubbles drifted over his head and toward the roof before popping on the rain gutters.

Mark ran his fingers through the hair over his eye, pushing it back. Without a word, he turned and walked into his apartment.

I groaned in frustration and glanced back at my kitchen window. Phyllis's branches were jerking in what I suspected were spasms of laughter. I gave her a dirty look and followed Mark into his house.

This was not my first foray into the apartment of a single man. They all seemed to have the same underlying funk, like sweat socks and leftovers long past their expiration date. Not so in Mark's house. It smelled like furniture polish and window cleaner. The living room still had a few newspapers on the table, and an empty pizza box sat on top of the kitchen trash can, so he wasn't a neat freak. But he wasn't a pig, either.

I didn't see him right away and searched down the hall to the bedroom. Even in there it smelled like clean laundry instead of gym shorts. Mark sat in a corner at a desk, sketching out a three-dimensional hexagon with the sides built up like we were looking down into it.

I frowned. "I really wish you'd just tell me what we're making." Before he could slip away and go outside into the wind again, I blew a bubble at him from a foot away. It landed between his eyes with an audible plop.

"I don't have enough wood or paint for something this size." He rose from his chair and nearly walked into me—not that either of us would feel it.

I followed him through the apartment like a puppy. When he dropped his tool belt on the floor next to the door and grabbed his keys, I threw my arms in the air. "I give up. This is ridiculous. It's as if they want me to fail."

He went out the door toward the parking lot, and I marched in the other direction, across the courtyard and into my apartment, scowling the entire way.

"What happened?" Phyllis sounded as exasperated as I felt.

I flapped my hand at her as I kicked off my shoes. "I think he went to the store to get more materials."

"Well, what's he making?"

My scowl deepened. "I haven't the faintest idea." I dug into my purse and pulled out the assignment to show her. "A *hexagon*. He's making a damn hexagon." I hit the button on my belt to become visible again, then unhooked the belt and hung it over the back of a kitchen chair. "It was going to be a square, but now it's a hexagon, and he doesn't have enough wood. Or nails. I don't know."

I left the kitchen and flopped onto the sofa.

The apartment wasn't large. Phyllis could still see me from her perch on the windowsill. "You're not giving up, are you?"

I shook my head. "No. But I'm not about to try to ride in his truck with him while I'm invisible. That would be weird. I'll try again when he comes back."

But he didn't come back. Not until long after I'd fallen asleep on the couch in an uncomfortable position. Around two thirty in the morning, I unfolded myself and went to bed, irritated and with a cramp in my neck.

Phyllis didn't say anything. I suspected she was asleep, too, which surprised me. I hadn't thought about it before, but she ate, drank, and breathed, in her fashion. I supposed she slept, too.

I dozed off wondering if she'd always been a houseplant, or if she'd been put under a spell by an angry god. Gods loved doing that sort of thing.

~*~

On Thursday morning, I stood in front of my desk and rubbed my eyes in disbelief. I glanced over my shoulder at Polly's office, then back at my inbox.

It was empty.

I muttered a vague prayer of thanks to whatever god was listening and headed for the elevator. Maybe three was all they would assign me. Honestly, if I had another client, I'd probably snap. I had a full plate.

The elevator doors opened to let me in, and there he was. Rick stood with his arms folded, eyes sparkling, and a grin making a dimple in his left cheek.

He was dressed as a Roman gladiator.

"Hey, New Girl. Coming to get some coffee?"

I inhaled deeply and stepped into the elevator. He smelled ridiculously good. "Sure. I've been going every morning on my way out." I paused. "Haven't seen you for a few days." I hoped I didn't sound petulant and whiny.

Or desperate.

The doors closed, and my stomach dropped a little as we descended. I wasn't entirely sure it was the elevator that had caused the sensation.

He gave me a sheepish look. "Not all my assignments are…human. I wouldn't want you to see me looking like a giant lizard or a monster covered in fur."

I frowned and looked him up and down, then felt my cheeks grow hot when I realized I was blatantly eyeballing his bare chest. I looked away as the doors opened and let us out on the second floor. "I'm not sure I follow. Why don't you just take off the costume?"

We walked together to the cafeteria, and he held the door open for me. His smile had disappeared. "It's not that simple. Let me get us settled and I'll explain. Do you have time to talk today?"

I shrugged. "Apparently, nobody is keeping tabs on me here. I can take all the time I want."

His grin was instantaneous, and this time it formed a second dimple. "Good. Have a seat. I'll get our drinks."

I opened my mouth to object, but he'd already spun around and started ordering. Nothing made me feel more awkward than having somebody I didn't know well pay for my order. If I objected, was I being rude? If I let it happen, was I thoughtless? Something about this guy made my insides go mushy and the neurons in my brain misfire.

Not sure what else to do, I found us a table and settled in to wait.

A few minutes later he slid into the booth across from me, bearing two large cups filled with steaming, cinnamony goodness. He set them down, then readjusted his bare legs against the vinyl seat.

I pulled my cup closer. "Thanks for the coffee." I took a sip and sighed in appreciation. "Will you let me get the next round?"

He shook his head. "Absolutely not. I'm being a delightful host right now." He shifted and winced as he peeled his leg free to move it. "Aren't I delightful host?"

I smiled. "You are a delightful host." I tipped my cup at him. "Thank you again for the coffee."

He squirmed a bit, then settled. "So, how's the Muse gig? Are you finding your footing?"

I grimaced. "I'm doing my best. Are all the departments so reluctant to train their new hires?"

"You're not getting training?" He took the plastic lid off his cup and blew into it to cool the liquid.

I shook my head. "One day. Since then, I've been completely on my own. No one will even talk to me. I just keep finding new assignments in my inbox."

His eyebrows rose in surprise. "Damn. So you're, like, flailing around by yourself?"

"Something like that. But I'm figuring it out." I paused. "Sort of."

"So, how many clients do you have, now? You've only been there a week."

I scowled. "Less than a week. I have three clients. I think I can do this, as long as they don't throw any more at me."

He put his coffee down. "Wow. Baptism by fire, I guess."

I nodded. "I have two of them under control, but the third one is stuck, and I have no idea what he's even supposed to be doing." I glanced around to see if anyone was watching—I had no idea if this would break any rules no one had told me about—and pulled the assignments out of my purse. The night before, I'd scrounged an old folder with Lisa Frank unicorns and rainbows all over it. The folder might not be dignified, but at least it kept my assignments together without causing further wrinkles. And it fit in my bag.

Rick smirked at the brightly colored sticker of a purple and white panda. "Nice."

"Do *not* make fun of my stickers. These are vintage." I flipped the folder open and pulled out the three pages, fanned them across the table, and pointed at the one on the left. "See how Mark's description is left blank? What the hell is *urban development*? How am I supposed to help him if I don't know what he's making?"

The frustration in me had built worse than I'd realized. As I spoke, my voice was louder than I'd intended. And a little more shrill. A couple of women wearing white, feathered wings glanced in our direction, and I slammed my mouth shut.

Rick reached out and took my hand. His fingers were warm and the middle finger had a callous on the side of the top knuckle. Interesting. He was left-handed, too.

"Look," he said. His fingers stroked the inside of my wrist and made me shiver. "You're doing the best you can. And according to this, you've got a whole month to get him sorted out. Don't worry. You can do this."

He pulled his hand away, and my disappointment was almost physical.

"Thanks." I looked away so he wouldn't see how much I wanted contact with him again.

Rick glanced at his phone. "My shift is done, so I need to go get out of this ridiculous get up." He peeled the backs of his legs free and slid out of the booth.

"You never told me why you were dressed that way." I wanted him to stay. Maybe if I stalled him, I'd get a few more minutes.

He drained his cup and tossed it in the trash. "That will have to wait, I'm afraid. But I'm off tomorrow. Can I convince you to play hooky?"

"My first week?"

He shrugged. "Nobody's keeping an eye on you. You could check in first thing in the morning, then meet me."

I bit my lip while I considered. He was right. Nobody was keeping an eye on me, and I could keep the belt and bubbles and check on my clients over the weekend. Who would know? Who would care? "I could meet you here, I guess."

"Great! I look forward to it." He grinned at me, then spun around to walk out the door, leaving me with a memory of bare chest, the smell of leather, and smiling green eyes.

Wait. Green? I'd have sworn they were blue the last time I'd seen him.

Chapter 13

To my surprise, both Missy and Alex needed no help with their projects when I looked in on them.

Alex had assembled the basic structure of two separate sections of the outside of the house. Presumably, once he was done, they'd fold together to form the whole or swing open to show the detailed inside. He was building a dollhouse, of sorts.

I didn't hang around long. He whistled to himself as he glued, and I sat on a box nearby to watch. After some initial hesitation, Oscar hopped up next to me for head scratches and cocked his floppy ears toward me every time I made a comment.

The Beastie Dust hung unused on my belt. If there was some terrible consequence of not keeping a client's pet unconscious while I worked, then someone should have damn well told me what it was. Leaving me to my own devices to figure out my job meant I made my own rules. Screw it. Oscar wouldn't rat me out.

I gave him a squeeze. "Gotta go, buddy. Your human is doing fine without my help. I'll check in on you two in a few days."

Oscar gave his tail a quick shake, then hopped off the box to go lie in his bed next to Alex. Alex never paused, his face tense with focus. He'd be perfectly fine on his own. I left, feeling confident.

When I stepped through the door into Missy's apartment, I didn't see her right away. I followed her voice down the hallway into Cassie's room and found mother and baby giggling together while Missy changed Cassie's diaper. Missy tickled the baby's belly and kissed her toes, then finished getting Cassie dressed. I leaned against the wall and watched, amazed at how carefree and relaxed my client was.

She put her little one in the crib and flipped the switch on a musical mobile that dangled snowflakes. Music from the movie *Frozen* played while the snowflakes rotated above the baby, just out of reach.

I followed Missy out of the room, both of us humming "Do You Want to Build a Snowman" with the mobile in the baby's room.

In the living room, Missy made a circuit, putting away toys, picking up tiny bits of paper from a shredded magazine Cassie must have gotten ahold of, and collecting dirty glasses and an empty baby bottle. I trailed behind and watched her throw away the trash and set the empties in the sink.

She puttered around for a few more minutes, then turned on the television.

"Oh, hell no." I fumbled to unhook the bottle on my belt. "Enough with the screwing around. It's time to get to work." I opened my bottle of Thought Bubbles and dunked my wand.

Before I had a chance to blow, Missy plopped on the floor in front of the coffee table and pulled out her box of supplies. She placed what she needed on the table, chose a fresh page and a photo, and got to work.

I stood with my arm bent, dripping bubble juice on the carpet. "Well, okay then." I felt sort of useless, fully prepared to inspire only to find I wasn't needed. "I must be better at this than I thought."

Taking a day off on my first week had seemed irresponsible. But now it seemed like no big deal. If at least two-thirds of my clients didn't need me, what was the point? In fact, maybe the entire point of my job was to get people started. I was the queen of getting stuff started. Maybe I wasn't so great at finishing, but these people seemed to be.

I'd continue checking on them in the weeks to come, but it seemed I'd already done what I'd been assigned to do.

Mission accomplished.

Watching someone cut paper and glue it in place was about as mind numbing as watching someone glue toothpicks together on a bed of wax paper. I didn't stay much longer at Missy's than I had at Alex's.

One stop left for the day, and I'd have a three-day weekend. Sort of.

Since nobody had said anything to me about taking my belt home before, I had no intention of going back to the office after I checked on Mark to drop it off. I wasn't done working for the day, but I was home for good.

I popped my head into the kitchen. "Hey. Is he doing anything new?"

I'd left Phyllis in the window to keep watch for me. Since Mark was proving to be my most difficult client, having a second set of eyes on him throughout the day couldn't hurt. Or whatever it was Phyllis used for looking at things. Magic of the gods, maybe. I didn't want to think about it.

"He went out once to get the mail. That's all I've seen him do until he left in a huff about an hour ago." She dropped her voice to a near whisper.

"Terwilliger was banging on our door. You might want to check. She's on another crusade and left a note. Mark had his crumpled in his hand when he went out."

I groaned and whispered back, as if the landlady might be standing outside with an empty water glass pressed against the wall and her ear. "Is she still out there?" I crept through the kitchen and eased the door open. Sure enough. A bright green slip of folded paper was taped to the chipped paint. I detached it and ducked back inside.

"What is it?" Phyllis shivered her branches in my direction. "Read it."

I unfolded the paper and cleared my throat. "Hear ye, hear ye…"

"She didn't!" Phyllis sounded scandalized.

I laughed. "No. I added that myself." I skimmed the page, then read it for my houseplant. "Management has received several complaints of people working on personal projects in the courtyard public area. Please refrain from using the courtyard in ways that will inconvenience other residents, cause excessive noise, or leave behind leftover materials or damage to the property. This includes but is not limited to: hammering, sawing, spray painting, and screwing." I giggled, then slapped my hand over my mouth.

Phyllis snorted. "Screwing? Did she really prohibit screwing in the courtyard?"

I nodded, dropping my hand. "Number one, she's hilariously stupid. Number two, that bitch! This is directed at Mark. People have been using that courtyard for projects for years. Remember when the McGinleys brought all that IKEA furniture outside so they'd have room to put it together?"

Phyllis's leaves lifted in what looked like a shrug. "I watched them screw up that bookcase. If I could have talked back then, I'd have sent you out there to tell them how to fix it. They had the side panel on upside down."

I smirked. "When did you get so wise about putting together furniture?"

"Sweetheart, I've been watching the world for a very long time. My roots go surprisingly deep. You'd do well to pay better attention to my advice."

"You're right." I folded the paper in half and tossed it in the trash. "And at the moment, you're the only one in the world who's got my back."

~*~

111

With nothing better to do while I waited for Mark to come home from wherever he'd gone, I pressed the button on my belt and headed over to his empty apartment. Maybe he'd left some drawings on his desk or something.

I was well aware I was in sketchy territory, spying on him while he was gone. But I was a Muse. That should give me immunity, right? I was trying to help.

The kitchen was tidy. Three ceramic jars in graduated sizes lined the counter, their lids secured with metal clips. There was nothing else on the counter but a toaster, coffee maker, and a single clean glass drying upside down on a dishtowel.

I ran my finger over the cheap, laminate countertop. It came away without any stickiness or grease, like it might at my house. Impressed, I concentrated hard enough to interact with my surroundings and peeked inside a cupboard. All the dishes and glasses were neatly stacked on clean, striped contact paper. The next cupboard was filled with food: jars of rice, honey, granola, olive, and coconut oil. Everything he had seemed to be either outright healthy or at least not bad for you. And it was so tidy.

I made a face and checked his fridge. "Holy crap." I stood in the light of the refrigerator, shocked. "How can any one person eat so many vegetables?"

It was like looking into my mother's kitchen. I took a look in the lower cabinet next to the sink, knowing what I'd find. I squatted for a better view. Sure enough. A big, shiny juicer shared space with one of those mini blenders that makes a single smoothie right in the cup.

I shook my head and closed the cabinet door. No wonder he had all those muscles under his tight shirts.

Ashamed of my lack of healthy habits in my own kitchen, I moved into the living room. I didn't linger long. Aside from a pair of socks under the coffee table and a home improvement magazine sitting on the sofa, it was pristine. I checked a drawer in the table, found three remotes, closed it, and moved on.

The bathroom was a little messier. A yellow bath towel lay discarded on the floor. I glanced up and found a hook on the wall. The towel had probably fallen. The shower curtain hadn't been pulled all the way shut, and a damp washcloth lay spread over the rim of the sink to dry.

I opened the medicine cabinet because that's what every good snooper was supposed to do. Toothpaste. Floss. Aspirin. Deodorant. Nothing interesting. The single drawer beneath the sink yielded nail clippers and a crap-ton of condoms.

"Now you have my attention, sir." Impressed, I closed the drawer and moved across the hall to the bedroom.

And that's where I found the mess. Discarded clothes. Work boots piled in the corner. Wadded sheets and blankets in the middle of the bed. And best of all, papers strewn everywhere. Crumpled balls covered the floor, and smooth pages spread across the desk. Whatever Mark was working on, it was frustrating the hell out of him. If I couldn't find the answer to what he was making here, I'd never find it on my own.

It was also a huge relief to find out my neighbor wasn't perfect.

I bent over the desk and tried to decipher the sketches he'd made. Most were seemingly random squares and circles. Some were a little more interesting, though. One featured what looked like a dinosaur made up of geometric shapes. It also could have been a dragon. I wasn't sure. Another looked like a tree with holes cut out at precise intervals.

The problem with being invisible was how much I had to concentrate in order to touch anything. Sitting on a chair was easy. Apparently, the gods who'd created this system had set it up so we interacted normally with our environment. This kept me from falling through stairs or sinking into the floor. Going through doors, now that I'd done it a few times, was possible without thinking about it. But individual items were a bitch to negotiate.

Obviously, I was doing something wrong.

Every time I tried to move one of the pages so I could look at one under it, my hand went through the desk. And forget about trying to smooth out the discards on the floor to see what secrets they held. Opening the cupboards had been difficult enough.

If I was going to get anywhere, I had to shut off the invisibility on my belt. This was probably a terrible idea. If I got caught, I'd have no way of explaining why I was there or how I'd gotten in. I'd only spoken to the guy a few times. Our next conversation really shouldn't have to be as he was calling the police.

But I had a deadline, and he was failing. Which meant I was failing.

I pressed the button on my belt and tested my solidity by tapping the desk. My fingers touched the polished wood instead of falling through.

Immediately, I panicked. "Fingerprints, fingerprints!" I tugged my blouse out from under the golden belt and used the material to scrub the desk in a vigorous motion. "And stop talking to yourself! You're not silenced anymore, either."

I took a step back and tripped, falling on my ass in the middle of the room, sending balls of paper rolling in every direction. For a moment I sat on the bedroom floor, trying to slow my breathing and get control of myself again. When I was a little less freaked out that I was sitting in my neighbor's house going through his stuff without the aid of magical camouflage, I reached for the nearest paper ball and smoothed it flat with hands that shook a little less than they would have a few minutes before.

I squinted at the page. Once I had the wrinkles ironed out enough to see the pencil lines, it appeared to be a fish. The series of three fins on its back were oddly flat, as if something was supposed to sit on it.

The next page showed a pirate ship with the Jolly Roger flying above it. Those strange circles dotted the sides, similar to the tree I'd seen before.

A third page yielded a picture of a two-headed animal of some kind— maybe a llama. One head was up and the other down. Both heads were flat, like the fins on the fish.

"You clever son of a bitch." I grinned at the pile of drawings. "You're trying to build a playground." I couldn't prove it, exactly, but *urban renewal* combined with these whimsical sketches told me I was right.

But Mark couldn't decide on the theme.

"Oh, honey. How the hell are you going to build something of this magnitude in less than a month if you can't even decide what to build?"

I examined each picture. He had great ideas. But they weren't cohesive.

A key rattled in the door and I froze. "No, no, no," I whispered.

In a burst of motion, I scuttled around the floor, wadding up the papers I'd smoothed and tossing them around in as natural a pattern as I could manage.

The front door opened and shut. Frantic, I reached to press the button on my belt, but the belt had shifted when I fell, and the fabric of my blouse was tangled from when I pulled it out to wipe off my fingerprints.

The kitchen faucet turned on and ran for a moment, then turned off. Shaking, I stuffed my blouse under the belt and tried to straighten the chain. The Beastie Dust bottle was caught, and the buckle I was searching for had migrated over my left hip.

Clunky footsteps strode down the hallway toward me. My fingers touched the button and I clicked it. Mark walked into the bedroom and looked right at me.

He frowned. "I thought I mailed those."

My eyes grew wide as he walked toward me. "I can explain." Why did people always say that? It was rarely true. I held my hands up, as if in self-defense, but he walked through me to the desk. I shivered from the weird contact—or lack of contact—and spun around.

Mark reached for two envelopes I hadn't noticed sitting on his desk. He shuffled them, then left the room. After a moment, the kitchen door opened and shut, and I was left alone to deal with an over-abundance of adrenalin.

I sat on the edge of Mark's bed and took a few deep breaths. "So stupid." I dropped my head in my hands. "Never again."

And yet, a small voice in the back of my head gave a little yip of excitement. I'd never really done anything dangerous or even slightly daring before. I was not a risk taker. I'd spent my life following the path of least resistance.

Pushing the envelope was kind of a rush.

I squashed the excitement I was feeling and waited for Mark to come back from the mailbox. No more risks for me. At least not for a long while. I would play it straight and follow the rules.

Whatever the rules were.

When Mark came back in, I had my bubble wand at the ready and my bottle open and waiting. He meandered from the kitchen to the living room and back again, avoiding the bedroom where I wanted him to go. He needed to work.

He needed to stop waffling.

I followed where he went, relentless. Small bubbles in a steady stream, large ones that glided on their own wind currents. I blew slowly and sent a large bubble to land between his shoulder blades.

If my Thought Bubbles had been made of the same substance as regular bubbles, Mark would have been drenched in sticky liquid.

"Come on." I blew another long stream at him. "Go sit down and hash this out. You know what you want to create. You just don't trust yourself. Unless you draw it, you can't make it." I blew a long squiggly bubble. "The thing in your head can be real. You know how to do it."

I doubted he heard me, exactly, but he did stop wandering around like he'd lost his wallet or something. He settled in front of his desk and took out a fresh piece of paper and a pencil.

I blew a massive bubble at his head. I blew so hard, it popped in my face, and I had to try again.

The resulting bubble was a great, ponderous blob that wobbled at him in a painfully slow line. I closed my eyes and put all the positive, encouraging energy I could into it. "You've got this, Mark. What's your fabulous idea? Be brave."

The bubble hit him on the back of the head and bounced. I blew a little air at it to make it change course and it returned to him, popped, and splattered.

Mark tensed as if he'd felt it, and I waited, fingers crossed. He blew out a lungful of air and touched his pencil to the page.

And the phone rang, breaking the spell.

"Son of a bitch," I said.

"Son of a bitch," he said.

I moved closer to his ear, hoping he would *hear* me, even if he couldn't hear me. "Don't answer it. Whoever it is will leave a message. We're *so* close."

The phone continued to ring. Mark sighed and answered it. "Hello?"

I smacked my face. "No, you knucklehead. I told you not to answer it."

Mark nodded. "Yeah, Pete. I've been working on some ideas to show you at dinner next week. Once we go over it together, I'll get the ball rolling." He listened for a moment, the fingers of one hand drumming on the desk. "No, yeah. We'll get it done before her birthday. No worries. I've got this. Yeah. You too, Pete. Take care." He disconnected the call and stared at the phone in his hand for a long moment. "I don't have this." He sounded miserable.

"You *do* have this, Mark. I saw these drawings." I gestured at the crumpled paper on the floor as if he could see and hear me. "I've never known anyone with half your creativity. You have to believe in yourself." I drew close to him, looking him in the eyes. "I do."

He sighed and put his phone in his pocket and rose from his chair. If he hadn't gone right through me, I'd have been knocked over. He clomped out of the room to the kitchen.

"Hey." I trotted behind him. "What are you doing? We're not done."

He opened the fridge, scanned the contents, then slammed it shut. He leaned against the counter and rubbed his face, looking tired and worried. With another deep sigh, he grabbed his car keys and headed for the door.

"Hey," I said, scowling. "Where are you going?"

"I'm out of beer," he said. "I need a drink." He shut the door and locked it.

I stood in the kitchen and watched him out the window until I realized what had happened.

Mark had answered me.

Chapter 14

Mark must have gone to Colorado for that beer, because he was gone all evening. I gave up after an hour and went home. I had to hope the work I'd done with him earlier had greased the gears a little. Maybe a few drinks would finish the job.

The truth was, Mark had stressed me out. And I didn't think I could help him unless I got myself in a better mindset.

Fortunately, I had a date with a gladiator the next day. That ought to do it.

I went into the office Friday morning before taking the day off. I was, after all, brand new. Maybe Fridays were a day of departmental meetings and I'd be notably absent. Maybe everybody brought potluck. Hell, I'd have been surprised if *anybody* had been there. But they weren't. And the biggest reason I'd come in was to check my inbox to be sure I didn't have a new assignment.

My inbox was mercifully empty.

I stopped in the prop room and refilled my Thought Bubbles. Mark had used up half a bottle with all the craziness the night before. I didn't want to get caught unprepared.

With nobody to stop me, I walked out with no intention of visiting any clients that day. My stomach had butterflies, but I didn't change my mind. At the end of the day, nobody cared but me.

I stepped out of the elevator and found Rick waiting outside the cafeteria. He wore totally normal clothes this time—jeans and a blue, buttoned shirt with the sleeves rolled up. He smelled clean like he'd stepped out of the shower five minutes earlier.

Rick grinned at me. "Good morning. You look beautiful."

I'd chosen a yellow print dress with a short, fluttery skirt and sandals with low heels, since I didn't know where we were going. Mom always told me yellow brought out the blue in my eyes and made my blonde hair shine like gold. Mom was weird like that. But she was surprisingly good at fashion advice.

"Morning." I smiled back. "And thank you."

His grin widened, and he held open the cafeteria door. "Shall we start with coffee and then go from there?"

I glanced up at him as I walked past, and my smile wavered. His adorable dimples were gone. And his eyes were definitely blue. How did a person change their eye color and lose their dimples?

For the first time, I wondered what Rick really looked like. Was this the real version?

He brought the coffee to our table, and I waited for him to settle into the booth. He handed me my cup and took a sip from his own.

"Rick?"

"Yeah?"

"Before we go any further with all this, maybe you should tell me a little more about your job. And, you know, your costumes. How they work."

This time, Rick's smile faltered. "It's all in the details, isn't it?"

I tilted my head and looked closer at his face. "The cowboy duds and the gladiator getup weren't really costumes, were they?"

His cheekbones were a little higher today, his nose a bit narrower. Both earlobes were pierced, but I didn't recall having seen them that way before. Both times before, his hair had been a shiny, bright blond, but now it was more of an ash blond. He was still attractive as hell, but he was also different. In fact, the previous versions of him had almost been too perfect. This Rick had a little razor burn on his neck, and his left eyebrow had a small scar. He wasn't nearly as intimidating with a few small imperfections.

Rick shook his head. "Not exactly, no." He leaned into the cushioned seat. "This is what I wanted to explain to you about my job. I am whatever I need to be for the dream role I'm cast in for the night."

"So, you're saying you don't have a wardrobe department."

"No. Not exactly. More like a graphic arts department." He took a long gulp of coffee. "And a spa treatment."

I smirked. "What?"

"It's kind of a long process. First, we receive the dream assignments from various departments. Sometimes they come from Fate, sometimes a client needs a shaking up from the Furies, and sometimes the dreams are assigned internally. They come from all over, really. We script it, cast it, then a designer pulls a character profile from the database and tweaks it or creates a new one altogether. The result is uploaded to a shower bomb."

I held my hand up. "Whoa. A shower bomb?"

He chuckled. "Not a bomb bomb. A shower bomb. Like a bath bomb, but for showers. The water hits it and the bomb dissolves, releasing the magical essence of the character rather than the smelly stuff in a regular shower bomb."

My eyes may have glazed over for a second as I imagined him in the shower naked every day in this very building. I shook myself and tried not to blush. "So, then what? You transform in the shower and walk out in a wet costume?"

"Well, the costume is dry, but yeah." He gave me a sheepish look. "So, that's why I didn't see you every day this week. Sometimes I don't look very much like myself."

I frowned. "How *much* not like yourself?"

"On Tuesday, I was covered in green fur, and Wednesday I kind of looked like a giant tuna with tentacles." His expression was serious, though his words sounded like a joke.

I blinked. "Not uh."

"Ya huh. And I can't wash it off, so I'm stuck here until it wears off. It's one thing to walk around in a black hat and chaps, it's another to scare people and put them off their breakfast." He paused. "Or, you know, chase you away before I'd even had a chance to take you out."

I gripped my cup in both hands and smiled. "I guess your plan worked then. So where are we going?"

The corners of his eyes crinkled. "Well, we can go through your portal or mine. I'm afraid mine's not exactly exotic, but if you'd like to see the capitol of Kansas, we can go through mine."

My eyebrows rose in surprise. "You live in Topeka?"

He shrugged. "Yeah. Like I said, not really exciting."

I grinned over the lid of my cup. "Oh, I don't know. Some of the best people live there. Me, for example."

He sat up straighter. "No!"

"Yes!"

"Well, then. I guess we're going through the Topeka portal. How do you feel about picnics?"

~*~

Apparently, Rick had been planning to talk me into a picnic all along. The fact that we belonged to the same portal made it easier on him, since he had everything we needed already in the trunk of his car.

We left my car parked up the street—I didn't want the fake homeless dude to report my hooky-playing ways if that's what his job was—and drove out to Perry Lake for the day.

119

My insides were at war with each other throughout the day. Here I was with this gorgeous, thoughtful guy, and I was having trouble relaxing with him. Just as he'd somehow known how much I loved cinnamon lattes, the contents of his picnic basket were strangely compatible with my likes and tastes.

The sandwiches were Swiss and ham on buttery croissants with mayo and a dab of mustard. Seriously, he'd nailed it, even down to the condiments. Nectarines, sea salt bagel chips, and white cupcakes with vanilla frosting. He'd also brought ice-cold bottles of water for after we drank the cans of strawberry soda he'd brought.

It was a little scary. My mother could have packed me that lunch.

I tried to tell myself I was holding back because I'd only broken up with Freddy a couple of weeks ago. It was probably too soon to start something new. But it was more than that.

We sat on a blanket together, listening to the waves lap against the rocks. My stomach was full of some of my favorite things to eat, the sun warmed my back, and a gorgeous guy sat next to me.

He sat so close, the hairs on our arms brushed. I shivered.

"Are you cold?" He rubbed the palm of his hand over my back. "I have another blanket in the car."

I shook my head. "I'm fine." I squinted up at the sky. "I should probably be getting back, though." I reached for my sandals and slipped them on.

"Oh." The disappointment in his voice was thick. "Alright." He reached for the empty water bottles and placed them in the carrier he'd brought.

"I'm sorry." I really was. I was torn between wanting to jump on him and wanting to back away. Backing away was usually my go-to position whenever I was in doubt. I'd have to work on that. "It's kind of a drive back, and then I have to get my own car. I've really had a good time, though."

He stood and helped me to my feet, then bent to grab the blanket. "I'm glad. I had fun, too." His tone was a little stiff.

I touched his sleeve. "Really. It was perfect."

His smile was slow, but it reached his eyes, and his shoulders relaxed. "Maybe we can do it again sometime?" He didn't look at me as he folded the blanket.

I couldn't believe a guy like this could be so unsure of himself. "Absolutely. We'll do it on a day when I'm not supposed to be at work. I can relax better that way."

He frowned and faced me. "I'm sorry. I shouldn't have asked you to do this on your first week. Next time, we'll do it legally. No shenanigans."

I looped my arm through his as we walked back to the car. "Well, don't get rid of *all* the shenanigans. There can be *some* shenanigans."

He held up two fingers and pinched them close together without touching. "A *little* shenanigans, then."

I laughed. "It's a deal."

~*~

I was still a little freaked out by the time we got to my car, although I was pretty sure my freaked-outedness was totally due to Wynter-itis—the inability to commit to anyone or anything. Freddy had been too recent a reminder of my inability to get out of my own way.

Hopefully, Rick would be patient with me. I wasn't ready for Mr. Perfect to swoop in out of nowhere. I was a work in progress and he wasn't. Slight razor burn and a tiny eyebrow scar were not enough to bring him down to my level of screwed up.

I nearly explained that to him when I gave him the cheek slide. He'd tried to kiss me goodbye, and I sort of panicked again. The hurt in his eyes wasn't lost on me. But I didn't have the words to explain it.

All the way home in my car, I mentally and verbally beat myself up. "Stupid, stupid, stupid. He's awesome. He's gorgeous. He anticipates your needs." I pulled into my parking space and glared at myself in the rearview mirror. "Get. A. Grip."

When I burst through the door, I slammed it behind myself, and threw my purse on the counter.

Phyllis sounded startled. "Wynter? What on Earth is wrong, sweetheart? You nearly scared the leaves off me." She wasn't exaggerating. Several dry leaves had fluttered into the sink below the windowsill.

"I'm sorry." I gathered the leaves and tossed them in the trash, then poked a finger at her dirt. "Are you thirsty? You're a little dry."

"I could use a drink. Thank you. But first tell me what happened."

I ran the faucet and adjusted it until it was the lukewarm temperature Phyllis preferred. "I'm an idiot. I'm broken. You can't fix me."

"Oh, honey. It can't be that bad. Did something happen at work?"

I shook my head and trickled water into her dirt. "I didn't go to work. I went on a picnic with a gorgeous guy. Then I freaked out and made him take me home because he's too perfect and I'm not." I shut off the water and burst into tears, still holding the potted plant.

121

"Oh, Wynter, no. Don't be silly." A leafy branch stroked the back of my hand. "Nobody's perfect. Any man would be lucky to spend time with you."

Her words and tone, combined with the surprisingly soft leaves stroking my hand calmed me. I wiped away my tears. "You think so?"

She patted my hand. "I know so." The soothing branch pulled back and whacked me where it had been petting me a second before.

"Ouch!"

"I cannot believe you spent the day with a boy instead of going to work. Are you trying to end up in the Underworld?"

I set her in the sink to drain, then rubbed the welt rising on my skin. "I've got it under control. It's only the first week, and two of my clients are well on their way."

If she'd had eyes, I wouldn't have been able to meet them. As it was, I looked away. She was sure to read the guilt on my face. I felt terrible enough already.

She tutted and shook her leaves. "Two. Two are on their way." One of her branches wagged in the direction of the window. "And what about poor Mark out there? He's running out of time. So what if you figured out he's trying to design a playground? Knowing what it's supposed to be isn't even halfway there. The poor boy needs an idea, Wynter."

I was getting lectured by a houseplant. And I was dangerously close to bursting into tears again because she was absolutely right. "I tried. He won't listen to me."

Her voice grew quiet. "Then you must make him listen. Not because it's your job and you don't want to fail. You must do it because you are a Muse, and he needs you. Without you, *he* will fail."

Chapter 15

Phyllis was right, of course. I'd lost sight of the purpose to all this. It wasn't about whether I failed or not. This was about getting Alex to the competition so he'd feel more in control of his life and less under his mother's thumb. It was about Missy giving her parents the perfect gift for their fiftieth anniversary.

And it was about Mark creating something truly special for some really lucky kid.

I washed the tears from my face and fixed my hair. It was time to get serious. Mark was getting my help in whatever capacity he needed it.

The ridiculous note from Mrs. Terwilliger was still in the trash. I rescued it and flicked half a grape off the edge.

"Wynter, what are you doing?" Phyllis sat draining in the sink, straining her branches to reach over the edge as if she couldn't quite see what I had.

I smoothed the page against the counter. "I'm going to see Mark about this stupid note."

"You can't go talk to him in person. Are you crazy? Where's your belt?"

I waved a dismissive hand in her direction. "It's in the other room. So far, it hasn't done me a hell of a lot of good."

"This can't turn out well. Isn't there a rule against it? What will your boss say?"

My hand was on the doorknob, and I stopped. "My boss hasn't had anything important to say to me all week. I'm doing this my way, now." I walked outside and shut the door before Phyllis could say anything else.

I stood in front of Mark's apartment and ran my sweaty palms over my dress. The memo in my hand slipped and dropped to the ground. I bent to pick it up, and when I stood straight again, Mark stood in front of me in his doorway.

"Hi." His eyes flicked to the bright note in my hand. "Are you here to complain about me, too? Don't worry. I'm done trying to build anything."

"No!" I blurted the single word a little too loudly. I made an effort to take it down a notch. "No. I don't want to complain. Well, I mean, I do. But not about you." I held up the note. "What the hell is her problem?"

He relaxed and smiled. "I don't know. Maybe she stole some of my spray paint and was huffing it."

I smirked. "That might actually improve her personality."

"That it might." He laughed and stuck his hand out. "I don't think we've really met. I'm Mark."

My eyes widened in surprise. "Oh, thank goodness. I thought we had met and I felt terrible that I'd forgotten your name. I'm Wynter." I took his offered hand, and he gave mine a warm squeeze rather than a shake.

"Would you…" He rubbed the back of his neck, as if he were nervous. "Would you like to come in for a drink or something?"

"I would love to." I wadded up Terwilliger's note and tossed it over my shoulder. "Oops. Don't you hate when people leave their stuff in public areas?"

He smiled and stepped aside to let me in. "I have no idea why we haven't been friends this whole time."

I walked past him, trying not to let him see my smile falter. I knew why we hadn't been friends before. I didn't have friends. I always thought friends were too much work.

Mark pulled a couple of beers out of the fridge, opened one and handed it to me.

I took a sip. "I've seen you out there building stuff. What is it you're working on?" I tried to sound casual, like it didn't matter to me. Like my entire world wasn't focused on it right at that moment. Like my future didn't depend on it.

He sighed and gestured toward the living room with his bottle. "I've been commissioned to build some pieces for a little girl's fifth birthday."

"That sounds fun." I followed him into the living room and sat in a squeaky leather chair.

"Fun. Sure. I'm running out of time, and I haven't come up with a theme yet." He sighed and took a sip. "Her name is Carry. She's got leukemia. I want to make it perfect for her."

I frowned. No wonder he was so stressed out. "What does she like? It's for her backyard, right?"

He froze with his bottle halfway to his mouth. "How did you know that?"

Shit. "I guessed. It looked like you were building a sandbox earlier in the week."

He nodded. "Yeah. Well, I took it apart."

"What was wrong with it?" I felt like I was approaching an antelope on the Savannah. I had to move slowly so as not to spook him. "I'm sure she would have loved it."

"It was all wrong. Too small. Too boring. I don't know." He sounded so defeated. "I want it to be something fantastic. She's been through so much. I want to give her back some of her childhood, you know?"

He really was sweet. I wanted to hug him and tell him it would all work out. "What about the tires you spray painted last week. Was that part of it?"

He shrugged and stared at his hands. "I was experimenting with the idea of doing an outer space theme. It didn't work." He shook himself and sat straight, looking right at me. "But I'll get it, right? I've got time." He snorted, then took a long swallow. "What about you? I see you come and go a lot lately during the day. What do you do?"

The question startled me. "Me?" I did a mental flail, trying to think of an answer that didn't sound like I'd had a psychotic break. Telling him I was a Muse was out of the question. "I'm a…consultant."

His eyebrows drew together. "What do you consult about?"

"Uh. Projects. Aesthetics. I'm a project manager. Consultant. An aesthetics project manager consultant." I wasn't sure there was such a thing. I was tanking in this conversation. If this had been a talk show, I'd have been begging them to cut to a commercial. I forced a smile and went all in. "For the government. I can't really talk about it."

"Okay." His expression was doubtful. "I won't ask."

The awkward silence that followed was broken only by the sound of each of us swallowing our beer. I lasted probably a full minute before I broke.

"So. What's got you frozen up? Why haven't you settled on a big idea, yet?" I tried to give him an encouraging expression, but it felt more like a thin film of desperation spread across my face.

He shook his head. "I don't know what's wrong. But time is running out." He sighed and ran his hand through his hair. "If I don't come up with something, we won't be able to get it built in time for her birthday."

I put my bottle on the table and strode over to him. "Come on." I stuck my hand out.

He looked at my hand, then up at me. "Where are we going?"

I gave my hand an impatient shake. "You need to remember what kinds of things kids like."

"I know what kids like. I don't need to go anywhere." Despite his protest, he took my hand and let me tug him to his feet. "Kids like video games and television marathons."

I led him into the kitchen and deposited my empty bottle on the counter. "Maybe. We'll see."

He frowned and grabbed his keys. "You're not going to tell me where we're going, are you?"

I grinned and shoved him through the door. "We're going to a toy store."

~*~

I'd been right not to attempt to hop into Mark's truck and follow him when I was invisible. The inside of the cab was small and crammed with blueprints, loose tools, and notebooks. If I tried to sit on top of it all in stealth mode, I'd have ended up with a screwdriver poking me in the butt at the very least.

"So, this is why your apartment is so tidy." I shoved an atlas and a map of Topeka to the floor. "You keep all your crap in here. Very clever."

"I wasn't expecting a passenger." He slid behind the wheel and started the engine. "This was all your idea."

I grinned. "It's a fabulous idea. You can thank me later."

He grunted and pulled out of the parking lot. "For someone who used to avoid talking to everybody, you sure are chatty."

I folded my arms across my chest. "Hey, I wasn't avoiding anybody."

"Uh huh. And you didn't duck behind your counter when I tried to wave at you through your window."

I'd really hoped he hadn't seen that. Apparently I wasn't as smooth as I thought. I grimaced at him and remained silent until we arrived at the store.

The store he chose was a family-owned place with all kinds of old-school games and timeless toys like hula hoops and yo-yos. We stuck together for a while, and I tried to help.

"How about this?" I held up a pair of hats, one with cat ears and one shaped like what a court jester would wear. "The whole playground could be done in giant hats."

He reached out and took the jester hat, frowning in concentration. "Maybe." He shook it and the tiny bells rang.

"The curly ends could be double slides." I gave him a hopeful smile.

"Let's keep looking." He handed it back.

After my third suggestion, I could see I was hurting his concentration more than helping. I wandered off and left him perusing the stuffed animals. I was sure the answer he was looking for could be found inside that store. He only needed to find it.

A few aisles over I found a woman about my age wearing a nametag and an apron covered in buttons. In one hand, she held a pink, plastic bottle. In the other, she held a stick with a hole on the end.

She was blowing bubbles.

Or at least, she was trying. As I came around the corner, she pursed her lips and blew. The liquid splattered everywhere. She dipped her wand in the solution and tried again with the same result.

At first, I was amused. Who doesn't know how to blow bubbles? She blew again, and the thin film almost formed a bubble, then sprayed backward into her mouth instead. I didn't know how that could even happen. She sputtered, stomped her foot, then tried again.

I approached with caution, not wanting an eyeful of liquid soap. "You know, if you lift your arm a little closer and a little higher." I moved her elbow into position. "There. Now try blowing more softly. If you blow too hard, it doesn't give the bubble a chance to form."

She tried again, and a perfect, medium-sized bubble drifted into the aisle. "Hey, thanks!" She tried again, and a stream of smaller ones pattered out of the plastic loop. Grinning, she dropped her wand into the bottle. "I've been trying to do that for days. I couldn't figure out what I was doing wrong."

I smiled. "Well, I'm glad I could help." What a weird skill to have to pass on to a stranger.

"I'm Amy." She tapped her nametag. "What can I help you find today?"

I started to tell her I was just looking. It's always the automatic response to that question. But I glanced at the shelves in the aisle where we were standing and gasped. "Are all these for bubbles?"

"Sure. Big ones. Little ones. Colored ones. Ones that land on you without popping." She touched the different wands of varying sizes as she spoke, her expression as animated as her hands. "We've got these trays so you can pour a bunch of solution into it and dip the really big wands. The bubbles are bigger than a person if you do it right." She shrugged. "Not that I could get them to work."

I was enchanted. There were so many choices dangling from pegs, taunting me. Inviting me. "I'm going to buy them."

"Cool. Which ones?"

I touched a bright green one with a flower-shaped loop on the end. "All of them."

She blinked at me. "How about I get you a shopping basket."

By the time she came back, I had an armful of wands, two industrial-sized bottles of bubble solution, and a book on the art of bubbles. Amy grabbed two of the smallest plastic wands as they slid off the book on their way to the floor, and we wrestled everything into the basket she'd brought me. As an afterthought, I added a green and yellow bubble gun that shot bubbles at the touch of a trigger.

"You really like bubbles," she said. "No wonder you knew how to help me."

I shrugged. "Everybody likes bubbles." I eyed the giant trays and grabbed one, then picked up a contraption that resembled a jump rope—two handles and a length of rope—but was far too short for anybody to jump. "What's this?"

"I watched a video of that, once. You hold the handles together and drag it through the solution, then sort of wave it with handles apart." She chuckled. "I tried it once. You can imagine the cosmic fail I experienced."

I dropped it in the basket, along with one last wand that was more hoop than handle. The circle was nearly the size of my head. "Okay. I think that's enough damage. Let's ring this up before I can't make my rent."

She rolled her eyes. "Try working here. If I'm not careful, I spend more than I make." With her free hand, Amy waved me to follow while she carried my basket to the counter.

The total wasn't nearly as bad as I'd expected. Turns out, bits of brightly colored plastic in weird geometric shapes were pretty cheap. The rope thing and the book were the most expensive items, and they weren't too bad, either.

Once I'd paid for it all, I went in search of my idea-deficient neighbor. He wasn't where I'd left him. After searching through the building blocks, the army men, and three aisles of Barbies, I finally found him standing in front of a rack of board games.

His face lit up when he saw me. "Wynter, you're a genius."

I suppressed a sarcastic reply. "Yeah?"

"Yeah." He gave a deep, satisfied sigh and held out the game in his hands.

"Candy Land?" I peered at the box. It hadn't changed much over the years. Bright colors, happy children, an exuberant king welcoming us to his kingdom—and a bazillion tempting pastries and sweets.

He grinned. "It's the perfect theme for a little girl's backyard playground. I'm going to build Candy Land."

Chapter 16

With all three of my charges chugging along on their own steam, I had an entire guilt-free weekend ahead of me to do anything I wanted. Normally, that would mean cleaning up the apartment, binge watching some television, or going to see a movie by myself.

Recent events had shown me how badly I was screwing up my life. It was time to make some changes.

I imagined a normal human wouldn't stare at a phone number and get queasy over the idea of calling it—unless it was a potential romantic partner. Sure. That's worth some butterflies. But calling a new friend to see if they wanted to hang out? Most people probably don't have to do mental exercises in order to talk themselves into it.

After a half hour of muttering to myself, setting down the phone, pacing, then coming back to pick up the phone again, I finally hit the button to call Jillian.

It only rang twice before she answered. "Wynter! Hey. I was going to call you in a few minutes. How weird is that?"

The tension ran out of me, and I sat on the couch. "You were? That *is* weird. What's up?"

"No, you first. How's the job?" She sounded out of breath.

"Is this a bad time? You sound busy."

"I'm on the treadmill, but I'm on the cool down. You talk. I'll be done in a minute." The pounding of her feet and the vibration of the treadmill were soothing in the background of the call. A slight echo let me know she'd put me on speaker.

I took a deep breath, wondering how much to tell her. "The job has its up and downs. I'm still learning. Met a cute guy. Don't know how that's going to pan out." I paused, then decided friendship meant sharing some of the crap, too. "Everybody in my office hates me, and I ran away from the cute guy when he tried to kiss me. One of my neighbors is a client, so I'm working even after hours. I don't know what I'm doing, and I'm probably going to fail. So, there's all that."

Once it was out there, I felt both better and worse. And to be honest, a little worried that she would decide I was one of *those* people, the sad-sacks that required constant handholding and far too much emotional commitment.

The hum of the treadmill stopped, and Jillian switched me off of speakerphone. "Well, crap. You've had a terrible week."

I smiled at how fast she'd cut to the chase. "Yeah. Terrible week."

"Okay. Well, what I was going to call about is even more important, then. We're going clubbing tonight."

"What?" My heart fluttered in panic. I'd only been to a few clubs in my life, and always with people from various work places. On the rare occasion that I joined in on something my colleagues were doing, I ended up in a corner nursing a drink while they all had a good time.

"Clubbing, honey. Dress hot. We will dance. We will drink. We will meet people. And we will forget this shitty week and the fact that, as a brand new Fury, I spent the week waiting tables in a fake restaurant. Being a Fury isn't as interesting as you might think."

I groaned. "Jilly, what the hell have we gotten ourselves into?"

"It could be too soon to tell. But in the meantime, we might as well make the best of it. Meet me in the Mt. Olympus lobby at eight. We'll go from there."

~*~

There are clubs, and there are *Clubs*. Having no idea which kind Jilly had planned for us, it took me over an hour to decide what to wear. In the end, I compromised and went with a simple black miniskirt paired with a flashy gold-sequined halter and a pair of gold strappy heels.

When I stepped into the lobby at Mt. Olympus, I was a little early. The lights were still on, but since the sun had gone down, the glass dome overhead didn't let in any ambient light. The lobby had considerably less traffic than during the day, but a few folks, human and otherwise, passed me while I stood there feeling awkward and alone.

My stomach was queasy, my palms were sweating, and I had to bully myself to keep from turning around and going back out the door to my car. Fortunately, Jilly was came in right behind me, and she grabbed me before I could chicken out.

The gold sequins had been a good call. Jilly sparkled like a shiny emerald, from the top of her glittery cheekbones to the tips of her spangled green pumps. I yanked on the edges of my top to make sure I wasn't flashing too much side boob. Not that anyone would notice a little pale skin showing on me when Jilly looked like a perky, green disco ball.

She looked me up and down, chewing her lip in concentration. "You look great." She slapped my hands away from fiddling with my top.

"You don't sound like I look great." The inside of my arm scraped against a sequin and made me itch.

A pair of centaurs clopped past, deep in discussion. I scratched the inside of my arm and tried not to stare. I didn't think I'd ever get used to all the strange creatures walking around the place.

"No, no. You do. Honest. It's just…" She rummaged in her tiny silver and green purse and pulled out a small, clear pot of gold glitter and a fat brush. "You're unfinished. You need some of this." She grinned, and twin dimples appeared in her cheeks.

I took a step back. "Oh, I don't think that's necessary. I've got sequins. That should be plenty of sparkle."

Jilly ignored my protests. She wiggled the brush into the container, tapped it to shake off the excess, and attacked me.

First my cheekbones, a little on my eyelids, then my collarbones. Just as I thought she was going to settle for subtlety, she spun me around and decorated my shoulder blades, then ran the brush down the outsides of my legs. I was never going to get all the glitter off of me when the night was over. They'd be finding glitter in my wrinkles when I turned ninety.

Jilly capped the body glitter and brush, but my relief was short-lived. Out came a tube of glitter lip gloss. By this time, she'd broken me, though. I held still and took it like a trouper.

It tingled and smelled like peppermint.

"Now am I acceptable?" I held still for inspection.

Jilly walked all the way around me, checking for flaws. "Almost." She tugged on my skirt, lowering it a few inches.

At first, I thought she'd decided my skirt was too short. Then I realized her real goal, once she went back for more glitter and dusted my newly exposed belly button.

I truly hoped we wouldn't get picked up for prostitution before the night was over.

My friend clapped her hands and bounced in excitement. "Yay! You're perfect. Are you ready to go?"

I sighed. At least I'd be in Seattle instead of Topeka. Nobody would know me. "I'm ready." I turned toward the door I'd come in, and she grabbed my arm.

"Not that one." She pointed across the hallway. "That one."

Puzzled, I followed her to a door I hadn't paid much attention to each time I'd come through the lobby. As we approached, I had a vague memory of Trina chattering about the door going to elsewhere in Mount Olympus proper, outside the Mt. Olympus business building.

Jilly took my hand and exited without pausing, but when I stepped through the door, I froze, too surprised to move.

"Jilly?" I'd expected a woodland scene or maybe a quiet village where all the non-humans lived. Instead, I'd walked into the drug-addled lovechild of Mardi Gras and the Vegas Strip.

Crowds bustled around us. Neon lights flashed up and down the street. A loud explosion made me jump and cover my head until I realized the shrapnel raining down on me was thousands of flower petals shot from an air canon located on one of the towering rooftops above us.

Jilly grinned at me and grabbed my elbow. "Welcome to the Mount Olympus Euphoria District. Next stop, Club Maenad."

She dragged me down the street while I gaped at the sights and sounds of the Euphoria District. Music from several buildings poured into the street, mixing in the open air in a cacophony of chaotic sound and vibration. A parade of donkeys carrying drunk people in togas passed us going the other direction. Another flower-petal canon went off and showered us in soft pink flutters. Jilly pulled me up the curb to the sidewalk to avoid a collision with a cyclops conga line.

We passed a club with a giant, pink neon sign that said Manticore's. Two guys holding hands stumbled out and bumped into a third guy who'd been on his way in. The three men shouted excitedly at each other, then broke out in an impromptu bump and grind on the sidewalk to the beat of the electronic music blasting from the club.

Two doors down from Manticore's, Jilly finally stopped yanking my arm and let go. "This is it!" She grinned at me and waved up at the flashing green sign that said Club Maenad.

We stepped inside, and the music swallowed us up.

The largest faun I'd ever seen stood in our path. I later found out it was because he was a satyr, not a faun. I still had a lot to learn.

The man half of the bouncer was decked out in a green satin shirt with a metallic sheen. The few buttons he'd bothered to use were shaped like fat purple grapes. He shouted something we couldn't hear over the music, then smiled and pointed to a sign over his head.

Every night is ladies night! No cover for ta-tas!

We sidled past him and he winked. I tugged at the sides of my top and tried not to wonder if "no cover for ta-tas" was supposed to be taken literally.

We squeezed down a long hall lined on both sides with people and other creatures hanging out or leaning against the walls. Thick, sweet-smelling pink smoke hung in the air and seemed to stick to my skin as I waded through. My skin tingled, as if the smoke was made of spices or mint oil.

Two identical men with silver eyes and jet-black hair watched us as we passed. Their heads bobbed to the music in a repetitive *yes* motion. At the end of the hall, a half-naked woman held a tray of glowing jewelry. An equally half-naked guy stood next to her, taking money from people and handing them their purchases from the tray.

Jilly stopped and pulled several bills from her tiny purse. She chose two small circles, one yellow and one green, then slipped the green one all the way to fit snuggly on her upper arm. She handed me the other to do the same.

Once we were properly glowing, she grinned and pointed. "Ready?"

I nodded, shouting to be heard. "I guess."

We turned a corner into the main room of the club and were nearly swallowed in the crowd of glowing, bouncing revelers. A bar ran along two entire walls. Dozens of bartenders in matching short togas bound with green leaves and purple grapes moved with perfect precision to keep the throng of partiers lubricated.

Cages dangled from the ceiling, swinging from the jerky dance moves of the scantily clad, barefoot women inside. All the women had crazy hair that stuck out from their heads in stiff dreadlocks. I assumed these were the Maenads—Wild Women—the club was named for. A haze of that same pink smoke hung above the dance floor, and colored lasers cut through the clouds in a glorious light show beneath the cages.

More cages rose up from the floor on pedestals, but these contained drunk men. Each wore a collar with a long leash attached, and the ends of the leashes were held on the outsides of the cages by dryads. The dryads swayed and undulated around the cages, their leafy fingers occasionally reaching in and stroking the cheeks of their willing captives. When the current song ended, the dryads swung the cage doors open, removed the collars, and the men reluctantly vacated the cage to make room for the next drunk guy.

It was nothing like any club I'd ever been to before.

Once we moved out of the doorway and waded through the people around the entrance, the crowd thinned enough for us to breathe. I followed Jilly to the bar. This I understood. I could order a drink, hold it in my hands, and watch the people without feeling too awkward. I might even be able to find a corner to stand in where I wasn't in the middle of everything.

When we reached the bar, I was stunned all over again. Hal and Elmore stood waiting for us, holding out golden cups.

"Thought you'd never get here," Hal said in my ear. "I am so uncomfortable."

I nodded and took the drink. "You and me both." I held up the cup. "Thanks." I took a tentative sip, not sure what it was. Then I took another. I still didn't know, but it was delicious. Refreshing, light, bubbly, and sweet. "What is this?"

Elmore leaned in to talk, his shoulders bouncing to the music. "It's called nectar. Not real nectar, like the gods drink. But it's good, isn't it?"

I took another sip and smiled. "I love it." The music was infectious. I felt the base in my bones, and my body started moving, too.

I drained my cup, and set it on the bar. Before I could stop him, a bartender swooped over and refilled it. He winked and walked away.

"Hey," I said. "He didn't wait for me to pay."

Jilly slid her arm around my waist and kissed my cheek, her curls bouncing as she bobbed. "Nectar's free. Hurry and finish it. I want to dance!"

I shrugged and drained my cup, then set it on the bar. The bartender spotted it and made a beeline, but Hal snatched the cup and turned it over. The bartender winked at me again and changed course to help someone else.

Things got a little blurry after that. Nectar may not have given us immortality, but it certainly gave the *feeling* of immortality. We danced a lot—something I wouldn't have guessed I'd enjoy. Even Hal had some wicked moves. Or maybe he danced like a middle-aged white dude, but in my drunken state, I admired him for it.

Both Hal and Elmore took a turn in the dryad cages. When they came out, they looked a little dazed, though how I could tell for sure in my own weird state left me questioning any of my observations.

For one thing, I most certainly couldn't have seen my ex-boyfriend, Freddy, at the other end of the bar when we went back for more drinks. At the time, though, I was sure of it. As weird as I felt that night, between the pink smoke and the steady supply of refilled golden cups, I couldn't trust anything I thought I saw or did.

At some point, I must have had one too many cups of nectar, because I woke up the next morning with no clue how I got home. I had a vague memory of all of us sitting in a diner and being waited on by a woman with the face of a pig. There'd been pie involved. I was almost sure of it.

I groaned, anticipating the splitting headache and wretched stomach that went with a night that can't be remembered. My eyelids slid open slowly, and I sat up. Nothing. I felt fantastic.

Frowning, I slipped out of bed, bracing myself for my body's inevitable objections. Still nothing. In fact, I felt better than usual.

I checked my phone and found texts from all three of my friends saying how much fun they had. I grinned and sent a quick text back to them.

After I hit send, it really hit me. I had friends. Real friends.

Maybe I wasn't a complete loser after all.

Chapter 17

At any of my previous jobs, Mondays were traditionally bad. And, sure, my first week in the Muse department had been rough, but most of that roughness had been my own doing.

If I ran into Rick, I'd apologize. Simple as that. And if nobody in my office liked me, maybe I needed to try harder. I'd never been the friendliest person. But Saturday night had proved to me I wasn't a total loss. I could make friends.

I was determined to make this Monday a good start to the week. My clients were getting along fine, so I was getting the hang of the job. It was my social ineptitude getting in my way.

If my heels were a little higher, my skirt a little shorter, and my cleavage a little deeper when I walked into the office, well, a girl likes to fit in, right? Maybe the preferred style of the other women was less sensible than I liked, but it didn't hurt me to loosen up a little to blend in.

Until I walked through the door and nearly collided with Dave and Jeremy on their way out.

Dave leered, making me regret leaving the top three buttons on my blouse open. "Nice rack."

Seriously. I was so shocked by his bluntness, I couldn't untangle my tongue enough to respond.

Jeremy's lip curled, as if in disgust before he dropped his gaze to my legs. "Nice legs." He brushed past me and out the door. Dave winked and followed.

I was both stunned and confused. Dave had been gross, but I'd understood his meaning. Jeremy was harder to read. Somehow, I felt like I'd just been slammed. Was he being sarcastic? And even if he was, why did I care?

After checking that no one was looking, I bent over and gave my legs a once-over. No runs in my hose. No toilet paper stuck to me.

What the hell did he mean?

"Asshole." I tried to shake it off, knowing I should've been at least equally upset by Dave's comment. But I wasn't, really. Some guys are immature little toads. If it continued to get worse, I'd find out the process and file a complaint with HR. Or maybe feed him to a minotaur or something.

For now, I was trying to fit in, not be the squeaky wheel.

My effort at dressing like the popular kids was wasted. Dave and Jeremy were the only ones to see it, and they were so not my target audience. I'd once read somewhere that women tend dress for each other, not for men. I was finally seeing the possible truth in that.

I refilled my bubbles, hooked them to my belt, and stopped by my desk to make sure I didn't have anything sitting in my inbox. Nothing. My desk was as bare as I'd left it Friday morning. The chair wasn't pushed in all the way. I readjusted it. Janitorial probably moved it to vacuum over the weekend.

Frowning, I rummaged through my purse. Something had to be in there that I could leave on my desk to make it more personal—less vacant looking. A yellow hair scrunchy from before I'd chopped all my hair off floated at the bottom of the bag. I left it there. Two plastic barrettes seemed like a more believable choice, so I arranged those under the monitor to look like I'd taken them out and left them for later. A stale pack of gum fit nicely on the top of the keyboard. The purse didn't give up anything else that might make it look like I worked there.

Had I been a different kind of person, I might have had pictures of old friends in my wallet. Pictures would have looked nice. But I didn't have any old friends. I had a few new friends, but no pictures of them.

In desperation, I opened the single drawer they'd given me and found pens and sticky notes. I scrawled *Pick up dry cleaning on Thursday* on the bright yellow pad, then stuck the note to my monitor.

I didn't have anything to pick up at the dry cleaners, but nobody needed to know that.

I took a step back. The desk was still pretty bare, but at least it didn't look like it was waiting to be assigned to somebody.

When did you start to care what the hell people thought, Wynter? I shook my head and wobbled out of the office in my inappropriately high heels.

Whatever failure I might be at the office, at least I was doing well with my clients. At least, I had been before the weekend.

First, I checked in to see how Alex was coming along with his toothpick house. He was right where he should be—in the basement, surrounded by piles of toothpicks and bottles of glue.

He was not, however, hard at work building his dream project like he should have been. He was reading a book.

I scooted around the basket of sleeping wiener dog and read the cover of the book Alex was reading: *Beekeeping—Save the Queen, Save the Planet.*

I shook my head. "Dude. What the hell? I left you alone for three days. You were doing great."

At the sound of my voice, Oscar's head popped up from the basket. He slapped his tail against the wicker a few times, then went back to sleep.

Alex's unfinished toothpick house had grown by maybe half a wall since I'd last been there. A separate section that looked like it might be the detached garage sat nearby without a roof or fourth wall. From the time I'd spent watching him build, I estimated he'd stopped working sometime Friday afternoon.

"Let's get you back on track, my friend." I unclipped my bubbles, dipped the wand in the liquid, and blew through the hole. "Time to get back to work, Alex. Works of art don't build themselves. You can do it."

The bubbles flew in a straight, steady line toward the side of his face and popped on his cheekbone and in his ear. Perfect.

Alex shifted on his stool and looked up, frowning, with his finger keeping his place in the bee book. He glanced around the basement and let out a heavy sigh. "I'd better get some work done, Oscar."

Oscar whined in response and wagged his tail. Alex bent and patted the dog on the head before heading toward the stairs.

I hadn't intended that. "Hey. Where are you going? Work's down here." I dipped my wand and blew at him.

He was a moving target, upping the difficulty level, but I managed to pop a few off his elbow.

"You have work to do. Inspiration awaits. I know you want to get this project done. Come back and work on it. It's fun!"

He scuttled up the steps, leaving me behind with a dripping wand and no client. I heard footsteps above me, a chair scraping, and he was on his way back down. Relieved, I took a seat on a box and waited for him.

When Alex reappeared at the bottom of the steps, he carried two kitchen chairs. I watched with growing trepidation as he spread a tarp on the floor, then set to work sanding the paint off the first chair.

"No," I said. "No, no, no." I crouched close to him and blew bubbles at him until I felt light headed. "This is not your project. You're building a house out of toothpicks for the competition in a few weeks. You're not fixing kitchen chairs. Go back to the toothpicks, Alex. Come on, man. Help me out here." He kept sanding, and I kept blowing until little stars sparkled around my head, reminding me that oxygen was important to staying upright. I stopped and caught my breath.

After what felt like forever, Alex stopped and wiped he forehead with the back of his hand. He glanced at the table where his toothpick creation sat untouched, then looked away with a pained expression.

He picked up a new piece of sandpaper, wrapped it around the wooden block he was using, and started on the back of the chair.

I threw my arms in the air. "Gah! Really? Okay. You do what you've got to do. I have other clients, you know. I can't sit here all day holding your hand when you're not even listening." I tightened the cap on my half-empty bubbles. "I'll be back tomorrow. Hopefully you'll have this out of your system by then."

I was a little nervous going to see Missy after the disastrous visit with Alex. But the odds of them both being in trouble were slim. Alex was probably overwhelmed with nagging from his mother. Missy would be fine.

Or not.

I found Missy stalled on page three of her scrapbook. She sat curled on the sofa watching *Golden Girls* and painting her nails. The scrapbooking supplies were scattered across the coffee table. The baby's car seat wasn't by the door like it usually was, and when I checked, she wasn't in her crib, either. Someone must have taken her out for the day. I had Missy all to myself.

Page three of the scrapbook lay in the center of the table, a half-finished tribute to a trip to New York City on New Year's Eve. At least, that's what I gathered from the photo of Missy's parents wearing hats that said 1966 on them. Missy had glued a silhouette of the New York skyline on the bottom of the page, and a cutout of an apple sat loose in the upper left-hand corner. That was as far as she'd gone with it.

A sheet of letters lay on the floor bent in half. A pile of colored paper collected a wet ring from the glass that sat on top of it.

Missy had given up.

I unhooked my bubbles and got to work. "I will not lose both of you today." I blew a stream of bubbles directly into her face. "Come on, Missy. You were doing such a beautiful job. Look at all those fantastic shapes and colors. Your parents will love it when it's done."

Missy paused in her manicure. I thought I'd made an impression, but she barked a short laugh at something Sophia said to Blanche, then went back to her nails.

"This is ridiculous. What are you doing?" I blew another stream at her. "You had this. The New York thing is inspired. Go back and finish it. It'll be gorgeous."

I was grateful she couldn't actually hear me. The desperation in my voice was alarming.

After a moment, she tilted her head and held out her splayed fingers, then blew on the nails to speed the drying process. To my relief, she leaned toward the coffee table and grabbed a pair of scissors and a thick piece of paper.

"There you go. Good girl!" I blew a fat bubble at her for good measure.

She cut something small from the paper, then set the scissors down with the leftover paper. She held a tiny scrap cut in the shape of a skyline. The New York skyline.

"Gorgeous. When did you learn to do that?" I sent a bubble to pop on the bridge of her nose. "It's so tiny."

She sprayed the back with adhesive, then, to my horror, stuck it over the nail of her ring finger, not on the abandoned scrapbook page.

"Missy, no. What are you doing?" My fingers tightened around the bubble wand, leaving an indentation in the skin.

She took out a second color of nail polish and used the tiny skyline as a stencil. After the polish dried enough, she peeled off the paper skyline and revealed a sunset over New York painted on her fingernail.

I held my head in despair. For two hours, I sat and watched her create an intricate design on each of her fingers. Shoes. Champagne glasses. Apples. I gave up blowing bubbles at her a half hour into it. There didn't seem to be any point. I was inspiring her to do the wrong thing.

Some Muse I turned out to be.

When she took her socks off and started on her toenails, I decided to call it a day. I couldn't watch her do a pedicure, too. Enough was enough.

"I'll be back tomorrow. Try to get all this business out of your system, okay?"

Missy didn't respond, of course. But the scowl on her face as she painted the first coat on her toenails told me, at least at some level, she was listening.

My stomach was in knots by the time I pulled into a parking space at my apartment complex. Two out of three of my clients had gone off the rails for no reason I could decipher. That didn't mean Mark had done it, too, but my gut said he had. Of the three of them, Mark seemed to be the most easily distracted. I braced myself and climbed out of the car.

There was no need to go invisible and sneak around. Nor did I need to knock on Mark's door to find out what he was up to. He was right there in the middle of the courtyard, hard at work.

Power washing the buildings.

I thought I'd prepared myself for his inevitable slide into procrastination. The other two had done it. Why not Mark?

Why not, indeed.

I was fuming. My job depended on three people completing three tasks. All three were acting like they had all the time in the world.

"Three weeks, people," I muttered. "You have three weeks or I fail."

I'd have thought failure would come naturally to me after the life I'd lived. But this was different. I didn't want to fail. I wanted to be good at this. Was that so much to ask?

"Mark!" I trotted across the courtyard and tapped him on the shoulder.

He shut off the water and turned toward me in surprise. "Oh, hey, Wynter. You're home early. Want to get some dinner?" His eyes flicked over my cleavage and then away. His cheeks turned a little pink.

He was soaking wet, and his white T-shirt clung to him like fresh paint. I swallowed and refocused, hoping my cheeks weren't pink, too. "What the hell are you doing?"

He blinked and stared at me, as if he didn't understand. "Just as friends, if you want."

"What?" Now I was blinking and staring.

"Dinner. If it'll upset you, I won't even try to pay for yours. Or my treat. I did suggest it. Whatever you're comfortable with."

I closed my eyes and took a deep breath. "Mark, I meant what are you doing out here washing the building? Why aren't you working on Carry's playground?"

His expression changed—one minute hopeful, the next, completely blank and unreadable. He turned toward the building and turned the water on again. "I'm just not feeling it today."

For some reason, a lump formed in my throat and my eyes burned from unshed tears. "But Candy Land. It was going to be epic. What happened?"

Mark didn't look at me. His shrug looked less carefree than I imagined he'd intended. "Nothing happened. I'm not in the mood today. Maybe tomorrow." He shut off the water. "I think maybe I'll take a rain check on dinner, if you don't mind. I'm pretty tired."

He went inside without another word, leaving me alone in the courtyard wondering what I'd said wrong.

And wondering how the hell I was going to fix all this with less than three weeks left.

Chapter 18

Tuesday morning I went into the office early. Somebody was going to help me if I had to camp outside Polly's door for the rest of the week.

My concern was unnecessary. For once, the office was filled with people. Dave and Jeremy stood outside the prop room, hands in their pockets and heads tilted toward each other in discussion. A general buzz of conversation came from the far end of the room. I couldn't see more than the tops of people's heads, since they were gathered in groups in a few cubicles, but they were there.

I headed for Polly's office and found Audrey and Kayla standing across from the door, whispering fiercely back and forth. A twinge of regret shot through me as I realized I was wearing sensible office attire again. The one day I tried to fit in, everybody missed it. Now I was back to sticking out again.

Audrey gave me a hard look, and Kayla snorted.

"If you're planning to talk to Polly, you might want to wait until tomorrow."

I knocked on the door. "I don't need her tomorrow. I need her today."

The door flung open, seemingly on its own. I poked my head in and found Polly sitting behind her desk and no one else inside.

"Yes?" Polly's melodic voice was icy. "Wynter, can it wait?"

Butterflies be damned. My stomach felt like an entire herd of wildebeests were trampling through. "For a few minutes, I guess. If you're busy, I can come back in a little while."

She pinched the bridge of her nose and sighed. "No, no. Come in. I've been meaning to check up on you for the last week. Today was bound to happen. I saw it coming. No reason for you to suffer for it. Close the door behind you."

Whatever was going on in the office, it didn't sound good. I shut the door and took a seat across from her, hoping I wasn't the cause of her shitty day. I'd only been working there less than two weeks. I couldn't already be in trouble.

147

Right?

Polly took a swallow of coffee and made a face. "Cold." She took another swallow anyway. "So. How are things going, Wynter? You finding your footing?"

Well, on the bright side, she didn't appear to be upset with me. Somebody else must've set her off.

I smoothed my skirt over my knees. "Well, I thought I was doing fine."

"Uh huh." A pair of glasses dangled around her neck from a chain. She placed them on her face and squinted at her computer monitor. "Toothpick art, scrapbooking, and urban renewal, yes?"

I nodded. "Yes."

She slid the glasses from her nose and let them drop to her chest. "And they're making adequate progress to make their deadlines?"

"Well, no. I mean, they were. Everything was great before the weekend. I checked on them yesterday, and none of them are working."

She shrugged. "Sometimes that happens on Mondays. Some clients lose their inspiration over the weekend. You may have to check out some supplies on Friday and give them an extra boost Saturday and Sunday to keep the momentum going. It happens." She wrote something in a notebook and tore off a sheet. "Here's a weekend pass so you can take the supplies home at the end of the week."

I took the piece of paper, my hand shaking. Was I not supposed to take stuff home without permission? Someone should have told me, since I'd been doing it a lot lately. "Thanks."

"That's what I'm here for." She folded her hands together. "So. You got them back on track yesterday, right?"

"Well, no. That's why I wanted to talk to you. They won't listen. I blow bubbles and think inspiring thoughts and they go off to do something completely different."

She did that nose pinching and sighing thing again. "Wynter, I can't do your job for you. No one can. Those three clients weren't assigned to you at random. They're your clients. The Fates department sent down the orders to go specifically to your inbox. These people are depending on you and only you to complete their tasks—their dreams. No one else can do it."

I sat in silence, staring at a smudge on the edge of her desk, letting her words sink in. My clients. Fate gave them to me for a reason, and nobody else could help them.

Holy shit. No pressure.

"So." I wasn't sure what else to say. Part of me wanted to bolt out the door and disappear. "Do you have any advice at all? How do I make them listen?"

She shrugged. "Just keep trying. You'll get through eventually. And if you don't, you'll do something else. Lots of people miss on their first department. If this isn't the right one for you, maybe something else will suit you better."

"Like the Underworld?" I bit my lower lip.

"Don't be silly. Legacy's don't go to the Underworld."

I tilted my head and gave her questioning look. "And?"

She frowned and put her glasses back on while tapping on the keyboard with her other hand. "You're not..." She blinked at the screen. "Oh. I see." The glasses dropped to her chest again. "You're a Legacy with an empty god file."

"So they tell me."

"Well, then. I guess you have two choices here." She leaned forward and fixed me with a hard look. "You need to either get your shit together or find out who your father is."

Not for the first time, I wondered how bad it must be to work in the Underworld. The more people talked about it, the more terrified I became of ending up there.

"I'll work on it." I dragged myself out of the chair and turned to go. "Thanks for your time."

I hoped there was no sarcasm in my tone. None that she could hear, anyway.

"Try to have a good day, Wynter. You'll get them back on track. Whatever the reason they were assigned to you, trust that there *was* a reason."

I nodded and reached for the doorknob. "Hey." I turned to face her again. "What's going on out there today? Why is everybody standing around like they're waiting for a fire drill?"

Her eyes looked sad. "Trina didn't make her deadline. Again. She's packing up her desk."

Trina was the only person in the department who'd been nice to me— besides maybe Polly. "She's still here?"

"You can probably catch her if you hurry."

I slipped through the door and down the hall. Audrey and Kayla stood sneering at me in the hall, and I brushed past them without comment. I turned a corner and walked into the box Trina held in front of her.

"Hey." She smiled, but some of her light had gone out. "I guess you heard."

I nodded. "I am so sorry. Are you okay? Can I help you carry anything?"

She blew her bangs out of her eyes. "I'll be okay. It's not my first time at this."

A small potted cactus teetered on top of her box. I grabbed the ceramic planter before it fell. "Got it."

We walked past Audrey and Kayla, and Trina gave them a little wave without letting go of her box. "See you around, I guess."

Audrey looked genuinely upset. "Sorry to see you go, Trina. Come back and visit once you get settled."

Kayla gave the first sincere smile I'd seen from her. "We'll miss you!"

Trina swallowed hard. "We'll have to do lunch some time."

As we walked past, Audrey looked at me with a curious, puzzled expression, as if seeing me in a different light.

I walked Trina out to the lobby, still carrying her tiny cactus. "Hey. You want to get a cup of coffee before you go?"

Asking a friend to get a cup of coffee gave me a nervous flutter in my stomach. Friendship was so *hard*. I had to actually *do* stuff.

Trina grinned. "Sure. They're expecting me upstairs, but they didn't say when. I could use a shot of caffeine first."

She probably could. The few conversations I'd had with Trina in the past had been a lot more…energetic. Getting booted from the Muse department must have taken a lot out of her.

We got settled with our lattes in a quiet corner of the cafeteria. I felt a twinge of Rick-related guilt when I smelled the cinnamon in my coffee. For the first time, I noticed Trina's hands were shaking.

I put my cup on the table. "You okay?"

She took a deep, steadying breath and put her hands in her lap. "Yeah. I'll be okay. Thank the gods I'm a Legacy. Maybe the next place will work out. I've got to be good at something, right?"

"You'd think all their assessments would get it right the first time. Where are you going next?"

Her expression was serious and intense. "All the way to the top. They're sending me to the Fates." She waited, as if I was supposed to gasp in surprise or draw back in horror.

The best I could give her was a slight raising of the eyebrows. "Is that good? Bad? I have to be honest. I have no idea what it means."

One side of her mouth drew up in a wry, half smile. "I guess I don't really know, either. I'm just going by the reactions everybody else gave me."

I shrugged. "I'm sure it's an office like any other." I held my coffee cup aloft in a toast. "And you will be fabulous at whatever it is goes on up there."

"I hope you're right." She sipped her drink. "So, how's it going for you? I never see you, so you must be busy."

I grimaced. "I suck. None of my clients are behaving."

She frowned. "How many do you have?"

"Three."

Her eyes widened in surprise. "Usually, they start people off slow. Somebody in Fates must have high hopes for you."

"Well, their hopes are wasted. I'm failing miserably."

She patted my hand. "You'll bring them around. I believe in you."

"Thanks." I picked at the sleeve on my cup. "Wish you weren't leaving. Everybody else hates me."

"You mean Audrey and Kayla? I wouldn't worry about them." She gave me a reassuring smile.

I shook my head. "I kind of get the feeling nobody there is too happy to see me." Not even Polly, if I were really being honest with myself.

Trina's smile faded. "Oh, that."

I sat straighter. "What?"

"I didn't want to tell you. I'd hoped everybody would forget about it." She fidgeted in her seat and looked distressed. "Here's the thing. There's only a set number of people who work in the Muse department in any given region."

"Sure." I nodded slowly.

"Somebody had to leave for you to take her place." She stared at me like she was waiting for me to understand some deeper meaning.

"Okay. So, whoever was there before me was somebody they all liked a lot. But I can't be somebody else."

Trina scratched her nose, took a breath, and tried again. "Your predecessor is named Phoebe. Everybody liked Phoebe. She was great at her job. Everybody gets a difficult client from time to time, but it takes three failed projects to fail the department."

"So, she wasn't so great at her job after all. Or really unlucky with the clients they assigned her."

"No," she said, drawing the word out. "*One* difficult client. Every few months, she'd get that same client assigned to her with a brand new project. And halfway through, the client would bail and stop working on it. After the third time, Phoebe got booted and transferred to the Underworld, since she isn't a Legacy." She gave me a pointed expression, as if waiting for me to pick up on something she wasn't saying.

"Well, I'm really sorry to hear that. Why would they keep giving her the same client, though? Obviously, this client wasn't a good investment. What kind of projects are we talking about, here? Life saving inventions? Setting up charity events? Building wells in Africa so people can have clean water?" I didn't know why certain people were singled out to receive help from a Muse, but to have help sent three times, the person in question must've had something important to contribute to the world.

Trina groaned. "You would think, but no. Cross stitch. Knitting." She paused and covered my hand with hers while staring into my eyes. "Quilting."

My face got hot, and my stomach felt queasy. That pattern sounded familiar. "No."

She nodded. "I'm afraid so, honey." She squeezed my hand. "You were Phoebe's client before you came here. And now you've got her job."

"No wonder they all hate me." Maybe being sent to the Underworld was all I deserved. And why was I so damned interesting that I warranted visits from a Muse on three separate projects? *Craft* projects, no less.

"I wouldn't take it too seriously. After you're there for awhile, most of them won't even remember anymore." She paused and looked around. "Well, except for Jeremy."

"What's up with Jeremy? He won't even look me in the eye."

"He was in love with her."

"Ew." I couldn't imagine the little toad involved with anybody.

"Oh, they weren't together. She did date Dave for awhile—gods help her—but Jeremy sort of mooned after her. Ha! Mooned. Phoebe, goddess of the moon. Get it? I'm hilarious!" She laughed at her own joke. "Anyway, he was kind of stalkery, but nothing came of it. She's probably lucky she got out of there before he got up the nerve to make a move."

"That explains so much." As horrible as I felt for my shitty life choices getting this Phoebe person fired, I felt better now that I understood what was going on in the office.

Trina glanced at her watch. "I feel so much better. Thank you for sitting with me so I could pull myself together. I should probably go upstairs now and get myself settled in my new reality—whatever it turns out to be."

Back to her usual self, Trina hopped up, gave me a hug, and disappeared before I could do more than wish her luck. She left me with far fewer questions than I'd had before, but a whole lot more guilt.

~*~

The day didn't get any better. Alex was halfway through painting the kitchen chairs a flamingo pink, and Missy was cleaning the oven. I couldn't even find Mark.

Though I should have been trying harder to blow some sense into one of the two clients I *could* find, I knew I needed to change tactics. I had no idea how to do that, though. I had no backup plan.

Crazy or not, my mom was always the best place to go when I was in trouble. I was pretty sure this more than qualified for trouble.

As I pulled into her driveway, a lot of the tension in my shoulders relaxed. I'd gone through with the whole Mt. Olympus thing so I wouldn't have to move in with my mom again. Maybe that hadn't been the best choice. Mom's house wasn't so bad. Nobody was trying to send me to hell, here, at least.

Because, honestly, that's what it felt like was happening in the Muse department. Whether it was my coworkers or somebody up in the Fates department, somebody wanted me to fail.

I found Mom in her bathroom, drawing on the walls with crayons. She had her long blonde hair tied in a knot on the top of her head, and it bobbed back and forth with her movements.

I rapped a knuckle against the open door so I wouldn't startle her.

"Hand me the burnt sienna," she said without looking up.

I found the crayon she needed and dropped it in her upturned hand. "Hi, Mom."

"Hi, sweetheart. Give me just a minute to finish this squirrel."

The last time I'd visited, the bathroom had been painted a light blue. It was still blue, but she'd been drawing trees and grass and birds in bright colors on every surface that the wax would stick to—walls, ceiling, wooden shelves and cupboards. Not even the floor had escaped. The crayons hadn't left much of a mark on the shiny blue tiles, but she'd colored the grout in between a deep cerulean.

I waited for her to finish shading the tail of the squirrel she was coloring right above the floor vent, trying to remember if I'd ever colored on the walls when I was a kid. Probably not. If I had, Mom would have made a day of it and helped.

When she was done, she pulled herself up from the floor and smoothed the wrinkles from her jeans. She wore a bright green T-shirt with the words *That's What She Said* printed in yellow.

She put away the crayon I'd handed her, folded the lid closed and smiled. "There. Let's get some juice." She brushed past me and took off for the kitchen, expecting me to follow.

After such a crappy couple of days, there was something immensely comforting in sitting in my mother's yellow kitchen, drinking fresh-squeezed juice and eating warm, homemade bread smothered in butter. For a little while, I felt like a little kid, untroubled and safe with a happy tummy.

After my second glass of kiwi-blueberry-pineapple juice and my third thick slice of warm potato bread, I sighed in contentment and pushed away my plate.

"Better?" Mom took away the dirty dishes and set them in the sink.

I nodded. "Better."

She returned with a dishtowel and wiped the table. "Want to talk about it?"

I shrugged. "I'm having a hard time getting the hang of my new job. Turns out, I may have been the reason the person before me lost her job, and everybody wants me to fail."

She paused and looked at me, her eyes narrowed in thought. "Well, then, you'll have to disappoint them, won't you?"

"I've tried everything they taught me to do, but I can't get the clients to listen to me."

"Then try something else." She moved to the trashcan and shook the towel to get rid of the crumbs. "Rules are only good if they work. If they don't work, change direction."

"Try something else." I brushed off a crumb she'd missed. "Okay. Yeah."

She sat in the chair across from me and tented her fingers under her chin. "You've never really been one to do things the way people expect you to. Find your own way."

I had no idea what I was going to do, but I felt a lot better. She was right. I was trying too hard to do it their way. I was trying to follow rules I didn't understand, with constraints I wasn't convinced were necessary.

Somehow, I had to figure out Wynter's way to solve this problem. And whoever was screwing with me was going to fail.

Chapter 19

I had to admit, I didn't feel as confident about things when I got up for work the next morning. It was one thing to decide to do things my way.

Figuring out what *my way* entailed was another matter.

As I got ready to start the day, Phyllis was uncharacteristically quiet. In fact, the lack of chatter was a little unnerving.

"Are you okay?" I poked her soil. "Do you need water? Maybe some sun in the courtyard?"

One leaf dipped and brushed the back of my hand. "I'm fine. A little worried about you, though. Any ideas yet?"

"Not a clue. I'll start by checking in on all of them. Maybe they straightened out on their own." I glanced out the kitchen window. "Maybe I'll stop at Mark's on the way out. See if I can jump start him before I go."

"It couldn't hurt, I suppose." Her voice sounded pinched, as if she were trying not to cry.

Which was weird for a plant.

"Are you sure you're okay?"

Several branches flapped. "Everything is fine. Go. Be productive. Inspire art. How am I supposed to people-watch all day if you're in my light?"

She was trying to make a joke of it, but I could tell something was bothering her. I was positive it was concern for me. The best I could do was get the job done. Then we could both be less stressed.

Before I left, I set her in the kitchen window like I'd been doing for the last few weeks. When I crossed the courtyard and stood outside Mark's door, I turned and gave her a wave.

He opened the door before I had a chance to put my hand down and turn around to knock.

"Who are you waving at?" He sounded amused.

I faced him, embarrassed, then saw he was standing in the doorway, soaking wet, with a towel wrapped around his waist. A small towel.

I shrugged in an effort to appear nonchalant. "My plant," I said. "We're very close."

He smirked. "Cute. So, what can I help you with first thing in the morning like this?"

My eyes watered at the strain of keeping them focused on his face. A drop of water dripped from his hair and rolled down his neck to his chest. I smiled harder and didn't watch. "I was on my way to work and figured I'd check and see how Candy Land is coming."

"Oh." He shifted from one foot to the other. "Well, that's not really a concern anymore."

"It's cancelled?" I felt like he'd punched me in the stomach. The Muse office probably didn't give a rat's ass if a project was cancelled by the client's employer. All that mattered was whether or not the project was completed.

He shook his head. "No. I decided to keep it simple. I appreciate your help trying to nail down a theme, but it's probably better if I just build her a sandbox and a couple of swings. She'll like it, whatever we end up doing."

"Oh." I tried my hardest not to look too disappointed. I wasn't even sure if that would count as completing his project. Probably, as long as it was done on time. Still, it didn't sit well with me.

He didn't give me a chance to object. "Listen, I'm feeling kind of exposed, so I'm going back inside. Thanks for stopping by, though. Maybe I'll see you later after you're done with work."

Count on it. I nodded. "Yeah. Have a good day." I gave him the same wave I'd given to Phyllis and turned away as he shut the door. As I made my way to the car, I mulled over what he'd said. Given the choice, no kid would rather have a plain wooden sandbox when they could have a candy castle. Was Mark giving up? Out of funds? There had to be a reason for scaling back after all the stress he'd put himself through to find the perfect theme.

I was still trying to sort it out when I got to work. Caught up in my own thoughts, I plowed right into that moody receptionist, Patrice, in the lobby.

The snakes on her head rose together in a chorus of hisses, a few striking in my direction. "Watch it," Patrice said. She patted the snakes to calm them. "I just got them settled down." She gave me an annoyed frown from behind her tiny sunglasses, then dismissed me as if I'd never existed.

Her mild reaction surprised me. I expected her to shriek at me, then turn me to stone or tear my heart out with her claws—though her claws were actually square-tipped nails done in a purple and gold French manicure. I'd noticed them when she fixed her snake hair. Maybe she wasn't so scary after all.

Maybe not, but my hands wouldn't stop shaking, and my knees were a little weak.

Because my day had already gone so well, the universe—or maybe the crazy people in the Fates department—had one more surprise for me before I could make it safely to my desk.

I got on the elevator, hit the button for my floor, and watched the doors close. One floor later, the doors opened on the second floor and there was Rick. I stopped myself before I groaned, at least. I retained that much of my dignity.

He was dressed in a pair of tight pants, a white shirt, and a black cape with red satin lining. He smiled, revealing fangs, then stepped into the elevator. "Hi." He held up his coffee cup. "I was hoping you'd be around for coffee, but I didn't see you."

I tried not to stammer, but I failed. "Oh. I…didn't…I didn't know."

His eyes looked sad, but hopeful. "Maybe tomorrow?"

"Well…uh…I don't know, Rick. I'm kind of having a rough week." The elevator opened on my floor, and I ran out before they'd finished clearing. "I'll call you, okay?"

The doors slid closed, but not before I saw the look of disappointment with maybe a touch of anger on his ghostly white vampire face. I felt like a horrible human being. It had only been two-and-a-half weeks since I'd seen that same look on Freddy's face. I was a serial dumper. And a coward, too.

What the hell was wrong with me?

As I entered the office, I didn't even look at Dave and Jeremy. They watched me walk past, and I had to refrain from rubbing the goose bumps from my arms. However, ignoring them seemed to work. After getting no response from me, they wandered off to the other end of the office, no doubt to attempt to make some other woman feel uncomfortable.

I checked my inbox and found it mercifully empty. A small, stuffed giraffe I'd brought from home made the desk a little less stark than it had been the day before, but it didn't help as much as I'd hoped. Then again, if I didn't turn things around, I'd be packing it all up to move to the Underworld in another two-and-a-half weeks anyway.

The prop room was quiet, so I slipped in and grabbed my belt and a full bottle of bubbles. I'd stopped bothering with the anti-doggy dust once I realized my only animal problem was Oscar, and he and I had become friends. However, remembering how tough the previous few days had been, I helped myself to a second bottle of bubbles. It couldn't hurt to have extra.

R.L. NAQUIN

Since there was a small possibility that taking two bottles was against some rule nobody had bothered to tell me, I slid the extra into my pocket, rather than attach it to my belt. At the last minute, I grabbed the Beastie Dust and added it to my belt. Better to have it and not need it.

I'd been thinking hard about what my mom had said—if their way wasn't working for me, I had to find my own way. I'd decided to give one last try at this the Muse way. If that didn't work, then let the crafty people of the world beware: Wynter was coming.

I bolted out of the building as quickly as I could and managed to avoid contact with anyone else. When I got to Alex's neighborhood, I parked up the street from his house and made my way up the sidewalk, invisible and ready to fight my hardest to get him back on track.

No matter what.

I barely thought about the process when I stepped through the front door. I'd done it enough times lately, it felt like second nature. When I entered the kitchen, Oscar let out a yip and hopped out of his bed. His toenails clacked on the floor on his way over to me.

I knelt to get closer to him. "Where's your Alex, sweetie? Is he downstairs?"

Oscar gave me a doggy smile and a short bark. He turned and went the direction I'd come, not toward the basement door.

"Okay. We'll go that way, instead." I followed him on the plastic runner down the hallway.

At the end of the hall, Oscar stopped in front of Alex's door and whined.

I wrinkled my nose. I knew from my initial excursion how that room smelled. "If you say so." I stepped through the bedroom door.

Alex was still in bed. The curtains were drawn, his clothes were on the floor, and the smell was worse than I remembered.

"Dude." I shook my head. "Dude, seriously." I unhooked my bubbles, prepared to use the entire bottle on him if that's what it took to get him out of bed. "What the hell happened to you?"

Oscar, unable to morph through walls like I could, was unhappy being stuck out in the hall. He clawed at the door and made a series of annoyed, sharp barks.

Alex groaned and pulled the pillow over his head.

Disgusted, I blew a string of bubbles at him. "Get your ass out of bed. What the hell is wrong with you?" Maybe that wasn't the most inspirational thing I could have said, but he did take the pillow off his head, so my method wasn't totally crap.

158

Oscar banged on the door, then continued scratching and barking.

Alex threw the pillow at the door. "Alright. I'm up. Knock it off." He sat up and swung his feet to the floor, then sat there, rubbing the stubble on his face. "Stupid dog."

I stood within inches of him and blew bubbles directly at his face. "Get moving, soldier. That dog's not going to walk itself."

He muttered something incoherent and stood to pull on a pair of pants that had been hanging over the end of the bed. He yanked off the tee he'd been sleeping in and replaced it with a fresh one from the dresser, along with a clean pair of socks.

I sat on the edge of his bed and watched, feeling like a voyeur with really bad taste. Once he ran his fingers through his sparse hair to set it straight, he open the door and scooped Oscar into his arms.

"I'm sorry, buddy." He planted a kiss on the dog's head. "Had some trouble getting moving today. Let's go outside."

I sighed. It was a start. Maybe the fresh air would do him some good and make him easier to work with—more suggestible.

I traipsed behind him blowing bubbles of encouragement. Occasionally, the wind picked up and the bubbles went wild, but mostly, the breeze was at our backs and my efforts smacked him in the back of the head as intended.

Oscar had a long leash, and he led us from tree to tree, across the street to sniff an intriguing bush, around the corner to snap at a dirty sock left in the gutter, then down a few blocks to a park where his little legs finally wore out and he dropped to his belly on a mound of grass next to a bench. Alex took a seat and got comfortable. I got the impression this was part of their regular routine.

"Guess this is it for us, Oscar." Alex stretched his legs out and crossed his ankles. "After this, I've got to make some changes."

I blew bubbles directly into his face. "Like building a replica of your house in toothpicks, perhaps?" I blew a few more for good measure.

He sighed. "No more screwing around, Oscar. Time for me to do something more with my life. He was right. I'm too old to live with Mom and play in her basement all day building models. It's time to do something with my inheritance. Investment banking isn't much fun, but it's respectable, I guess."

Oscar wagged his tail, lifted his head, and whined.

Alex shook his head, shoulders slumping. "I'm sorry, buddy. I won't be able to take you with me." He sniffed and looked despondent.

I scowled. "Who the hell have you been talking to?" I blew so many bubbles, I felt lightheaded. "You march back to the house and get back to work on your masterpiece, Alex. Come on, man. Don't give up on your dreams."

Alex leaned forward and scratched Oscar's head. "Real life isn't about dreams, I guess. Being an adult means giving things up."

"What? No!" My head swam from hyperventilating on bubbles, so I dropped to the bench next to him. "There's no giving up in toothpick art."

Alex pulled Oscar up onto his lap and massaged the little guy's floppy ears. "We had a good run, though, didn't we?"

The man was talking as if his entire life was over. Until that moment, I hadn't really wondered what he did for a living—he was always home when I got there. That he was living off his inheritance hadn't even crossed my mind.

The more I found out, the less I knew about him. But I did know this: the only time I'd seen Alex happy was when he worked on his building project. I was a Muse. I would not sit back and watch a man give away his soul to a nine-to-five job he didn't want or need while leaving his dreams behind simply because some asshat told him he should.

I rose from the bench and walked behind a nearby tree. The only other people at the park were a young mother and her twin toddler boys. Mom pushed a stroller under another tree and released her little ones, who tore off toward the sandbox. Nobody was paying any attention to me.

I flicked the button on my belt and became visible again, then clipped my bubbles to their spot. When I appeared next to Alex's bench, I did my best to look distressed and overheated.

"Excuse me." I panted a little, pretending to be out of breath. "Did you see a Pomeranian in a green bowtie come tearing past here?"

Alex glanced up at me, frowned, then shook his head. "No, I'm sorry." He sat up straighter. "Do you need help looking?"

I dropped to the bench in feigned exhaustion. "No. Thank you, though. He's an idiot. He'll come back home when he runs out of energy." I fanned myself with my hand. "I don't know why I bother to go after him. He does this all the time."

He patted Oscar and smiled at me. "I understand. It's dangerous out there. They don't realize how dangerous."

I nodded, then stuck my hand out. "I'm Wynter."

He gave my hand a firm shake. "Alex. I've never seen you around here. Do you live nearby?"

I took a deep breath. I've never been especially good at lying before. But I've never been especially bad, either. "About four blocks from here. Over on Brown. You?"

"Two blocks in the other direction. What do you do?" He wasn't flirting, exactly, but he did appear truly interested. As if he didn't get a chance to talk to other people very often.

Maybe he didn't.

We chatted awhile about my job as an operator at an answering service—not a total lie, since I did have that job once—and about his lack of a job, due to having inherited money when his dad died fifteen years earlier.

"But, what do you love, Alex?"

He gave me a sheepish look. "It's stupid."

"Nothing's stupid if it makes you happy. Some days, lime Jell-O makes me happy." I wrinkled my nose. "Unless it's got fruit or carrots or something chopped up in it. Jell-O is only good if it's smooth."

Alex chuckled. "Agreed. Well, my hobby's not as cool as Jell-O, but I build stuff with toothpicks."

I raised my eyebrows. "Seriously? Like, what, bridges and stuff? I've seen some pretty amazing things online."

Oscar shifted in Alex's lap, then moved to the space between us to rest his chin on my leg before going back to sleep. I smoothed the soft fur behind his ears.

Alex gave a small shrug. "I've built bridges before. Right now I'm…I mean, I was building a replica of my house."

"Was?"

He shrugged again and scratched Oscar's back. "I gave it up. I need to do more important things."

"Alex." I sat without speaking until he finally made eye contact with me. "What's more important in life than doing the thing that brings you joy?"

The cloudy, uncertain look I'd seen in his eyes for the past several days appeared to recede like a slow tide. "Maybe you're right."

I smiled. "Alex, I may not be able to catch my dog, but trust me. I'm always right."

Chapter 20

When I left, Alex had an excitement on his face he'd been missing since the previous Thursday. I was confident his enthusiasm for finishing his project was fully restored. I'd have liked to stay and watch, but I still had two more clients to reignite.

My fingers were crossed that Missy was back to work and not screwing around with her fingernails again, but I didn't hold my breath. The fact that all three clients fell off the wagon at the same time had me suspicious. Of what, I wasn't exactly sure, but something—or rather someone—could be working against me. Maybe.

Or maybe I just sucked at this.

Whatever the reason for my failures, Missy was hard at work on a Sudoku puzzle when I got there. The scrapbooking supplies she'd so painstakingly sorted last week were piled in a haphazard stack on the kitchen counter. Some of the pretty papers had rings on them from where she'd left a water glass or coffee cup.

Baby Cassie lay on her back on a blanket on the floor, bare feet wiggling in the air and hands swatting at the brightly colored safari animals dangling above her. That didn't bode well for getting Missy moving on her project. I may not have had any kids of my own, but I knew having a baby in the room wasn't the best way to concentrate on anything—except on the baby.

"Fine." I sat on the floor next to Cassie. "I'll wait until naptime. I've got all the time in the world."

Of course, that was a big fat lie. I had a little over two weeks. *We* had a little over two weeks. Cassie cooed and giggled at me. I hadn't noticed it before, but apparently babies could see me as easily as dogs could.

Interesting.

I unclipped my bubbles and blew them in Missy's direction. "Time to get back to work, Mama. You don't want to go to the party empty handed."

Cassie giggled and her eyes followed the bubbles across the room.

Missy sighed, and a fat tear rolled down her cheek.

Not the response I'd been looking for.

She unfolded her legs and climbed from the sofa. "Gabe!" She took a few steps toward the hallway that led to the bedrooms. "Gabe, I need to do a load of laundry. Can you watch her?"

A pale man with red hair and a headset poked his head out of the bedroom. "Yeah. Okay. Now? I was about to level up." He saw the look on her face and frowned. "Are you alright?"

"I'm fine. I just need to get out for a few minutes. Get some air."

He nodded and pulled off his headset. "Go ahead. We've got this." He grinned down at the baby. "Don't we, sweetie pie?"

Missy disappeared into the bedroom for a moment, then reappeared with a basket of dirty clothes and a bottle of detergent. She dropped a kiss on Gabe's cheek. "Thanks."

He grinned and picked up the baby, cuddling her against his chest. "You go get some air, Mommy. Daddy and Cassie will be here planning world domination." He blew a raspberry on Cassie's cheek, making her giggle.

This was the first time I'd seen Missy's husband. I liked him. He seemed sweet, and Cassie obviously adored him.

I followed Missy out the door.

She went down the steps, around the corner, and into a room lined with washers and dryers. No one else was in there, so she flipped the light on and got to work.

I backed out, trying to decide what to do next. After a moment, I turned and ran for my car. Breathless, I rummaged through the trunk and the backseat. Fortunately, I'm not the tidiest person in the world. I found three socks, a pair of yoga pants, two T-shirts, and a hoodie. Good enough. I shoved it all in a reusable, cloth grocery bag, grabbed a handful of change from the ashtray, and jogged back to the laundry room.

Before I stepped inside, I tapped my belt and became visible.

Missy looked up from her sorting and smiled. "Hi."

"Hi." My grin was probably a little too big. I was still getting the hang of this friend thing. A person can't erase a lifetime of habitual self-isolation in two weeks. Awkwardness was still a thing for me.

I opened a washing machine and tossed my bag full of assorted car discards into it, then lowered the lid.

"You forgot your detergent." Missy gave me a curious look, like she wondered if I'd ever done laundry before.

Of course I'd done laundry. But my apartment had its own washer and dryer. Laundromats were kind of foreign to me.

I opened the lid and peeked inside. "I did. I totally forgot." I fumbled with my bag, as if I might find some inside, a magical grocery bag that yielded any item I could wish for. Unfortunately, my bag remained stubbornly empty.

"Here. Help yourself." Missy handed me hers. "I hate when I have to go all the way back upstairs because I forgot something."

I nodded. "Me, too. Thanks."

She tossed the last of her whites into one machine and a pair of jeans into another. "I've never seen you around. Did you just move in?"

And…we were back to making stuff up. "I just moved here, and I'm staying with a friend until I get a place of my own."

"Oh. I wonder if I know your friend."

"Um…" I bit my lip while I measured laundry soap into its cap. "Do you know…Alfonso?"

She thought about it. "Dark hair, drives a blue Honda?"

My smile faltered and I returned her detergent bottle. "I'm staying with Alfonso's friend, Terrence."

She frowned. "I'm not sure I know Terrence."

I dropped quarters into the slot on the machine, bobbing my head cheerfully. "That's who I'm staying with. Terrence. Yep."

The back of my neck was sweating. Making stuff up was hard.

I hopped onto the machine and folded my legs. "Have you lived here long?"

She set her machines and fed them the obligatory quarters. "About three years. I'm living in 1117B with my husband and baby. We like it here." Once both her machines were running, she slid onto one of them and sat facing me. "Gabe's off today, so he stayed with Cassie."

I sat there looking at her, not knowing what to say after that. Alex had been a little easier, but women were tough for me sometimes, and small talk was my Achilles heel.

After a long, uncomfortable silence, I remembered how I'd handled Alex, and stuck my hand out. "I'm Wynter."

She shook my hand. "That's so pretty. I'm Missy. Which isn't a name at all, really, but it's all I've got. I always figured my mom was too startled by having a baby right after she turned forty to actually think up a real name for me."

"It's nice. And I'm sure your parents liked it when they gave it to you."

Her expression darkened and she looked away. "Yeah. Well."

"I'm sorry. I didn't realize they were a touchy subject." I could not believe my luck in finding a way to get her parents into the conversation so fast. Maybe I wasn't so stupid at this after all.

"Well, no. It's not like that. They're awesome. In fact, that's part of my problem." She pulled something out of her pocket. "Forget it. Want some gum?" She tossed me a piece before I could answer.

I unwrapped it and stuck it in my mouth. "Thanks." So much for guiding the conversation in a subtle, non-invasive way. We chewed in silence for a little while. "My mom's weird," I blurted, rupturing the silence. "And her birthday is next week. I have no idea what to get her. What do you get someone who clips coupons to use as decoupage on her coffee table?"

"A newspaper subscription?" Missy laughed. "I don't know. I'm the last person to ask for help on that one. My parents' fiftieth anniversary is coming up soon. I thought I had the perfect gift, but now, I have no clue." She blew out a dramatic lungful of air and pushed her hair out of her face. She looked miserable.

I chose my words carefully, afraid to spook her off the subject. "What were you going to get them?"

"I was making them a scrapbook." She shook her head. "But that's stupid. It's their golden anniversary. I should be doing something more—like a cruise or something."

I stared at her, incredulous. Was that the problem? She thought she should be buying them some huge, expensive gift instead?

"Don't you think your parents would rather you spent the money on their grandbaby?"

She popped her gum as she considered it. "Maybe. I guess. But the scrapbook seems so stupid. Like a six-year-old drawing a picture of her stick-figure family so Mom can stick the picture on the fridge with magnets."

I shrugged and blew a tiny bubble with my gum. Since the gum wasn't meant for it, I wasn't very successful. "The phrase 'It's the thought that counts' exists for a reason. Plus, scrapbooking is hard. It takes a lot of thought, creativity, and work. Anybody can go to a travel agency and buy tickets. Money isn't love."

Maybe I was laying it on too thick, but I was desperate to get her back on track. My machine was done and so were hers, so we worked in silence as we moved our wet things into dryers and fed more quarters into the slots.

While we waited for the clothes to dry, we switched to safer topics. If I hit the right note about her parents' anniversary gift, it would sink in and take hold. If I hadn't, well, poking it would drive her the wrong way.

Instead, I asked about Gabe. She told me all about their long-distance relationship built solely through phone and Internet exchanges working for different branches of the same tech company. Eventually, Gabe transferred to Topeka, they married, and Missy quit her job as an account manager to be a full-time mom.

That gave me a start. I'd viewed her as unambitious and unskilled, since finding her at home with a kid, messy house, and the television constantly on. I was ashamed to have judged her like that, even if it was an unconscious opinion. Stay-at-home moms came from all types of backgrounds.

Hell, I wouldn't be able to stay home by myself with a baby every day, and I didn't have any real skills.

Having actual conversations with people gave a lot more insight into their lives and their needs than skulking around invisible did. I'd learned that with Alex, and now I was learning it with Missy.

When my clothes were dry—I had a much smaller load than she did—I thanked her for the laundry detergent, gathered my folded gym clothes, and left. If I'd done things right, Missy would be back to work on the scrapbook. If not, I'd think of something new tomorrow.

Because I still had Mark left to badger. And he'd been the most difficult of the three from the beginning.

~*~

By the time I was finished with Missy, the day was nearly over. Now that I knew I was supposed to have written permission to keep my stuff home over night, I figured it was best to drop it off before I tackled a heart-to-heart with Mark. The pass Polly had given me was only for the weekend.

The lobby was kind of crowded, since most people were heading home, but I was going up, and most people were coming down, so the elevator was empty when I stepped in. As the doors closed, a blond head that looked familiar bobbed above the crowd out in the lobby. The man stopped and turned, and my breath caught in my throat. The doors closed before I got a good look.

I rubbed my eyes as I rode to the fifth floor. I couldn't have seen Freddy. That would be too weird. I'd never seen him here before. Was he related to a god, too? Could he have hit rock bottom on the loser scale? If so, was that my fault?

The doors opened, and I headed into the office, still arguing with myself. It couldn't have been Freddy. Surely I'd have seen him before, especially since, coming from Topeka, he'd be using the same portal into the building that I used. I hadn't seen his car in front of the abandoned warehouse where I parked every day.

I hung my belt under my name and placed the bottle of bubbles in the supply closet.

Didn't I have a moment in Maenads when I'd thought I saw Freddy at the other end of the bar? Was I losing my mind? Was I obsessed with my ex?

Had I made a mistake breaking up with him?

I didn't see Freddy when I went out through the lobby, nor did I see a guy who *looked* like Freddy. Mine was the only car parked outside the building.

When I got home, I was still mulling over the possibility that Freddy was working at Mt. Olympus. The problem had such a deep hold on me, I walked right past Mark and into my house. I didn't even notice him.

Phyllis, however, had seen us both. "Wynter, how could you not stop? He's been sitting on his front step waiting for you for over an hour."

"What?" I peered out the window. Sure enough, Mark was sitting on his porch, looking a little forlorn, and holding a bottle of wine and a bouquet of flowers. "What makes you think it was me he was waiting for?"

She flapped a leaf at me. "He was looking right at you and tried to get your attention."

I frowned at her, but stuck my head out the door anyway. "Hey. I didn't see you out there." I stepped outside. "You okay?"

His pout turned into a smile. He pulled himself up and held up the flowers and wine. "I owe you an apology."

I shook my head. "For what?"

He crossed the courtyard and handed me a bouquet of purple irises and fat yellow tulips. "I was short with you last night, and I nearly flashed you my junk this morning before kicking you out." He looked ashamed. "I haven't been very neighborly."

I cradled the gorgeous flowers in my arms and smiled at him, still shaking my head. "Totally my fault. I've been too nosy." I eyed the bottle of wine he still had. "I don't suppose you'd want to come inside with that and we can both be more neighborly."

I wasn't even sure what that meant. I hoped he didn't take it to mean I was inviting him in for sex—or worse—a date.

"That would be perfect." He held the door open and followed me inside.

I handed him two glasses and a corkscrew so he could handle the wine while I put the flowers in water. With the flowers in a tall vase in the center of the table, we each grabbed a glass and sat in my kitchen like old friends and not awkward acquaintances.

We talked about a lot of things during our first glass—Mrs. Terwilliger's latest tirade about the volume of everyone's televisions after 10 PM. Construction on the turnpike. And whether I actually had any friends.

I hadn't been expecting that one.

"Seriously," he said. "In all the time you've been here, I've never seen a single person, other than you, walk through that door." He finished his last sip and refilled both our glasses. "You must have a boyfriend because..." He waved his hand at me. "Well, look at you. Yet, I've never seen you bring anyone home."

I chuckled at him and gave him a long look. "So, are you asking me if I have a boyfriend? Is that what this is about?"

He shrugged. "That wasn't my intention, but sure."

I twirled the stem of my glass between my fingers. "I've been single for, oh, about three weeks or so."

"Oh. Well." He took a nervous swig. "I'm sorry. I hope it wasn't a tough breakup."

I sighed. "No. Not especially. Pretty typical. I'm not so good at the long-term thing. Probably tougher on him than it was on me, since I'm the one who pulled the plug." I neglected to tell him I was having ex-boyfriend hallucinations.

"Gotcha." He sat in silence for a moment, running his fingers over the rim of his glass. "Want to get a pizza?"

~*~

We were halfway through a large with pepperoni, sausage, and extra cheese, and already into our second bottle of wine, when his project finally came up. We'd moved to the living room and sat on opposite ends of the couch.

"I just feel like such a chump," he said. "The guy gave me this huge sob story about his little girl having leukemia and wanting to do something special for her. I gave him a really cheap price for my design expertise and

169

agreed to build it myself, too. That way, I could control costs and keep it super cheap for him."

I frowned. "Well, what's wrong with that? I'm sure he's got a lot of hospital bills to pay, right? And it's a nice thing to do for a sick little girl. That doesn't make you a chump."

He sat with his head hanging down, staring at an uneaten crust on his plate. When he looked up at me, his hair fell over one eye. The other eye looked so sad. "I just found out the guy scammed me."

I gasped. "Not uh."

He nodded. "Ya huh. I ran into this guy in the hardware store. We got to talking, and he said he'd been through the same exact thing with my client. Made-up daughter with leukemia, awesome playground for cheap, then, apparently, Pete turns around and sells the house for a profit. I'm not helping a little girl. I'm helping a scumbag flip a house."

My heart sank. "No. I can't believe that." The pizza I was chewing lost all its taste. "Did you call him? Double check?"

He shook his head, and I wanted to push that hair out of his face.

He reached into his pocket and pulled out a black leather wallet. "Here." He handed me a business card. "That's the guy I met in the store."

The card felt thin and flimsy, as if it had been printed on a home computer. "Did you check him out?"

"He's got a business card."

I stared at him. Nobody was this sweet, gullible and naïve, were they? I let out a long sigh. "Let's see what we can find out before you take a side, okay?"

I ran into my room and grabbed my laptop. When I returned, he was refilling our glasses. I took a sip, then settled in to boot up and see what I could find out. If my client's project was a scam, maybe somebody up in the Fates department was being a dick. Somebody should know about that. I suspected, however, that something else was going on.

First I searched for the Dwight McDougal from the business card. I was not surprised to find nothing on him. Not even a Facebook page. Mark's client, however, was easy to find. He *and* his adorable little girl were in the paper.

I turned the laptop around so Mark could see the screen. "Is that your client?"

His eyes widened. "Yes. He does have a little girl."

I nodded and closed the laptop. "And she's pretty sick, too."

"Wow. I don't know what to say." He looked horrified. "I screwed up."

"Why on Earth would you believe a random guy in the hardware store over your client, then not verify it?" I touched the back of his hand.

He looked so intelligent. In fact, I *knew* he was intelligent. This made no sense.

"I'm an idiot. I've been taken for a ride before." He shook his head. "I didn't want to look stupid a second time, so I guess I jumped to conclusions." He ran his hand through his hair, and his face looked pale. "Holy shit. I nearly screwed up that kid's birthday."

I understood that he was focused on the client and trying to get things back on track. But I had a more important concern he didn't seem to be worried about. "Who the hell was the guy in the hardware store, then?"

The question seemed to startle him. "I have no idea. Why would he try to interfere like that? Why would anybody care?"

I stared at the card in my hand, turning it over and over. "What did he look like?"

Mark shrugged. "I don't know. Like any guy. A little taller than me—maybe six-two. Blond hair, short on the sides, kind of spikey on top. Blue eyes, I think. Nothing really memorable about him."

My stomach dropped, and I tried to keep my face neutral. It had to be a coincidence. That description could apply to just about anybody. I was being paranoid.

There was no way Freddy was hijacking my clients.

Chapter 21

I didn't see Freddy at work the next morning, though I didn't expect to. I still thought he had nothing to do with any of this and I was making connections where there weren't any. That was the reasonable explanation.

Rick, however, made damn sure I saw him. He sat in the lobby for me and hopped up as I walked by. "Hey. Thought I'd try to catch you on the way in so we could get some coffee."

I stopped and counted to five in my head. This was a problem I couldn't put off. I would have to deal with it. But it was also a problem that smelled like an invitation to a sweaty, loud, life-changing night. It was a problem wearing a thick layer of guy-liner and a pirate costume. His eyes today were brown, as was his normally blond hair. The hopeful quiver of his lower lip made me want to press my mouth against it and see if it tasted like a cinnamon latte.

This would take every bit of resolve I had in my body to set things right and not make them worse.

I nodded. "Okay. Coffee. But I have to be quick. I've got a lot going on."

His worried face relaxed into a grin. "I'll take it."

We rode the elevator to the second floor in silence. The presence of so many other people—and a small sphinx that smelled a little like a wet skunk—made it less awkward than it might have been. When the doors opened, we were the only ones who stepped out on that floor, so we were alone. The pressure and warmth of his hand against the small of my back was both familiar and troubling.

He ordered a cinnamon latte for each of us again, and we took them to the table in the corner we'd used before.

This time, the silence was definitely awkward. He looked incredible. He smelled fantastic. He looked at me like he really liked me. A lot. A guy who looks at a girl like that is likely to treat her like a princess.

But I wasn't ready. It was too much too fast.

I took a deep breath and let it out. "Look," I said, not meeting his eyes. "I really like you. In fact, maybe I like you a little too much."

He touched my chin and raised it so I would make eye contact. "I don't understand why that's a bad thing."

I took a gulp of coffee and burned my mouth. "It wouldn't be if I'd met you later. But I just got out of a relationship. I mean *just* got out."

He raised his eyebrows. "You still have feelings for this guy?"

I shook my head. "Well, no." I couldn't possibly tell him I kept seeing my ex pop up in unlikely placed. "But I'm not..." I trailed off, thinking about how ridiculous and impossible it would be for Freddy to have been the guy in the hardware store trying to sabotage Mark's project.

"You're not ready?" Rick's voice was gentle. "I didn't mean to rush you into anything. I can back off until you're more comfortable."

I gave him a weak, worried smile. "You're not mad?"

He leaned forward and tapped his paper cup against mine. "I've got all the time in the world."

Rick agreed to give me time, then said something about being out of time himself and ran out the door. One of his eyes had turned blue, and blond streaks had appeared on the top of his head.

As I watched him go, I wondered for the first time what would happen if his costume ran out in front of me. Would he be naked? Was he really that good looking?

In the end, I was more confused and distressed than I'd been before I'd had coffee with Rick. But I did know I'd done the right thing. Somehow, I wasn't done with Freddy yet. A new boyfriend wasn't in the cards until I sorted myself out first. In fact, most of the trouble I'd had with men in my life was because I jumped into relationships too fast.

I needed to figure out how to handle Wynter before I could take another stab at having a boyfriend.

Having figured out this deep, spiritual truth, I waltzed into the office with a little more confidence than I'd had before. Dave's leer and Jeremy's ugly smirk barely touched me as I squeezed past them in the hallway. I grabbed my gear, dropped a framed picture of my mom on my desk, and squeezed past the Ass-clown Brothers on my way out.

I had more important problems on my plate than a couple of mouth breathers who resented their inability to get laid.

My nerves were pinging all the way down the elevator, expecting Freddy to step in from a different floor or be walking away in the lobby when the doors opened. Since I'd stopped for a little while to have coffee, it was already late enough that, when I left the elevator, traffic in the lobby had died down.

Patrice glanced up at me as I passed her reception area. She raised a dark green eyebrow from behind her glasses. I lifted a hand to give her a half wave. She didn't wave back, but one side of her hot-pink-painted lips lifted in a tiny smile.

I hid my own smile as I ducked out the door. I was betting underneath all the grumpy attitude was a much gentler soul than she wanted to show.

Who knew? Maybe in my quest to learn how to be a good friend, I'd acquire a gorgon as well as some humans. Stranger things had already happened to me in the last week or so.

I headed straight to Alex's house to see if yesterday's pep talk had stuck or if I'd have to build the damn thing for him. To my relief, he was hard at work in the basement. The detached garage had taken shape, and he was working on the garage door. He whistled as he glued, a weird, perky song I couldn't identify until the third time through.

"Dude." I blew bubbles at him and crossed my fingers. "The theme song to *Gilligan's Island*? Really? How about a different song?"

The bubbles must've taken hold because he switched in the middle of the song. I grinned until I realized he was whistling the *Brady Bunch* theme now.

I groaned and rose from the box I'd been perched on. "Well, at least you're working." I screwed the cap on my bubbles and reattached them to my belt.

I endured his whistling for a few hours, relieved that he was finally back in the zone. Around noon, he climbed off his stool and stretched, and I did the same. I wandered over to see how he was doing. The garage door was drying, but it looked as if he'd made it functional, so that when he finally attached it to the rest of the building, it would actually roll up and down.

Without thinking, I patted him on the back. He must have felt it, because he startled and looked around.

I took a step back embarrassed. "Sorry! Sorry! Nobody's here. We're fine." I backed into the table. Now that I remember what I was doing, though, I walked right through it without affecting the surface. I glanced down and found the pamphlet for Alex's big toothpick architect competition.

It was a glossy page covered in photos of toothpick bridges, castles, and ships. Happy people held up trophies with golden toothpicks on them. At the bottom of the page, it gave information about the convention space in a moderate-quality hotel, ticket prices, and the dates.

I turned to follow Alex up the stairs and stopped. It felt as if all the blood had left my head and gone to fuel the quicker pace of my heart. I returned to the table, afraid to look, but I did anyway. What I'd seen was crazy.

I still had two-and-a-half weeks until my deadline was up. But the competition was in a week and a half. Somehow, I'd lost a week. Or the Fates had screwed up.

Alex had made it upstairs already and had Oscar's leash in his hand to take him for a walk. That was great, since I really needed to talk to him in person, but I was seriously freaked out about the deadline.

Did Alex know it was next week? No, I was sure he knew. His paperwork had the right date on it. I had to get to my car so I could check the paperwork stashed in my purse.

I wanted to vomit.

But I couldn't. If I was going to get a chance to talk to Alex, I had to do it now. The paperwork would be there when I finished.

I tore off ahead of Alex and Oscar, my invisible feet clomping on the sidewalk. I made it to the park before they got there, plopped onto the bench, and switched off my belt so I'd be visible. I had about a minute and a half to catch my breath.

"Hello." Alex took a seat on the other end of the bench. "Lose your dog again?"

I shook my head, still breathing heavily. "My…um…sister caught him and took him back. I'm just trying to catch my breath."

"Ah. Well, I'm glad I caught you. I owe you a thank you."

"Yeah? What for?"

"Talking to you really helped the other day. I'm back to creating my project. You said just what I needed to hear. I found my joy again."

I smiled. "I'm glad to hear that." I tilted my head and gave him a serious look. "How did you lose it in the first place, though? It sounded like maybe you got some bad advice from somebody."

He nodded. "It was stupid. There was this guy I met at the craft store. We got to talking, and he found out I live with my mother." He paused and searched my face, as if I might reject his friendship with that revelation.

"Nothing wrong with that." I shrugged. "I very nearly moved back in with my mom last month."

His eyes brightened. "Well, this guy didn't think it was reasonable at all. By the time he finished talking about prospects and accountability and ambition, I felt about two inches high. I decided I needed to make a change in my life."

I scowled. "He didn't even know you. How dare he?"

"Well, he wasn't terribly wrong."

I bent over and scratched Oscar's head. "He wasn't right, either. What's this guy look like? Shriveled and bitter?"

Alex chuckled. "No. Nothing special. Young guy. Mid-twenties, I guess. Weird haircut, kind of almost shaved on the sides, but sticking up on top."

I most definitely wanted to vomit now. "Blond? Blue eyes?"

"I think so, yeah. Why? Do you know him?"

"God, I hope not."

~*~

The paperwork, it turned out, wasn't in the car. I'd left it on the kitchen counter at home. I had to decide whether to go home or head straight to Missy's. In the end, I did neither. I stopped at the craft store.

By the time I did get to Missy's, I'd calmed down considerably. Whether it was Freddy or not, somebody was sabotaging my clients' projects. And there was a good chance somebody—likely the same somebody—was sabotaging me so I couldn't help them in time. Whoever was screwing things up missed one important fact.

Wynter Greene was nobody's bitch.

I wrapped on the door of 1117b and waited. Missy opened the door with a cloth diaper over one shoulder and a baby on her hip.

It took her a minute to remember who I was, but when she did, her face broke into a delighted grin. "Wynter, right? Come in!"

I handed her the package in my hand. "I thought this might help with your project. It sounded so gorgeous, I wanted to help."

She had a puzzled look on her face, but shoved the baby into my arms and opened the bag. "These are beautiful." She pulled out stacks of adhesive jewels in a rainbow of colors. "They're perfect. Here, I'll show you."

We sat on the sofa, and she slid the partially finished scrapbook from a box under the coffee table and flipped it open. Several pages were done. She'd been working harder than I'd realized.

Each page was a celebration of a different significant day in the lives of her parents. She'd done a fantastic job so far.

"Check this out." She flipped to the wedding page and placed a string of adhesive pearls around the edges. "See? The one thing that was missing and you brought it." Her face was flushed with excitement. "Thank you,

177

thank you, thank you!" She leaned close and hugged my arm, then gathered Cassie in her arms to kiss her cheeks. Cassie giggled.

I laughed. "You're very welcome. These pages are incredible. This is *art*, Missy. I don't know how you could have doubted yourself. You have so much talent." I flipped through the book. She'd added at least three pages since I'd last seen it.

She shrugged. "Yeah. I think this guy I met was trying to sell me a trip for my parents. He was a travel agent. I was stupid to listen. I guess he just got under my skin, you know?"

I nodded. "Yeah. I get it." Knowing exactly what she'd tell me, I asked her to describe the guy.

"Cute as hell. Nice butt. Long eyelashes and twinkly blue eyes. Cool haircut, too. Like yours, only shorter on the sides."

Somebody was going to get his pretty face punched when I found him.

I pulled myself from the couch. "I need to get going. I just wanted to give you that stuff and see how you were doing."

She gave me a one-armed hug. "Thank you again. They're perfect."

"Glad you like them." I stepped out the door and stopped. "Missy, when's your parents' party?"

"About a week and a half. If I work really hard, I might be able to get it done in time."

Chapter 22

Phyllis was livid. I hadn't expected that part.

When I got home, I went straight to the folder on the counter, muttering to myself about deadlines and booby-traps.

"Are you alright, Wynter?" Phyllis sat in the kitchen window, her leaves perky with interest.

I flipped open the folder, my lips in a tight smile. "Nope. I'm not okay. Not at all." I scanned the assignment for Alex till I got to the deadline. I ran my finger over the number twenty-eight, and the ink smeared, leaving behind a one where the eight had been. "Nope. Not okay at all." I repeated it on the other two assignments with the same results.

"What's wrong, honey? Talk to me." Phyllis's branches were shaking.

I slammed the folder shut, though it didn't make a very satisfying sound. "Somebody changed the dates on my deadlines to make me think I had more time."

"No!" Her braches whipped around so hard I moved her to the counter for fear of her slipping off and spilling in the sink. "You have to report this, of course."

I nodded. "Oh, I will. But there's more. Some guy has been talking to each of my clients and throwing them off their projects. All that crazy stuff you watched Mark do? Mystery Guy caused it."

"Oh, Wynter. What a disaster. Who did this? You take me with you tomorrow. I'll find out who's behind all this. Don't you worry."

I took a deep breath. "I think…well, this is going to sound crazy, but I think maybe the person doing it could be Freddy."

Phyllis laughed. "Don't be ridiculous. Why would—okay, I do know the why—but *how* could Freddy do anything? You haven't even talked to him."

I chewed my bottom lip in thought. "I know. But I have a feeling Freddy was working at Mt. Olympus all along."

"Well, that much we can find out first thing tomorrow."

I nodded, distracted by Mark's light across the courtyard. I should've gone over and checked on him, but I was physically and emotionally drained. All I wanted was a good night's sleep.

"You're right. First thing tomorrow, we'll get to the bottom of it. But you know what?"

"What, honey?"

"I'm not letting these people miss their deadlines, no matter how hard someone's been trying to make that happen."

Phyllis patted the back of my hand. "That's my girl."

~*~

Despite her insistence that I take her with me, I left Phyllis at home to keep an eye on Mark out the window. I considered knocking on his door and asking him to keep her with him for the day, but she wasn't a dog or a sick kid. I couldn't come up with a convincing reason why my houseplant needed constant monitoring. She was coming down with root rot? Her water consumption was too high, and I was worried she might be diabetic? Maybe I could tell him she'd been hanging out with a bunch of bad seeds and I was afraid she'd run away.

That would be weird. Even for me.

"Just watch and see if anybody goes in or if he goes anywhere, okay? I need your help, Phyllis. I can't be everywhere at once."

Phyllis sounded pouty. "You need me at the office where I can set everything straight. They'll listen to me."

I placed her on the window ledge. "I know they would. But I need to do this myself. And I really do need you to watch in case Freddy—or whoever it is—tries to contact Mark again."

"Fine. Go." She shook a few branches in my direction. "But if you get in over your head, come back and get me."

I smiled. "Thanks, Phyllis. You're the best."

She really was. For a plant, she was a pretty loyal companion. I was lucky to have her. Not for the first time I wondered what her story was—and how she'd ended up as my guardian.

~*~

In the lobby, I checked for any men who were my past or present love interests. Unless I had plans to date a minotaur in a business suit, the lobby was clear. I took a calming breath and stepped into the queue in reception.

This was the part Phyllis could have made easier, but I felt like I needed to do it on my own.

The line wasn't long, probably because it wasn't a Monday, so there were no new hires needing to be checked in. Still, those five minutes or so gave me plenty of time to get worked up into a solid case of sweaty nerves.

"Next." Patrice eyed me through her tiny glasses.

I inched forward to the edge of her counter. "Hi."

She grunted. "Hi. You need something already? Didn't you just get here a few weeks ago?" The two snakes that hung over one of her eyes squirmed and flicked their tongues at me.

My mouth felt dry. "I was wondering if you could help me find someone."

One of her eyebrows rose. "Did you try lost and found?"

"Ha. Yeah. No. I think someone I know works here, but I don't know where to find him. I was wondering if you could look it up or tell me where to go to find out." I cleared my throat. "Please?"

Patrice smirked. "A guy?"

I nodded. "Yes."

"A guy you're interested in, perhaps?"

I let out a rush of air. "Oh, gosh, no. I already…I mean. No. Not someone I'm interested in."

The second eyebrow jumped up with the first. "An ex. Ah. So, let me get this straight. You think you saw your ex somewhere and want to know for sure if he's here? Is that right?"

"No!" I frowned. "Yes. That's exactly right. And I think he may know I'm here and he's been screwing with me. Or I'm paranoid and delusional. And if that's it, I'd kind of like to know that, too."

Patrice nodded. "Men are idiots." She tapped something on a tablet and it came to life. "What's his name?"

"Freddy Mossman." I shifted my weight from foot to foot. Now that I wasn't so nervous about Patrice—okay, still nervous but no longer terrified—my anxiety shifted to what Patrice may or may not find.

"Mossman." She scrolled through the list on her screen. "Arnold, Carl, Cathrine, Erika, Fredrick, Harold. Hmm. You said Freddy?"

The sweat on my skin grew cold. "Yeah. You said Frederick."

"Could be him. Maybe you're not delusional." Her snakes curled around her head and settled into a new style. It was flattering—kind of like a casual updo.

"Only one way to find out, I guess. Can you tell me where he works?"

She tapped on the screen and a new page came up. "Dreams and Nightmares. Fourth floor."

I nearly choked. "Really?"

She nodded. "Mean something to you?"

"Maybe. It makes sense. Now, I think I know who's been helping him."

She backed out of the screen and set the tablet aside. "I guess you've got your work cut out for you, then."

"I guess I do. Thanks, Patrice."

She smiled. "Good luck." She shifted her attention before I stepped away. "Next!"

I went to the elevator fuming. Freddy had been here the whole time, and he'd been working in the same department as Rick. I stabbed at the button inside the elevator for my floor. All that time, Rick had been playing me. And to what end? So Freddy could…

The final piece slid into place and I nearly choked on it. Freddy. Rick. Fredrick. Fred. Rick.

"I am a total moron."

A harpy—the only other person in the elevator—shook her feathers. "Did you say something?"

I shook my head. "Nothing. Sorry. Just talking to myself." The doors slid open on my floor and I stepped out.

"First sign you're delusional." She smiled at me as the door slid shut.

I shivered. Nope. I knew I wasn't delusional. I still didn't know all the hows and whys of what the hell Freddy/Rick was up to, but I was going to find out.

When I entered my office, the atmosphere was similar to the previous Friday. In an office where I rarely saw anyone, people were clustered in groups everywhere, whispering and looking worried. Dave and Jeremy actually stepped out of my way as I passed them to get to my desk.

The air was thick with murmurs from every corner.

I set my purse on my desk and pulled out a small decorative candy dish I'd brought back from a short time I spent living in Albuquerque. The bottom of the dish was painted in bright colors and featured a hot air balloon. I dropped the hair clips and old gum into it and set it next to my keyboard.

Little by little, I was moving in.

As I adjusted the position of the dish, someone behind me tapped on my shoulder. I turned to find Audrey looking at me with uncharacteristic emotion. What emotion it was, I couldn't tell. But it wasn't a sneer on her face. More like guilt or as if she'd swallowed a bug.

"Can I talk to you for a minute?"

I folded my arms and leaned against the desk. "Sure. What's going on today? Everybody's all agitated again."

She glanced away, not meeting my eyes. "I need to apologize to you."

I wrinkled my forehead. "Oh?"

I wasn't sure what else to say. "It's okay, some people are just naturally bitches" probably wasn't the way to go.

Audrey rubbed her palms over her skirt, as if her hands were sweating. "I'm sure you don't know about this, but your predecessor was my friend."

"Phoebe." I dropped her friend's name, and it lay between us like a rock.

Her eyes widened in surprise. "Okay. Maybe you do know. Well, I blamed you for getting her fired, then taking the job opening she left. I'm afraid I wasn't a very good trainer as a result. Then you were so nice to Trina when she got booted. You didn't report Dave to HR, even though he's been a pig. And I've watched how determined you've been, even working extra hours. I feel terrible."

I sighed. "I figured most of the job out eventually. Don't worry about it."

"I wasn't very nice. And I made everyone else ignore you. I hoped…"

"That I'd quit?"

She nodded. "Maybe."

I chuckled. "Look. I've recently figured out that I'm not the best at being friendly myself. No harm done."

She relaxed a little. "I figured, once you read your handbook, you wouldn't really need me for much, anyway. It's all there. But I'm sorry for isolating you."

I frowned. "What handbook?"

She froze. "You can't be serious. You didn't read the handbook?"

"I didn't get a handbook. I got paperwork, and you threw out most of the stuff that came with it. What was leftover was hardly worth looking at. Did I miss something?"

She gave me a gentle push to get at my computer. "It's on your desktop. You can't miss it. It says Muse Handbook. Sheesh."

My stomach churned. How could I have missed something so important? I hadn't used the computer for much—research and mapping— but I'd totally missed the handbook.

"Well, that's weird." She stood over my monitor, her expression puzzled.

"What's weird?" I leaned closer. The little icons lined up neatly on the desktop. There weren't very many of them. I didn't see the one she'd been referring to.

"It's not here. How can it not be here?" She clicked through several folders and they all came up empty. As a last try, she clicked on the trashcan icon.

And there it was—*Muse Handbook* in large, clear letters.

"Why is it in the trash?" I honestly couldn't understand what was going on.

"I'm assuming you didn't throw it away." She looked up at me for confirmation.

"I've never even seen it."

"Well, despite my poor behavior, I never would have tried to sabotage you like this. Breaking some of these rules can be serious. You need to tell Polly about this. It might change her mind."

"Change her mind about what?"

Audrey straightened and turned toward me. "Polly wants to see you. She sent me to get you. She looked pretty upset."

I sucked in a long breath. "Well, crap. So, that's what everybody's talking about?"

She nodded. Her expression was filled with compassion. "I'm afraid so."

I lifted my chin. "Okay, then. I'm going in. There's a lot more going on here than you know."

"I'm so sorry, Wynter. I never would have screwed with you if I'd known." She paused and her voice dropped to almost a whisper. "Who did you piss off?"

I sighed. "I have my suspicions, but I don't know for sure yet." I pulled my shoulders back and left her standing there, wringing her hands.

Polly's door was wide open. I didn't even have a chance to knock before her melodious voice greeted me from deep inside.

"Come in, Wynter. Close the door and sit down." The voice was still melodic, but it sounded more like a funeral dirge than an aria.

I sat in the chair opposite her and placed my hands in my lap so she couldn't see them shaking. I still wasn't sure what I'd done wrong. I knew a lot had been done *to me*, though, so I was prepared for a fight. "You wanted to see me?"

She rubbed her fingertips over a tiny spot between her thick eyebrows. "Please tell me it's not true that you've been speaking with your clients in full-flesh mode."

My stomach tightened. "Full-flesh mode?"

"Visible. Solid. Out in the open." She gave me a pinched look, as if she would be angrier if she weren't so tired. "Don't make this more difficult than it already is. Please."

I took a deep breath and let it out. "Okay. Yes. I've been working with my clients in person. But there are circumstances you don't know about."

"Wynter, you broke the cardinal rule." She shook her head and pushed a sheet of paper toward me. "What's more, you've been observed breaking several rules. Really important ones."

I took the paper from her desk and read it. "Turned off invisibility belt while alone in a client's home." I thought about it. "Yeah. Okay. I hadn't learned how to interact with objects very well, and I needed to see his notes. He didn't catch me." How the hell did they know about that? "Since my paperwork failed to tell me what the project was, I had to get creative."

Polly frowned. "That's odd. But go on."

I consulted the list. "Interacted with clients while corporeal. Yeah. I had to undo the sabotage someone else had been doing." Looking at the list, I felt my blood pressure rising as I grew angrier. "Took home belt and supplies without proper authorization." I looked up from the list, scowling. "First of all, one of my clients is my next-door neighbor, and I wasn't about to drive all the way back to work at the end of the day to put it back when I was already home. Second, I had no idea it wasn't allowed until I talked to you a few days ago and you gave me a pass."

Polly watched me with an unchanging expression. "Go on. Read the rest."

"Touched a client, drove a vehicle for three blocks while still invisible, used more than twice the recommended dose of Beastie Discombobulator Dust on a client's dog. Hey, nobody even trained me how to use that stuff. Totally not my fault." Despite my anger—and admittedly, a good helping of fear—my hands didn't shake anymore.

Polly folded her hands on her desk. "It sounds as if you've got an excuse lined up for everything. All of those rules you broke were in your handbook." The disappointment in her voice made the melody of it sound a little flat. "Audrey came to me earlier and admitted she didn't give you as much training as she should have. However, you could have learned it all from the handbook. Did you not even bother to read it?"

Despite my effort to remain cool and calm, a short bark of laughter escaped   me.
"The handbook? I didn't even know about it until this morning. Ask Audrey. We found it in my trashcan on my desktop. So, not only did I get

lousy training, I had nowhere to go for answers." I pulled my folder from my pack and placed my three assignments in front of her. I poked a finger at the various fields. "You see that? No explanation filled in for Mark's project. I was flying blind. See the deadlines on all three? Take special note of the smudges on the numbers where someone changed them so I'd think I had a week longer than I actually did."

Polly rubbed her finger on the numbers, making the smudge more apparent. "What the hell?"

By now I'd worked up a pretty good rage. My voice was shaking. So much for cool and calm. "You ready for the best part?"

"Mighty Aphrodite, I have a feeling I'm not. But go ahead."

"It turns out my ex-boyfriend works in the Dreams and Nightmares department and he's been sabotaging my progress. He had all three of my clients talked into quitting their projects. The only way to figure that out and talk them back around was by breaking the stupid rules." I paused, thinking I was done, then remembered one last thing that upset me—because, hey, if you're going to blow up your career, you should be thorough, right? "And what is wrong with this office? Nobody would help me. Dave and Jeremy are a couple of pigs. And you're never in your office. I've never been so alone in my life—and that's saying something, because I'm pretty much a loner. I needed help and there was no one. So, yeah. I did what I had to do."

I felt cleaned out, emptied. She could do what she wanted to me, now. I didn't care. At least I would go to the Underworld knowing I'd done my best. I sat again, folded my hands, and waited.

Polly stared at the paperwork in her hands. "Wynter, I'm so sorry. Word came down from higher up that I was to keep an eye on you but to let you get on by yourself. I had no idea why. I do know they don't usually give three clients to a Muse on her first week." She rubbed the spot on her forehead again. "But the rest of this is too much. I can't allow someone to sabotage my Muses."

"So, now what? Do I just go back to work?"

Polly rose from her chair and walked around her desk to lean against it. "No. That's not even an option. I called you in here to give you orders to pack your desk and report to staffing in the Underworld."

Despite my earlier bravado, my stomach felt queasy. "But circumstances…"

She nodded. "Yes. Circumstances. I'm going to need your ex-boyfriend's name. I'll look into all of this. And you are going home to wait for my decision."

I blinked. "Home to wait? You mean...a suspension?"

"You still broke rules, Wynter. Go home. Let me get to the bottom of this. Shouldn't take more than a week or so."

"What about my clients? What about their deadlines?"

She pursed her lips. "No longer your concern." She went back to her chair and settled in. "Make sure you leave your belt on the hook."

And with that, I was dismissed. It was as if I were no longer in the room. How people could turn compassion on and off that quickly was beyond me.

I exited through a sea of anxious faces. Audrey, especially, looked upset. I stopped at my desk to see if I needed to take anything, but the only things there were the kitschy candy dish, photo of Mom, and the stuffed giraffe. I left them there. It made me feel better to still have a claim on the desk.

Somehow, I managed not to cry until I was halfway home.

Chapter 23

By the time I got home, my tears had dried up, as had my anger and my self-pity. Phyllis was so angry, she lost big handfuls of leaves, and I had to sit with her using a damp cloth on the remaining leaves to get her to calm down.

"I told you I should have gone with you." Once she was calm, she sounded more miserable than I'd felt in the car. "I can't do my job if you won't let me."

"What exactly is your job?"

"To keep you out of trouble. Obviously, I'm doing a terrible job."

We sat like that for some time at the kitchen table, Phyllis drooping her branches in defeat and me stroking her leaves with a soft cloth. The repetitive motion was as soothing to me as it was to her, so it took me a moment to notice Mark tapping on the window.

I waved him toward the door, and he let himself in.

"Wow," he said. "Doesn't look like you're having the best day ever." He pulled out a chair and sat. "You okay?"

I put the cloth on the table and sat up straighter. "Unexpected time off work. It'll be okay." I tried to give him a cheerful smile. "How's the project going?"

"I've got the designs all done. It's going to be gorgeous. I lost some time though. Those days I spent screwing around have put me behind. I still have to build it all. And her birthday's next weekend."

I frowned. "Will you make it in time?"

"I think so. Might be some late nights, but I'll make it work." He scooted his chair out and stood. "Anyway, I just came by to say thanks for your help. Without you, I'd still be sitting around feeling sorry for myself."

This time my smile wasn't forced. "I'm glad I could help." I tilted my head. "Hey, I'm not going to work next week anyway. Could you use an extra pair of hands?"

His eyes sparkled. "That would be amazing."

~*~

I had a number of things I wanted to take care of while I was suspended from work. My number one priority was to make sure all three clients made their deadlines. Screw my deadline. This was no longer about me. My future didn't hang on their successes anymore. In fact, my future was out of my own hands. I could cry about it some more, or I could use the week off to make damn sure my garbage didn't stick to them.

I had no access to the invisibility belt anymore, but there had been that day I'd taken an extra bottle of bubbles and slipped them in my pocket. I'd completely forgotten about them until now. I found my jacket in the corner of my bedroom, and the bubbles were still there. Nobody knew I had them.

The collection of crazy-shaped wands I'd bought at the toy store were still in the bag in the corner, forgotten and unused. Keeping the Thought Bubbles with the wands would've made sense if I wasn't so worried the Muse police might try to come in and search for my ill-gotten booty. I stuffed the bag of wands in my closet, then hid the bubbles in my bookcase behind some old Nancy Drews. Its presence both comforted me and scared me. But I wasn't going to give it up unless somebody caught me. As much as I'd been screwed with over the last three weeks, I figured I deserved to have a little magic to keep, even if it was only a souvenir.

Before I could focus on my clients, though, I had a certain ex-boyfriend to deal with—and I needed to do it before he went into work that night and found out he'd been ratted out.

I dialed Freddy's number and wasn't surprised by how fast he answered. "Wynter?"

"Hi Freddy. Are you busy?" I knew he wouldn't be. He never was during the day.

"Why?" The question came out slow and wary. "You haven't talked to me in three weeks."

"Well, I'm ready to talk now. Do you have time for a cup of coffee?"

There was a long pause. For a minute, I thought he'd hung up.

Finally, he took a breath. "I'll meet you at Jerry's Java in half an hour."

"See you then."

I hung up feeling a little sick and a lot nervous. But I was determined to confront Freddy before he found out at work what I already knew.

"Kick him in the balls," Phyllis said. "The little worm."

I laughed. "I won't be kicking, punching, biting, scratching, or karate chopping today."

Phyllis's branches rubbed together, making a grumbling sound. "Fine. I'd want to watch anyway."

~*~

Freddy was already there when I arrived, and he had coffee waiting for me—a cinnamon latte, of course. The fact that I hadn't questioned Rick on knowing what to order bothered me, now. I'd been an idiot.

I sat in the big comfy chair opposite Freddy and smiled. "Thanks for the latte. How've you been?"

"Okay, I guess. I missed you." He widened his blue eyes to look sad and miserable.

I had to bite my lip to keep from laughing. Rick's hair and eyes had changed shades a few times, and he was bulkier through the shoulders than Freddy. Also, Freddy had a longer nose with a bump in the middle. Even when their coloring had been the same, they didn't look at all like the same person.

The Dreams and Nightmares costumes were more than cowboy hats and vampire capes—they went more than skin deep. Even Rick's voice had been different, deeper.

While I examined Freddy for clues—anything that looked or sounded like Rick—he told me about his cat Dallas, who missed me a lot, how his car had been in the shop for the last several weeks after he'd wrapped it around a telephone pole, and how happy it made him that I'd called.

I cleared my throat. "I have to tell you something, Freddy. I never meant to hurt you, but..."

His face went pale. "What?"

"Well." I took my time, smoothing my skirt, taking a sip of my coffee, then looking up at him with as much guilt and sadness as I could fake. "I've met someone else."

He frowned. "You...you have?"

I nodded. "I met him at my new job. Nothing's happened, yet. Not really." I smiled and looked away. "Well, we did go on a picnic once. I really like him."

Freddy relaxed a little. "I see." He took a sip of his coffee, but I could see the satisfaction dancing in his eyes.

"Please don't be upset."

"Oh, I'm not."

I leaned forward and put my hand on his knee. "Will you excuse me? I'll be right back."

191

"Of course." He sat back in his seat with a self-satisfied look on his face that I kind of wanted to scrub off with a loofa.

Or a phone call.

I left him reveling in his perceived success at getting me to fall for Rick. Once I was in the bathroom where he couldn't see or hear me, I dialed Rick's number.

Now, everything rode on this part. If Freddy had separate phones for the two personas and had left his Rick phone at home, this wasn't going to work. But I knew Freddy. I was betting he'd forwarded Rick's number to his phone.

It rang three times before he answered. Which made sense. Rick was way cooler than Freddy, so he'd never answer on the first ring.

"This is Rick."

"Hi, Rick. It's Wynter." Because caller ID didn't exist, and he couldn't possibly know who it was, right?

"Oh, hey, Wynter. What's up? I missed you this morning in the cafeteria."

I opened the door to the ladies room and peeked at the back of Freddy's head. He sat in his comfy chair chatting on the phone. I stepped into the coffee shop and let the door close behind me.

"Well, I'm going to have some time off next week. I was wondering if you might want to do something."

"Absolutely." His grin was almost audible through the phone.

I walked toward Freddy while I talked. "I promise not to freak out on you this time."

"Well, I'm glad to hear it." Freddy shifted in his seat, but didn't turn around.

"I know what I want now." I stood directly behind him, now, but he was so full of confidence, he didn't realize what was going on.

"That makes me really happy. What would you like to do next week?"

I stopped talking and stood over him, waiting for him to notice me.

"Are you there? Hello?" He took his phone from his ear and checked the signal, than put it back. "Wynter?"

I hung up.

He checked again and saw that I was gone.

"In your excitement, you forgot to disguise your voice," I said.

He froze for a second, then slowly tilted his head back to see me. "How long have you been there?"

"Quite awhile." I moved around him and returned to my seat. "So, any last words?" I took a long sip of my latte, savoring the cinnamon. I might never have one again after this. Maybe I would try hazelnut next.

"How did you figure it out?" His face was pinched with disappointment.

I shrugged. "Doesn't matter. What matters is why. Why would you do this to me? What did I do that was so wrong? I broke up with you. I'm sorry that I hurt you, honestly I am. But what was I supposed to do? Wait until we'd picked out china before I did it? We weren't right for each other. It happens."

He gave me a dark stare. "Once I could take. But I gave you someone else—a whole new person. Rick was cooler and better looking, but he knew all the things you liked without being told. I made myself into your perfect guy, and you still rejected me."

I rolled my eyes. "Freddy, *I* don't even know who my perfect guy would be. How could you possibly create him? That's crazy."

"I'm not crazy."

"Dude. Seriously. You might want to take a closer look at everything you've done over the past month or so. And in case you're wondering how my clients are doing, thanks for your help, but I got them back on track anyway."

He opened his mouth to say something, but nothing came out but a series of stutters.

I smiled and nodded. "Yeah. That, too. Anything I'm missing? Anything else you want to tell me about?"

He shook his head. His face looked a little green.

I sat forward, perched on the edge of the cushion. "Can you just tell me why? I get that you wanted a redo. That explains the Rick thing—at least in *your* head. But why the hell would you mess with my job? Why try to get me fired?"

He looked away, unable to meet me gaze. "I'm really sorry about that. After you bolted from our picnic, I kind of lost my mind. I'd tried to give you everything you wanted, and you still dumped me. You'd shown me your assignments in the coffee shop, so I spent the weekend tracking down your clients and sabotaging your work." He scrubbed at his face with the palms of his hands. "I was so angry. But then I saw you again and thought you might give me another chance. I felt terrible."

I shook my head. "Shit, Freddy. I've been suspended. They're deciding whether or not to send me to the Underworld. And what about changing the dates on my assignments so I couldn't make my deadlines? And you

193

threw away my handbook so I would break rules I didn't know about. How did you even get into my office? What the hell is wrong with you?"

He paled. "Wynter, I swear, I never set foot in your office. I never touched your stuff."

At this point, I had to believe he wasn't lying. He'd confessed to everything else. I couldn't see a reason for him to lie about this. I frowned. That meant somebody else—probably someone in my own office—was also screwing with me.

Mt. Olympus was turning out to be a giant clubhouse for people who hated me. For once in my life, I refused to accept it was my fault. Other than having crappy taste in men, of course. That was all me.

I finished my coffee and stood. "Well, Fred. It's been a slice. Good luck at work tonight. My boss was pretty pissed off. I'm sure your boss won't be too happy either." I walked toward the door, then stopped and turned my head. "If things don't go real well over the next week, I guess I'll see you around. In the Underworld."

I walked out without looking back.

~*~

When I got home, I felt drained, but at peace. Whatever was going to happen would happen. Polly had taken me off the job and said the clients were no longer my concern. But she was wrong. I cared about them, now. I cared about their dreams. And I wasn't going to let petty people who were angry with me derail the dreams of Mark, Missy, and Alex. It wasn't fair, and it wasn't right.

I'd have to help them the old-fashioned way. With my own two hands. The next week would be a busy one.

Once Phyllis heard the sad story of Freddy and Rick in the coffee shop three times, she was satisfied that justice had been and would be served and went quiet for the night. I, on the other hand, was still too wound up to sleep.

I opened the hall closet and stared at the big black garbage bag tied shut with a knot so final, I'd have to cut it open if I wanted to get inside. Despite my decision to throw it out, I'd never managed to haul it off to the trash.

Did I dare try again to finish it? What if pieces were missing? What if it was ripped?

I pushed at the bag with my bare toe. "You're the reason I ended up in this mess, you know. You're the proverbial last straw." I prodded it again, and it prodded back with a sharp pin to the foot.

My uninjured foot twisted beneath me, and I fell to the floor, landing on my butt in front of the bag. I squared my shoulders and ripped the plastic open. Pins and satin and batting spilled out to the floor. I collected the stray pins and stuck them in a pincushion, then gathered the material to spread on the living room floor.

It wasn't as bad as I'd expected. Some of the squares needed to be re-pinned, others had been sewn but needed their stitches ripped out and re-sewn. Once the squares were all together, I'd attach the binding on the edges, the backing, and the batting to make it fluffy and sew it all together.

All in all, a simple project likely to take me about a bajillion hours to complete. But I was determined to do it anyway.

Getting the whole thing laid out, assessing the damage, and getting everything organized took the rest of the energy I had. I fell into bed and slept hard.

~*~

The next morning, I was up early and back at the craft store. I purchased four cases of toothpicks, two bottles of glue, and a brand-new collection of decorative scrapbooking paper that had arrived in the store that morning.

I made it to the park bench in time for Alex and Oscar to find me sitting there.

"Tell me you didn't lose your dog again. That's the third time in a week." He plopped down next to me. "Maybe you should try obedience school."

I grinned. "We tried that. You know, no matter how many classes I take, I just won't listen."

Alex had the decency to laugh at my lame joke. He was a pretty good guy.

I leaned down for a bag I'd shoved under the bench. "I got you a present."

His eyes widened in surprise. "Why on Earth would you want to go and do a thing like that?" He peered inside and found the toothpicks and glue. "How did you know I was running low?"

I shrugged. "A hunch. How's it coming?"

"It's coming. Nearly done with the main structures, though it's slower going now since I have to hold the walls up until they dry. After that, I'll be working on the inside—all the furniture and fiddly pieces."

"Would you like some help?"

"Oh, I couldn't ask you for that. You've got plenty of your own things to do with your time."

I held up my hand. "Alex, are you going to get this done in time for the competition?"

He looked away from me. "I think so."

I dipped my head so he'd look at me. "If I helped, would you know so?"

His reluctance faded, and he grinned. "Yes. I think I would."

"Then let me help you? Please?"

He rose from the bench and stretched. "Wynter, I don't know where you came from, but Oscar and I are grateful. Aren't we boy?"

Oscar gave a sharp bark, then led us back to Alex's house.

I spent all day with him in his basement on Saturday, except for when we came up from time to time for lunch or snacks. His mom insisted on feeding me, once she'd pinched my arm and decided I needed more meat on my bones.

We worked hard down there. Sometimes I held pieces together for him, like a human clamp, until the glue set. Other times, he'd snip a toothpick to a specific size as an example and have me cut an entire box to the same length. I opened boxes, unclogged glue spouts, and mostly kept him going until we were both too tired to continue.

Before I left, I promised I'd be back on Tuesday to see if he needed any more help.

After a glass of wine and a quick sandwich, I spent the rest of the evening working on my quilt until I couldn't keep my eyes open. Phyllis sat beside me, murmuring encouragement and singing '80s power ballads.

I didn't mind her throaty rendition of Bon Jovi's "I'll Be There for You," but by the time she sang Poison's "Every Rose Has Its Thorns" for the third time, I was ready for bed.

"I think that's it for me." I tied a knot, cut the thread, and stuck the needle in my little stuffed tomato pincushion. "Thanks for the serenade."

"It was my pleasure." Phyllis sounded as tired as I was. "I could sing you a lullaby if you like."

I gave her a weary smile. "I won't even be awake long enough to change out of my clothes. But thanks for sitting up with me tonight."

"It's what friends do, sweetheart. Sleep well."

On Sunday, I knocked on Missy's door and surprised her with the new paper collection.

"You're spoiling me," she said as she took the package. "I only gave you a piece of gum and some laundry soap." She looked more closely at the paper and gasped. "Is this velvet? Oh, wow." She dropped to the floor in front of the coffee table and pulled the sheets out of their plastic cover. "I can't believe how gorgeous this is." She ran her fingers over the velvet-embossed patterns. "I want to use all of them. Thank you so much!"

Cassie gurgled from the next room, hiccupped, then started to cry.

Missy groaned. "So much for that. Gabe's working this weekend. Babies don't take days off."

I waggled my hand at her. "No. Sit. I'll get her."

"She'll need a fresh diaper." She gathered her legs under her to stand.

"Seriously. I've got this. I've been a professional babysitter before."

"Really?"

I rolled my eyes. "Trust me. I've done just about everything at one time or another."

My past experience came in handy. Cassie was a mess. I got her cleaned up and in fresh clothes and diaper, changed her crib sheet, and put all the wet clothes in the hamper. By the time we came out, Missy was in the zone, cutting, clipping, arranging and gluing.

And that was what it turned out Missy needed from me to help her get her work done. She needed a nanny. Cassie and I spent the day together, playing in her bedroom, having snacks in the kitchen, and rocking in a chair watching her mommy make art.

When Cassie went down for another nap several hours later, I ran a load of laundry downstairs and brought it back clean and folded. I washed the dishes, cleaned the bathroom, and dusted. The only thing I didn't do was run the vacuum, since nobody can concentrate with that much noise.

For the first hour or so, Missy tried to object, afraid she was taking advantage of me. Eventually, when she realized how much she was getting done, she allowed me to help and tuned out what I was doing unless I had to interrupt with a question.

Around five, she stretched and looked up at me. "I can't believe I got so much done. I think I'm going to make it in time for the party." She gave me a hug. "Thank you so much, Wynter."

I picked up my purse. "It was my pleasure. Sometimes moms need an extra hand."

She hugged me again. "You were amazing. Thank you."

"I'll come back Wednesday and see how you're doing. Okay?"

She grinned. "Awesome. See you then!"

By the time I got home, I was almost too tired to work on my quilt. But I did it anyway.

Chapter 24

At least on Monday I didn't have to work to convince Mark to let me help, since I'd already done that. I did, however, have to work a whole lot harder on the project itself.

I lifted and carried. I hammered and painted. I dug, mixed, screwed, and drilled. I even went on a beer run.

We weren't the only two people there, but the other guys were hired to be there, and their work ethics weren't so great. When I left to get beer, I stopped at the apartment and grabbed my illicit bottle of bubbles and a few of the wands from the bag in my closet. From time to time, when I thought no one was looking, I used the heart-shaped wand from my collection to blow bubbles at their backs. As the bubbles popped around their heads, I told them what a great job they were doing.

It didn't work well, but they didn't take quite as many breaks as they'd been taking.

At the end of the day, the hired guys went home, and Mark and I kept at it until we didn't have light left. The end result was disappointing. I'd seen the plans he'd drawn up, and this was only the skeleton. We had a whole lot more work to do.

"Don't worry." He patted me on the back. "We'll make it." His voice was full of confidence, but his expression was anxious.

I was way too tired to work on the quilt. I was almost finished sewing the squares together, though, so I felt I deserved a night off.

I hit the pillow hard.

~*~

When I knocked on Alex's door, his mom answered and let me in.

"We're so glad you're here, aren't we, Oscar?"

Poor Oscar was bundled up in a green vest dotted with daisies. He looked uncomfortable.

"I'm…uh…happy to be here, Mrs. Meyer. Is Alex downstairs already?"

She shuffled into the kitchen in her daisy slippers, waving for me to follow. "He went down right after breakfast. Here." She shoved six pieces of bacon into a napkin and handed it to me, then balanced a cinnamon roll on top of the pile. "Take that down with you to eat. You look half-starved."

"Oh, thanks." I kept the roll balanced while I opened the basement door, then escaped downstairs.

Alex saw my mountain of bacon and laughed. "Sorry. If you're not hungry, you don't have to eat it."

I shrugged. "She's very sweet." I licked icing off the roll. "So. How are you doing? What are we working on today?"

He waved me over to the table. "See for yourself."

The house was done. It was an exact replica of the house I was standing in, even down to the crazy lawn ornaments. He turned the house around and showed me the inside. Tiny toothpick furniture decorated the rooms. There was even a miniature Oscar down in the basement.

I gasped. "Alex, it's fantastic. Is it done?"

"Just a few touchups to do. I'll probably work on it right up until the judging, but it would be fine even if I entered it right now."

I grinned. "You did it. I'm so happy for you."

His expression was serious. "Thanks to you."

I chomped a piece of bacon. "I didn't do much."

He shook his head. "You did a lot more than you know. If you ever need anything, you let me know."

I had a similar experience the next day with Missy. She was still fussing with individual pages, tweaking things here and there, but the book itself was done. All the pages were complete.

"It's so beautiful, Missy." I flipped from page to page, following the story of two people who fell in love, married, had children, went on adventures, and never stopped looking at each other with so much love the camera couldn't miss it in every single shot Missy had chosen.

"Do you think they'll like it?"

"Oh, honey, they're going to be so happy with this."

She hugged me. "Thanks for making sure I finished in time. You're a good friend."

That was probably very much against the rules. And I didn't care one bit. "I'm glad I could help."

I would have loved for things to have gone the same with Mark as it had the other two. But it didn't.

The two guys who'd been helping picked up another job and didn't show for work on Wednesday. Mark had worked hard, but he'd been by himself. When I showed up to help on Thursday, he looked so forlorn, I wanted to put my arms around him and cry.

He sat on a half-painted teeter-totter that was supposed to look like gumdrops balanced on peppermint sticks. Instead, it looked like a wooden pole with two purple blobs.

"What happened?" I stood in the middle of all the chaos, wondering if I'd ruined things for Mark by going to help the others.

"I failed," he said. "I should have kept it simple or started sooner. I can't do this."

I sat next to him on the center beam. "Can we hire some new guys to finish?"

He shook his head. "I tried. Not enough notice to get anybody out here. I have to have it done by tomorrow night." He waved his hand at the yard. "I figure I could finish it up in four days by myself. Three, maybe, with your help. But I can't do it by tomorrow."

At first, my eyes welled with tears. How could things have gone downhill so fast? Then I thought about it, and anger burned away the tears. How did this happen? Well, first, Fate gave a new hire too many clients. This caused my boss to assume Fate was up to something, so she stepped aside and didn't notice when my trainer failed to train me properly, my paperwork wasn't in order, and my dates were changed. To top it all off, my ex dropped in to sabotage the whole thing.

How did it happen? The poor guy got a bad Muse, through no fault of his own—or mine.

"I've got an idea." I stood to face him, my face serious. "Remember how I told you I work for the government?"

"Sure. Top secret. Can't tell me anything."

"Yeah. That." I ran my fingers through the top of my hair, which probably spiked it into a weird punk thing I hadn't intended. "I think I can get you some help. But I was undercover with them, so they think I'm someone else. If I can get them out here, you have to promise to go along with anything they say about me, and you have to try to keep them working in different areas so they don't compare notes. Think you can do that?"

One of Mark's eyebrows went up. "What the hell do you do for a living?" He held his hand up. "No, never mind. I get it. You can't say." He smiled. "If you can get me some help, I'll do anything you say."

I had to swallow a saucy retort. The way he'd said it sounded so dirty. "I'll be back in a few hours to help. And with any luck, I'll have a couple of people here first thing tomorrow morning."

Both Alex and Missy were surprised to see me again so soon, but when I told them a friend of mine was in a bind with a project for a little girl with leukemia, they were more than happy to help. Well, Alex was happy to help. Missy was willing to come out and help, but her husband, Gabe, insisted on taking over.

"You helped Missy out when she needed it. And what kind of dad would I be if I let someone else's little girl be disappointed when I have the day off anyway?"

So, Thursday, I did some painting for Mark, then Friday, we were a team of four, finishing all the unfinished pieces, getting last coats of paint on the brightest pieces, and putting banners and ribbons on the tallest peaks.

Halfway through the day, Missy and baby Cassie showed up with lunch. Missy and I sat together on the ledge of a pink, green, and yellow marshmallow castle, swinging our feet eating sandwiches.

"So," she said, tipping her head toward Mark on the other side of the yard. "He's cute as hell."

I chewed slowly. "Yes. Yes, he is."

"What's the story there?" Her eyes were lit with amusement.

"No story. Just a friend." I braced myself. I knew it was coming.

"Why not? He obviously likes you." She jabbed me with her elbow.

"He does not!" I startled myself with how loud I'd spoken, and lowered my voice. "He does not. Besides—I'm currently off the market for awhile for maintenance."

"Ah. I see. Bad breakup." She took another bite.

I nodded. "You have no idea." And I'd had to do it multiple times for it to stick.

She swallowed and grinned. "Well, when you're done with maintenance, you might want to come back to this conversation."

I watched Mark stretch and bend over to pick up a screwdriver from the grass. "Maybe. I've got a whole lot of maintenance to do first, but I'll keep it in mind."

Cassie fell asleep in the stroller, so there were five of us to work on the remaining project—laying the squishy, interlocking playground tiles on the ground. A path of brightly colored tiles led from the marshmallow play castle, beneath each licorice swing, around the gumdrop teeter-totter, over the rock candy mountain slide, and through the lollipop forest of wobbly climbing springs. The rest of the yard was laid with regular, light-gray tiles to protect from falls and to make the game-board tiles stand out. The last touch was to paint the words *start* on one end of the colored tiles and *finish* at the other.

It was magnificent.

I had less than two minutes to admire it before my phone rang.

"Wynter, it's Polly. I need you to come in and see me. The Muse Board has a decision."

~*~

I sat in the same chair in Polly's office I'd sat in before, hands folded in my lap to keep them from shaking, ankles crossed to keep my feet from tapping. I remained still while Polly handed down a decision about my future.

It occurred to me that no matter what the verdict, I was already in hell.

"All nine Muses met to discuss your situation," Polly said. Her gaze scanned my face. "The charges are pretty severe. Rules get broken sometimes, but no one's ever broken so many of them—especially in such a short time."

I was almost proud of that. If I was going to screw up, at least I did it better than anybody else. Finally, I was good at something.

Polly tapped a stack of papers against her desk and glanced at the top sheet. "There were, however, extenuating circumstances, and that was taken into account."

I relaxed a little. Maybe they'd let me off with time served.

"Audrey has been reprimanded, and a mark has gone into her record for the part she played in all this."

I nodded. "Don't be too mad at her. She didn't know all the other stuff that was going on. She apologized."

"I am aware of that. She'll be fine." She consulted her paperwork again. "Jeremy, on the other hand, has been transferred to janitorial. For the remainder of his contract, he'll be cleaning toilets. We went over the security vids, and the changes to your paperwork and the erasure of you handbook were his doing."

My eyes widened. "It was Jeremy?" I frowned. "It's because of Phoebe, right? Because I was her client, and I failed." I still felt guilty for that. Because I was such a screw up, some other Muse lost her job.

Polly leaned forward, her expression intense. "Wynter, Fate doesn't send my Muses to the same client more than once unless it's an ongoing project. I've never seen someone get a Muse for three different projects— especially not the same Muse. Be careful. The Fates have been watching you closely since long before you came here, and they seem to have made you their special project."

A shiver ran up my back. "I'm nobody. Why would they mess with me like that?"

She shook her head. "I have no idea." She cleared her throat. "In addition, you'll be happy to know that, while we were viewing the security vids to catch Jeremy, we observed Dave's behavior. Because he's a descendent of Aphrodite, he's been given several chances. He's been…removed."

I didn't say anything. Nothing I could say would be appropriate—certainly not punching the air and yelling "Woohoo!"

"Your boyfriend has been dealt with by his own department. I've been assured that he will be quite uncomfortable in his new environment, though they wouldn't tell me where he's been transferred."

I felt a twinge of guilt for getting him into trouble after breaking his heart. I didn't owe him any guilt but still felt bad. But maybe only a little bad.

"Which brings us to you, my rule breaker."

My stomach clenched.

Polly stared at me across the desk. "Is it true that, even during suspension, you continued to break the rules and assist your clients in person, even going so far as to convince them to help *each other*?"

I lifted my chin. *That* was something I would *not* feel guilty about. "Yes. And all three of them finished their projects. *Before* the deadlines." Admittedly, Mark had cut it close, but the deadline was tomorrow morning, so he was early, too. I met her gaze with a steady stare.

Polly sighed. "I told you they weren't your concern. Why would you risk what little chance you had left for your future by breaking more rules?"

I chose my words carefully. "Polly, those people had dreams. And their dreams affected other people's dreams, too. Alex, with his toothpick sculpture, made his mother happy by building the house she loves. Even if he doesn't win the competition, it's brought him closer to his mother. Missy's parents will be so happy with her scrapbook. Missy knows she made something wonderful with her own hands for people she loves, and Gabe is proud of his wife."

I paused, gathering my thoughts. "Mark built something so breathtaking, it will change his life by boosting his self-confidence and bringing in better projects in the future. And that little girl will have the joy of seeing her new backyard and then playing there with her friends. And if she doesn't survive her illness, her parents will have the comfort of knowing they gave her those wonderful memories. That's why I couldn't just walk away. These projects were too important to let them go. If that meant breaking rules to get it done, then I don't care. I was the best damn Muse I could be."

Polly was so silent, I almost expected her to start a slow clap.

Finally, she sighed and nodded her head. "Good. That's what I wanted to hear. I made the right choice, then." She shuffled the papers on her desk, then handed me a page. "You'll be reporting to the Underworld by 8:00 PM tonight."

"What?" I was stunned. "I thought..." I stared at the paper in my hand, tears making it difficult to read. All I could make out was the same flaming gate icon I'd seen on Hal's paperwork.

Polly held up her hand to stop me. "Despite your extenuating circumstances, rules are rules. You're still being sent to the Underworld to work off your sentence." Her expression softened. "But you won't be going through the staffing office. This is a special assignment. It's a six-week residency assignment, and you'll be filling in for someone on maternity leave. Then you'll return here with a clean slate."

"Oh." I smoothed my fingers over the paperwork. "Personal assistant to the CEO of Underworld LLC. Okay. What's that mean exactly? Wait. Residency assignment?"

"It's exactly what it looks like. You'll be assisting Hades."

"Hades the guy?"

"God. He's a god, Wynter. So, remember to be respectful." She rose from her desk. "Go home. Say your goodbyes. Pack a suitcase." She handed me another sheet. "Here's a packing list. They'll provide you with a uniform, but you'll want something for your days off. Be back in the lobby before eight, and someone will be there to escort you."

I sat there staring blindly at the instructions, not processing what was going on. Polly took my elbow to get me to stand and walk out the door.

"Don't worry about packing up your desk. You'll be back soon enough. Safe journey." She closed the door behind me and left me standing in the hall confused, relieved, and terrified all at once.

~*~

I stood in the lobby, shaking like a leaf, one hand clutching the handle of my suitcase, and the other wrapped tightly around a potted philodendron. A duffel bag containing my pillow and my newly finished quilt was slung over my shoulder.

"It's going to be alright, Wynter."

"But my car—"

"Syd is going to watch it for you."

"Mom. What if Mom gets into trouble?"

"Shhh." Phyllis stroked my hand with a low-hanging branch. "Your Mom's going to be fine. And Mark's going to take care of your apartment. Don't fret so much. This is a grand adventure!"

My knees were shaking so much I was getting nauseated. I dropped into a chair in the waiting area. Few people walked by at that hour. "We're going to the Underworld to work for the boss. That's not an adventure. That's hell."

"Don't say that word. They hate when you call it hell."

I wondered how far I'd have to run before they couldn't find me. I wondered if everything smelled like sulfur down there. I wondered if the boss dude would have a maniacal laugh and make me torture people.

I wondered if I had time to run to the bathroom to be sick.

Someone tapped me on the shoulder, and I jumped.

"Wynter?"

I turned and found Hal standing behind me, his familiar face split in a grin.

"Oh. Hi, Hal." I patted the seat next me for him to sit. "You won't believe what happened to me."

He grabbed my hand and pulled me to my feet. "I know exactly what happened to you, and I'm really excited." He took my suitcase and duffel bag, then led me to the elevators. "We'll get to hang out more, now."

"Wait, they sent you?"

Phyllis chuckled. "Of course they did. He's a ferryman, isn't he? That makes him part of the Travel and Welcome crew."

I looked at Hal for confirmation. He nodded and inserted a keycard into a slot on a panel inside the elevator. The doors closed and we went down.

Hal put his arm around me and gave me a hug. "Don't look so worried. It's not so bad down there. Especially when you've got a friend to show you around."

I held my breath as the doors opened for my first look at the Underworld.

I could stay out of trouble for six weeks, right?

Sure I could.

"Undercover Gorgon"
A Bonus Mount Olympus Employment Agency
Short Story

At 12:01 AM on my twentieth birthday, I lost my humanity.

Okay, maybe that was a little dramatic, especially since I was never human to begin with. I'd thought I was human. Clearly, I was not.

I didn't notice at first. I sat on the foot of my bed, drying my hair with a towel and watching Kathryn Hepburn toss a withering look at Humphrey Bogart as they drifted down the Amazon. I glanced at the clock. One more minute of being a teenager. I tried to think of something immature to do in my final seconds of pre-adulthood.

I couldn't think of a damn thing.

I'd never been a very good teenager anyway. I didn't drink or smoke, slam doors, sneak out at night, or moon over boys. Twenty wasn't likely to be much different from any other age. I'd still go to class on Monday, I'd still be working a shitty job at a drug store, and I'd still be living in my old bedroom in my parents' house.

At least, that was my thought at midnight. At 12:01, everything changed.

I gave my hair a last rub, then dropped the towel on the foot of the bed. My wet hair hung to my shoulders in heavy strands. Once it dried, it would lighten to a dishwater, nothing color, which went well with my eye-colored eyes and my pallid skin. Not a looker, as Bogie might have said. I wasn't ugly, exactly, but I wasn't noticeable—which was fine with me. I didn't care if anybody noticed me. Most people pretty much irritated me anyway.

Shadows moved on the wall in the flickering light of the television. My hair brushed my bare shoulder, and I scratched where it tickled.

My hair licked my finger.

I froze and peered at my hand where it hovered over my skin. A thin, emerald snake slid over my knuckles and flicked its tongue. I frowned and glanced at the terrarium across the room.

"Daphne, how did you get out?" I let the little grass snake weave between my fingers and headed toward the habitat I kept for her. "The lid is still closed. Did you slip out when I fed you?" I lifted the hinged door and tried to place her inside.

Several things occurred at once. First, I spotted Daphne already tucked in a corner behind an artificial rock. Second, the snake in my hand wouldn't come loose from my head. And third, several more snakes slithered across my hand.

Had I been a typical human, I might have lost my shit. But I'd loved snakes since I was a little girl, and I was studying to get a degree in herpetology. I was all about the snakes, reptiles, and amphibians. So, yes, I had a buttload of snakes crawling on me, but my initial reaction was that Daphne had somehow managed to lay a clutch of eggs when I wasn't looking.

"Okay, kiddies. You've had your fun. Time to get in bed with Mom. My parents will freak if you're running around the house." I took careful hold of several at once and gave a gentle tug to disengage them from my person.

They wouldn't come lose. In fact, I felt the tug all the way to my scalp.

With my left hand, I held out a snake, and followed it with my right hand to its origin. My fingers prodded the base. It appeared to be attached to my head. This was, of course, stupid. Snakes couldn't grow out of my head, even in the weirdest of Internet urban legends. Still, my entire head squirmed with them and, as many heads as I found, I could find no tails.

My heart raced and my mouth went dry. This was the worst nightmare I'd ever had—way worse than the dream about the rabid squirrel with the eye patch and the tiny hooked paw.

"Okay. Breathe. Wake up, Patrice. Just a bad dream. Wake up." I hit the light switch in an effort to get a better look in the mirror by my bedroom door. Pain raced through my head like someone had shot me through both eyes with a Daisy Red Ryder BB gun. I covered them with one hand and slapped at the light switch with the other until I got lucky and flipped the lights off.

Dream or not, the pain had been real. The snakes attached to my head squirmed and writhed in agitation, as if they, too, had felt the stabbing pain. I threw my bedroom door open and ran out in my cotton nightgown, yelling for my parents.

I was halfway down the hall when they heard me. Their light flashed on and I spun around, shielding my eyes. "Turn off the light! Turn it off!"

The light went out and my parents stepped into the hall, the low light of my television giving us enough to see each other. I rose and stared at them, waiting to see if they saw what I thought I'd felt—hundreds of snakes growing from my head.

I expected either bewilderment at my odd behavior or horror at what they saw. They gave me neither. I certainly hadn't expect an apology.

Dad took a step toward me. "Sweetheart, I can explain."

Mom gave me a watery-eyed smile. "I am so sorry, honey."

I frowned. "Sorry? I have snakes on my head. How is that something you did?"

Mom glanced at Dad and back at me. "It's not exactly something I did, but it did come from me."

The snakes settled over me, curling around each other and laying still.

I gave a nervous laugh. "What? You planted snake seeds in my scalp?"

I was still going with the idea that this was a terrible nightmare. Even worse than the one about the blood-filled water balloon fight with Christopher Walken.

She shook her head and walked toward me. "It's a recessive gene. Somewhere in my family, way back, we're related to gorgons."

I snorted. "What are you saying? Medusa is my great-grandmother?"

"Something like that." She took my hand. "Come sit down."

In a daze, I followed my parents into their room. Dad turned on the bathroom light and closed the door enough to shield my eyes from the light, yet give us enough to see each other.

A terrible thought occurred to me, and I squeezed my eyes shut. "Don't look at me! I might turn you to stone if you look me in the eyes."

Dad patted me on the arm. "You wouldn't do that to us. We trust you. Just don't look straight at us."

This was insane. I noted, as if from a far off, detached sort of way, that in the more natural bathroom light, my skin was a sort of translucent, sea-foam green. It was kind of pretty.

"I don't understand." I twisted my arm in the light to see the color better. "Why am I only seeing this now?"

Mom and Dad glanced at each other again, then Dad looked down at his hands. "We were contacted when your mother was pregnant. The situation was explained that you wouldn't appear human. They gave us a choice between giving you up to be raised as a gorgon in a foster home for mythological creatures, or raise you ourselves with you having no knowledge of what you really were."

I pointed at my head. "But I didn't look like this."

Mom brightened. "The man who originally contacted us sold us Deity Springs Stealth Insurance for you. It disguised you so well, no one would ever know. Including you."

I scowled. "You bought me a disguise that was mousy and unattractive? Thanks a lot." I shook my head and the snakes hissed in objection to the movement. "So, why am I seeing this now? What changed?"

Dad took a deep breath. "Your insurance lapsed. We can't legally cover you anymore."

~*~

The next few days were pretty rough. The light sensitivity was an easy fix. Sunglasses did the trick, and it kept me from turning anyone to stone by mistake. But no hat was big enough to cover all those snakes, and I wasn't about to do a full-body spray tan every time I left the house.

So much for my degree in herpetology.

Dad called the stealth insurance company and got the runaround. Since my parents had let the insurance lapse instead of actually telling me what the hell was going on so I could transfer it to my name, getting the insurance started again was enormously expensive. I didn't have enough in my account, and neither did Mom and Dad.

I'd have to save up for months to have the money. The catch to that was I couldn't go to work anymore, not without the insurance. People prefer to buy hand lotion, mints, and toilet paper from people who don't have green skin and a head full of snakes. I had no choice. The life I'd been living was over. I'd have to go to wherever non-human folks lived and start over.

Oddly enough, I wasn't too upset by that. Sure, I'd miss my parents. I couldn't think of too many other things I *would* miss, though. And this might sound crazy, but once I got a good look at myself in the mirror, I was thrilled. Seriously. For the first time in my life, I was *hot*. Maybe not the kind of hot that would get a guy's attention or make other women jealous, but that never mattered to me. I liked what I saw. The skin color. The snakes. The curve of my cheek and the fullness of my lips.

I was finally comfortable in my own skin—proud, even. Ironic that I couldn't go out in public like that.

So, when Garmond Schumacher, the six-foot tall minotaur, showed up at my front door in a snazzy business suit, I was ready to leave with him before he'd finished his spiel.

The bull-headed man sat on my sofa and cleared his throat. "Temporary housing will be provided for you, and you'll meet with a career consultant to find you a good match." He braced his hands against his knees and gave me an earnest look with his large cow eyes. "I know this is all new and difficult. We'll do everything we can to ease you—"

"I'll go pack my suitcase." I leaped from my chair. "How much stuff can I bring?"

He flicked an ear and blinked. "Pack a bag, and we'll send for the rest once you're settled."

My parents gave him sheepish smiles.

"She's been cooped up for a few days," Mom said.

I ran up the stairs and tossed clothes into a suitcase as fast as I could pull them off hangers and scoop them out of the dresser. I threw my toothbrush, toothpaste, and shower gel into a toiletry bag and stopped. What else could I possibly need? Hair products were out. I'd never need those again. I never wore much makeup before, and now that I wanted to, nothing was appropriate for my new coloring.

I shrugged and zipped the bag. Fairyland—or wherever the hell I was going—had to have drugstores, right? Oh, gods. I truly hoped I didn't get stuck working at a supernatural drugstore for the rest of my life.

Once my suitcase was packed, I paused and looked around my room. With the exception of the snake habitat in the corner, the room looked more like a guestroom or a motel room. It was as if no one had ever lived there.

In a way, I never really had.

I pushed my sunglasses up the bridge of my nose. "I'll send for you, Daphne. I promise."

~*~

The bull guy had promised me housing. He hadn't promised I'd have it to myself. Two giggling nymphs and a siren shared my dorm room with me. The nymphs were afraid of me and stayed clear whenever possible. The siren used up all the hot water while she sang entire operas in the shower.

Other than that, though, she was pretty cool. Her name was Lizzy, and she helped ease me into my new life from the first day of my arrival.

"One thing's for sure, we need to get you some better clothes," she said, wrinkling her nose. She flipped through the hangers in my closet, scowling at the sensible skirts and blouses. "Clothes are meant to decorate your body, honey, not hide it." She took a sip from her wine goblet, one finger sticking out toward me. "And we need to get you some makeup. Seriously. Look at that gorgeous complexion. I've got some lavender lipstick that will totally pop against that lovely green."

I perched on the edge of my bed and watched her scurry around, humming softly to herself. She snagged a huge cosmetics case and dropped it on the bed next to me. Her face screwed up in concentration as she dragged a chair close to me.

"Okay. First, I need you to take off those ridiculous sunglasses." She reached toward me to take them away.

I pulled away from her reach. Several head-snakes hissed and drew back. "What are you doing? I could turn you to stone."

Her eyes widened in surprise, and she stared at me. "What?"

I pointed at me head. "Hello? I'm a gorgon!"

Her lower lip quivered. "Honey." She put her hand on my knee and pressed her lips together while she inhaled through her nose. "Oh, honey."

"What? Don't you know anything about mythology?" I sat straighter, offended. She wasn't laughing at me, exactly, but she was close. "I can't take these off when people are around." I paused as she pulled herself together. "Besides. The light hurts my eyes."

She nodded. "Okay, that one's legit." She waved her hand. "The stone thing? Totally bogus. That was specifically Medusa's curse. Haven't you ever met another gorgon before?"

I folded my arms across my chest. "I only met *me* a week ago."

"Ah." She patted my leg. "I see." She tapped her finger on her thigh, thinking. "Okay. You need a makeover and a full tour. Have you met with your career counselor yet?"

"I just got here. I have an appointment tomorrow afternoon."

She snapped open her makeup case. "Good. We've got a lot of work to do before I can take you out in public. Let's get started."

~*~

I began my new job looking fabulous. The lavender lipstick was a great contrast to the green eye shadow Lizzie taught me to use as blush. We found some small, round shades that shut out enough light to protect my eyes without covering half my face. The slit in my pencil skirt showed off a whole lot of hot green leg. I learned to coax the snakes into a side part with a few of the smaller ones hanging seductively over one eye. Never in my life had I felt so confident.

And it was all wasted on the shitty receptionist job they assigned me in the career center.

I glared through my glasses at the skinny girl in front of me. "Yes?" I pressed my lips together as if she'd done something terribly wrong. The only thing she'd done wrong was have the bad luck to be there when I was there.

One of my snakes hissed, and the girl twitched and slid paperwork toward me. "I think I filled it out right." Her voice quivered and her hand shook.

I felt sorry for her and glanced over the page. "It'll do."

I regretted my grumpy tone and offered a small smile. "Follow the gold line on the floor to Athens. Orientation begins in ten minutes." I stamped her paperwork with a flourish and dropped it in the outbox. "Next."

There wasn't much to the job. I sat behind a desk and handed out maps of the building, registered newbies for orientation, took complaints, and answered general questions. Better than retail, I supposed. At least I got to sit down.

But it wasn't what I wanted to be doing with my life. I wanted to study reptiles and amphibians. I wanted to learn things. I wanted to go back to school. The moment I turned green and sprouted snakes from my head, my options became limited.

It turned out, the job did not actually require me to be nice to people. That was at my own discretion.

Within a month, I ruled the reception desk and all who stepped inside the brightly lit, domed atrium of the Mount Olympus Employment Agency. If someone wanted something done, they had to go through me to get the proper paperwork. If a new hire showed up, they couldn't get to orientation until I stamped their application. How long it took to accomplish anything depended solely on my good will.

If I couldn't have the career I wanted, I'd take what I was stuck with and make it mine.

"Next." I always kept my voice low and cool, sometimes adding a little hiss where I could. It made people nervous.

A human guy, kind of cute but nothing remarkable, stepped forward and placed a pile of paperwork on the chest-high counter. I gave him a long look until he squirmed, then picked up the papers, slowly tamping them on the counter.

213

"I filled in what I could," he said. His voice shook a little. "I didn't know the answer to a lot of the questions."

Of course he didn't. No one knew the answers to all of the questions on the intro-forms. Questions like "Which parent is the dominant deity?" and "What powers have you manifested?" weren't meant to be answered by the majority of newcomers. Most of them had no idea what was going on. They'd hit rock bottom in their lives, which propelled them into Mount Olympus. They had no idea they had the blood of a god or hero in their ancestry. Like regular humans, they didn't know any of this existed. The paperwork was meant to give them their first clues in order to ease them into their new reality.

I grunted and pretended to examine his paperwork. Frankly, as long as his name, address, and social security number were on the form, that's all that was required. Anything else was bonus.

"I didn't understand half of what's on it," he said. "What do my parents have to do with any of this?"

I looked down at him through my glasses, and he shifted from foot to foot. "You'll have to ask someone in personnel, sir." I leaned forward. "Did you want me to give you the form to fill out for an appointment?" There was no form for that. But I made it sound so ominous, he'd never ask for it.

He took a step back—they usually did that when they were afraid I'd take off my shades and turn them into stone with my stare. I loved that part.

"No, no. That's fine." He stuffed his hands in his pockets and pointed his gaze somewhere over my left shoulder. "I was just wondering, that's all."

I grunted at him again, then slammed a stamp on the top page of his paperwork and dropped it in the outbox. "Follow the copper line to Thebes for orientation and further instruction. Next."

My favorite part was always the way the finality of my words fed the confusion and panic on their faces.

After a moment of hesitation, he spotted the colored lines on the floor, chose the thick, copper one, and followed it out of the atrium down a hallway. Three more new hire humans stood in line behind him. I sighed and gave the next one an impatient signal to step forward.

The morning dragged in what felt like an endless stream of newbies to be sent to orientation. By ten, though, even the stragglers were checked in and on their way. Mondays always went that way—an influx of brand new humans bound for training for the first few hours, then everything went back to business as usual.

I dropped a *Be Right Back* sign on my desk and took my ten-minute break without saying a word to the four people standing in line. I heard a centaur clomp one foot in agitation, but I ignored him. I couldn't intimidate a Mythic with the threat of turning them to stone, since they knew I didn't have that ability. But I still had all the power. I was the receptionist. If they wanted me to straighten out whatever their problem was, they'd have to suck it up.

I might have liked the job more than I let on.

After a quick trip to the ladies room, I refilled my coffee cup and took a few minutes to watch the other folks meandering in the Mythics cafeteria. Two satyrs sat hunched over a game of checkers, laughing at some joke or other. A minotaur in a jogging suit blew on a cup of ramen noodles, then tipped it back and drank it all in one gulp. The snuffling noises he made were…unlovely. I wrinkled my nose, a little grossed out. A stray noodle had squirmed from the side of his mouth and lay flat against his hairy cheek. I took a sip of coffee and looked away.

A naiad and a dryad sat in a corner together, the naiad drinking water through her graceful blue fingertips, and the dryad with both green hands buried in buckets of soil. The naiad's cerulean hair shimmered as if wet, and the dryad's hair sprouted flowers as she ate.

I tried to take another sip of my coffee, but it was gone. While I'd been otherwise occupied, my snakes had dipped their tiny faces into my cup and drained it.

Fantastic. Now my hair's all caffeinated and won't stay in place.

I poured a second cup of coffee and returned to my desk. It turned out, spazzy snake hair was far more disconcerting to the clients than when I gave them the stony stare. I'd have to consider saving up for an espresso machine.

First in line when I came back was a cyclops with corrective lenses—lens. Really, it was a monocle. It was held in place around her head by a string of pink and yellow beads. She had her hair pulled into three pigtails, one on each side and one on top.

I made no attempt to hide my smirk. "Next."

She slapped an employee ID card on the counter. "I need this changed."

The card had a picture of a similar cyclops, but with a little goatee and a black plastic frame around the monocle.

I pushed the card toward her with two fingers. "You can't make changes to another employee's card. This person…" I bent closer to look at the name and my hairsnakes gave a warning hiss at everyone near enough to scare. "Charles Leech. Charles will have to come in himself if he wants a new ID card."

The cyclops's single eye grew wide, and the single eyebrow rose. She slammed her fist on the counter, her voice rising with each word. "I *was* Charles Leech. You're not listening. I'm Charlize Leech now, and I need the name changed and a new photo taken. I've been getting the runaround for weeks." With each word, the pigtail on the top waggled and bobbed.

The entire atrium had fallen silent. If I didn't take back control of the conversation, every person who witnessed the situation would take advantage of me from then on. I blinked. "Ma'am, in order to process your request, I'll need to see some photo identification."

Charlize groaned in frustration. "The only photo ID I have has the wrong information on it. That's why I'm here."

"I see." I reached under the counter and thumbed through a file. "Fill out these forms and follow the red line to Crete. Please make sure you answer all questions completely or they won't be able to help you." I slid the forms into a clipboard with a pen dangling from a string. On top, I added a yellow sticky note on which I wrote "Ask for Peg." Peg would make the transition go smoothly, and the cyclops wouldn't get the runaround.

What? I did nice things for people all the time. I just didn't make a habit of letting everyone know about it. I had a reputation to uphold.

"Did you say the red line?" Charlize asked.

"Yes, I said red." I handed her the clipboard and dismissed her. "Next."

She hesitated—they all did when I wanted them to leave—and I ignored her. She glanced at the clipboard, then found the red line and stomped off.

She'd be fine. But seriously, how often do you get such a perfect opportunity to roll out the red tape? She was lucky I didn't draw out the situation.

I should have drawn it out. The rest of the day droned on forever with nothing quite so interesting as a transgender cyclops in a beaded monocle. Plumbing complaints, transfer requests, lost time cards—it all had to go through me before I funneled it through to the correct department.

I glanced at the giant clock embedded in one of the enormous pillars across from my desk. Ten more minutes and I could bug out of there. All the clients had been taken care of, and with a little luck, no one else would come in. Five minutes later I bent over to grab my purse from a built-in shelf. Maybe I could cut out early. Who would care?

My headsnakes hissed, alerting me to the presence of another person at the desk. I sighed, bracing myself, and sat up. "Yes?"

A small woman with nervous eyes clutched her bag against her chest. "I need an exterminator."

I frowned. "Pardon me?"

"An exterminator. You're new." She glanced past me, standing on her toes. "Is there someone else here? Where's the man who was here last month?"

"Samuel?" I gave her a polite smile. "He was reassigned. What sort of exterminator do you need?"

She gulped. "I have a basilisk living under my porch. The exterminator came out to take care of it, but there must've been more than one. All the grass around the house is dead, and I'm afraid to let my cat out."

"Uh huh." I reached for a form in a cubbyhole under the desk, only half listening. I stopped and blinked. "Wait, basilisk?"

"Yes. Apparently, there were two."

My heart pounded in excitement. "What happened to the other one?"

"The exterminator took care of it"

I frowned. "Took care of it?"

She nodded. "Chopped its head off right in my yard. I doubt anything will grow there now. Might as well pour cement and make a patio in that spot."

My pulse pounded in my ears. Basilisks were small, peaceful creatures. I'd read about them—roosters with poisonous spurs on their heels and the long tails of snakes. *Snakes*. I couldn't let another one be harmed. I had to do something.

I pushed the paperwork into a clipboard with an attached pen. "Fill this out for me, please. I'll see to it the basilisk is removed and does no further harm to your property."

"Thank you." She sighed with relief and went to sit in a chair while she wrote down her information.

Five o'clock came and went, and I watched people from other departments brush through the atrium and out one of the two doors, off to wherever they lived in either the human world or in Mount Olympus.

As the last of the stragglers exited the building, my client returned to the desk with her completed paperwork. "You're sure they'll take care of it this time?" The skin under her left eye twitched. "I'm so afraid it's going to come out and bite me or turn me to stone."

I glanced at the paper she'd given me. She lived in New Mexico. It figured. Basilisks liked warm, dry places. "I'll see to it myself," I said. "Everything's going to be fine."

~*~

A lot of logistical problems stood between me and saving my first real, live basilisk. The first being location.

Mount Olympus was in a separate dimension from the human world. The front door led to wherever a person came from. I'd originally arrived from downtown Philadelphia. The building I'd entered looked, on the outside, like an abandoned department store. Once I walked through the door, I was in the atrium where I worked. All major cities had an access building that looked abandoned but led to Mount Olympus. If I walked out that door, I'd be in Philly, not New Mexico.

Now, of course, I didn't leave through that door. I didn't live in the human world. I left through the other door on the other side of the atrium. It led to other parts of Mount Olympus, like the residential and shopping districts.

The only ways to go to a different human location were to apply for a transfer, go with someone as a guest, or work in the courier department.

Since transfers took weeks and I couldn't let anyone see me, that only left one option. I'd have to become an unofficial member of the messenger branch.

After hours, the building was dark and echoed with every footstep I took. The ding of the elevator and the sound of its doors opening bounced around the atrium and made me cringe. My hand shook as I pressed the button inside, and I held my breath when the doors opened for me on the seventh floor. Nobody stood waiting to catch me.

I stuck my head out and peered both ways, then stepped into the tiled hallway. A directory on the wall across from the elevator advised me to turn left, and I followed the arrow until I reached the correct door. Gold letters on frosted glass read *Courier and Travel*. Beneath that was a picture of a pair of gold, winged sandals.

The problem with breaking into a god's office is you can't whisper a prayer before trying the doorknob to see if it's unlocked.

To my surprise, the knob turned and the door swung open. I ducked inside and closed the door behind me. A bead of nervous sweat trickled from my temple, and my headsnakes shifted and coiled tightly against my head.

The room's overhead lights had been turned off, but all along the far wall pockets of ambient light kept the room from total darkness. I crept over to inspect the light's source and found a row of glowing sneakers hung on pegs by their laces.

Perfect.

Every department had specific tools its employees used to do their jobs. Cupids had their wings and arrows to encourage love, muses had their bottles of thought-bubbles to offer inspiration, and messengers had their sneakers for travel.

I found a pair in my size, tucked them into my purse, and got the hades out of there.

On the way back downstairs, I nearly ran into a harpy pushing a mop bucket and humming to herself off key. I ducked behind a potted plant as she passed by, then made a run for the elevator. By the time I made it back to my desk, I was out of breath and panicky.

I'd only been a part of this world for less than two months, and I'd already stolen something from a god. I'd never done anything wrong in my life. I'd never so much as stolen a stick of gum. This was insane.

I berated myself for my terrible behavior the entire time I was changing into my ill-gotten sneakers. I lectured myself thoroughly all the way across the atrium, out the door, and out into New Mexico.

I glanced at the address on the paperwork the woman had given me and rebuked myself for risking so much without a thought to consequences as I flew over Albuquerque and landed at Mrs. Swanburg's house.

And then I forgave myself. No use ruining a perfectly good adventure.

The minute my magic-covered feet touched the dry earth, my headsnakes became alert. Something under the porch had their undivided attention.

One of the advantages of using one of the departmental tools—like the traveling shoes—was they disguised the user. What I'd lost when my stealth insurance had lapsed was returned when I put on the shoes. I looked human. The only difference was, I wasn't human. My headsnakes were still present and, to my eyes, my skin was green. But to anyone else, I was the mousy, unremarkable girl I'd always thought I'd been. At least, that's what I'd read would happen. Fingers crossed the material I'd read in training hadn't been outdated or incorrect, because I was in a New Mexico suburb pretending to be someone—something—I wasn't. Eileen Swanburg was obviously a part of the Mythos world, but I was betting none of her neighbors were. If a gorgon showed up and crawled under her porch, that would be bad for everyone.

I glanced around. A blue, four-door sedan pulled in across the street, and a man got out. He gave me a smile and a wave, then turned and went inside.

Obviously, he hadn't seen a green-skinned woman with a head full of hyperactive snakes. I was in the clear, so I turned my attention to the Swanburg house.

Four painted steps led up to the wraparound porch. A pair of whitewashed wooden chairs with pink cushions sat beneath a picture window, and hanging plants and wind chimes swayed from the overhang. Pretty in a kitschy, overdone sort of way.

The space beneath the porch was skirted in flimsy latticework, and one corner on the right hung loose. I assumed it was where the exterminator had gone in the last time. I tested it and found the decorative barrier came off without any resistance, so I set it aside and took off my glasses to peer into the darkness under the house.

Something moved in the shadows. I tapped a flashlight app on my phone and used the light to get a better look.

Two tiny eyes like liquid tar stared back. Silky black feathers glistened, and the creature snapped its beak open and closed several times. It shook its crimson rooster wattle at me and scraped its clawed, poison-spurred feet in the dirt, then ruffled two dark wings.

"Don't be silly." I kneeled in the dead grass and ducked my head inside. "I'm here to help you." I crawled inside on all fours, hoping the dirt wouldn't ruin my skirt.

The rooster bobbed its head up and down, then it stretched its neck toward me, beak clacking in warning. But the front half of the basilisk was a distraction. Aside from the venomous spurs, the rooster portion was no more harmful than its barnyard cousins. The problem was the back half. It slithered next to me in silence, fangs dripping with the same poison that had killed the grass outside.

My hand touched something wet and stiff, and I shone the light at it. A dead rat lay curled in on itself, as if it had died in agony. I wiped my hand on my skirt. I'd probably have to toss it after this anyway.

I turned and addressed the snake as it crept closer. "Look. I really don't want to hurt you. Give me a second." I sat up and removed the stolen sneakers so the basilisk could see my true form. "See?" My snakes coiled and uncoiled, the movements making my scalp itch.

The snake end of the basilisk pulled back, its eyes wide in surprise. The rooster stepped toward me, head turned to the side to examine me with one piercing eye, and the snake's tongue flicked to taste my arm.

I smiled and held still while the creature judged me. I must have passed the test. A moment later, my lap was filled with scales and feathers. The rooster end buried its head under my arm, and the snake end climbed my body to commune with my headsnakes.

"There you go." I cuddled the rooster with one hand and rested my other hand against the snake's skin. "Everything's going to be okay, sweet boy. I know. This was scary. I don't know how you got out here, but I'll get you someplace safe."

We sat like that for a while, until the basilisk was ready to go.

If I'd had a choice, I'd have taken him back to my dorm room. But I doubted my roommates would appreciate him the way I did. As it was, they already didn't like having my Daphne there in her tank. Besides—basilisks weren't pets, and certainly not indoor pets. I'd already thought it through, though. I knew exactly where to take him.

"Now, I have to change how I look before I we can go. Don't be alarmed, okay? It's still me."

The basilisk's rooster head bobbed a few times, and the two ends climbed from my lap and waited while I put the sneakers back on. Once I'd tied the shoes, the snake portion drew closer and flicked my cheek with its tongue to verify it was still me.

The rooster portion of the basilisk followed me out from under the house with the snake riding patiently on its back. The gods were a strange bunch, making such awkward creatures.

The sky had turned dark, so no one saw us emerge. I scooped the basilisk into my arms, replaced the lattice work over the hole, and flew into the sky.

The only way back to Mount Olympus from the human world I knew of was through the front door to the main building, right past my desk in the atrium. Despite my earlier expedition to steal shoes from the courier department, I felt pretty ballsy walking into the empty building with a basilisk tucked under my arm. Still, I strode through the door and across the atrium like I owned the place, then exited through the opposite door out into the rest of Mount Olympus.

Five minutes of flight later, I was in a clearing in the wilds of the land of the gods.

"This is it." I gave the basilisk an affectionate squeeze and set him on the ground. "You'll do a whole lot better here. I promise."

The basilisk nudged me with both its heads and gave me a sorrowful look from four eyes.

I hunkered down so I could get closer. "Now, don't be like that. I'll come visit when I can. I promise."

The bushes across the clearing shook, and clicks and hisses came from within it.

Another basilisk stepped into the clearing, this one with a purple rooster wattle and green tips on its wings. It hesitated, then stepped forward. My creature met it in the center of the clearing, and they eyed each other, circling and ruffling their feathers.

The two snakes slithered toward each other, tongues flicking.

After a moment, the two roosters crowed, the snakes twisted together, and the two creatures settled in a patch of grass to doze.

My heart gave a little tug, but I left, satisfied that I'd done a good thing.

That satisfaction carried me all the way back to the atrium and up to the seventh floor.

"No exterminators today," I whispered, as I hung the magic shoes back on their peg in the courier office.

~*~

The next day, I sat at my desk feeling particularly smug as I stamped unnecessary paperwork and directed people the long way to their appointments.

I'd totally gotten away with it. I'd broken several huge rules, stolen the shoes of a god, and robbed some exterminator out of a job. Not too shabby for a shy girl who'd never even driven over the speed limit in her previous life.

A lot more had changed than my skin color and a head full of snakes. I had a lot of catching up to do. I barely knew who I was yet. But I had plenty of time to find out.

"Next!" I bent my head and glared at the nervous man standing at my counter. "Can I help you?"

"I need a supernatural pool cleaner." He glanced past me, then at my desk, at his hands, the ceiling—anywhere but my eyes. "Or something."

I crooked an eyebrow, and the snake hanging over my left eye hissed at him. "What seems to be the problem?"

He bit his lip and looked at my hairsnakes. "I have a hydra in my pool, and it won't come out."

My heart sped up in excitement. "Did you ask it nicely?"

"Yes, but then it tried to bite me. My son threatened it with a knife, you know, to scare it off. He accidentally cut off one of the serpent heads and two more grew back. I don't know what else to do. Please. My mother-in-law is coming to visit next week. She doesn't know anything about this stuff."

I smiled and pushed a form toward him. "Don't you worry, sir. I think I can help you."

Relief spread across his face. "You can?"

"Sure. I think I might be able to get someone out there tonight." I checked my watch. Two more hours till everybody went home.

Maybe my job wasn't so bad after all.

"Undercover Gorgon" was first published by Bottle Cap Publishing in the short story collection *Transmonstrified*, available now.

About R.L. Naquin

Rachel writes stories that drop average people into magical situations filled with heart and quirky humor.

She believes in pixie dust, the power of love, good cheese, lucky socks, and putting things off until the last minute. Her home is Disneyland, despite her current location in Kansas. Rachel has one husband, two grown kids, and a crazy-catlady starter kit.

Hang out with her online:
Web: www.rlnaquin.com
Facebook: www.facebook.com/rlnaquin
Twitter: www.twitter.com/rlnaquin

Visit her website to subscribe to her newsletter.